PARADISES

PARADISES

Iosi Havilio

Translated by
Beth Fowler

Introduced by Alex Clark

LONDON · NEW YORK

First published in 2013 by And Other Stories

www.andotherstories.org
London – New York

ISBN 9781908276247
eBook ISBN 9781908276254

A catalogue record for this book is available from the British Library.

This one belongs to Mirko, Loli and Zlé

INTRODUCTION

'I dream of toads, skirts, orgies and horses,' recorded the unnamed narrator of Iosi Havilio's first novel, *Open Door*, whose story is reprised in *Paradises*. Then, the wildness and surrealism of her sleepscape represented the complications that were multiplying in her waking life: having quit the city following the disappearance of her lover, Aída, she had come to rest in a small countryside town that was also home to a lunatic asylum, formed a fragile relationship with a taciturn farmer, begun a strange, unpredictable liaison with a young local girl and become pregnant. These seismic events suggest a certain self-determination, or even agency, but almost the reverse is the case: our protagonist appeared to drift in and out of places, attachments, states of mind, occasionally allowing herself to be directed by sexual desire or an appetite for experiment, but largely content – or at least prepared – to let events unfold without her intervention.

Havilio uses a correspondingly blank, affectless prose style to describe his creation's progress, or lack of it, although it is also studded with fragments of imagery and curious juxtapositions, as with the toads and orgies above.

Its power is undeniable: we are gradually and stealthily drawn into this peculiar, disturbing story, intrigued by the narrator's inner and outer lives and wrong-footed by the parallels between the disjointed community she has found by chance and the wider world of the patients at Open Door who, as its name suggests, are free to come and go as they please. The novel's close – the apparent arrival of a UFO – is both determinedly odd and unusually cheerful: 'I feel happy' are its final words.

At the beginning of *Paradises*, it emerges that life has cohered, only to fall apart again. A few years have passed, and the narrator has built a relatively stable life with the farmer, Jaime, and their son, Simón. But Jaime is killed in a hit-and-run accident, and things begin to unravel; evicted from their farm, burdened with too many possessions to carry comfortably but too few to make a home, the narrator and Simón make their way to Buenos Aires. They have little money and fewer plans. Survival is, clearly, their first priority.

The landscape is demonstrably different – flooded streets through which pedestrians guide themselves by a rope, crowded bars and cheap hotels with communal kitchens – but it would be simplistic to see *Paradises* as the city sequel to *Open Door*'s rural beginnings. Both are about contingency, and about the connections between people, but they are also about boundaries: between stability and disintegration, the real and the imaginary, the sane and the insane. They probe the extent to which autonomy and independence are illusions. Despite its urban setting, which could conjure vastness and anonymity, *Paradises* is notable for its enclosures: el Buti, the squat in which the narrator and her son go to live, named for a young man who died resisting eviction; the zoo, and more specifically the reptile house, in which she goes to work; and the underground shelter in a palatial house.

This last is part of the family home of Axel, a quasi-boyfriend of Eloísa, the sexually uninhibited young woman from Open Door, who makes a characteristically dramatic reappearance in Buenos Aires. Once again the narrator is caught between resisting her attractions and being unable to, although she seems to have gained some perspective, remarking astutely that Eloísa is 'exhausted from always having to be the same. So theatrical. And yet again, as in the past, as with her adventures in the country, my attention is grabbed by that capacity of hers to re-emerge as though nothing has happened, burying everything, without blame or remorse, like an animal.'

Eloísa's oddness is not unrivalled, though: the reader is also presented with Tosca, a monstrous and mysterious woman who presides over el Buti and whom the narrator injects daily with morphine; with Canetti, the zoo's janitor, whose former life as a bank treasurer collapsed when he attempted to deceive his employers; and with Iris, a secretive Transylvanian woman stranded in Argentina after her boyfriend's departure. These are lives in the process of some kind of complicated collapse, or stalled and circumscribed – and they are the people to whom the narrator, once again despite any outward sign of volition, is drawn.

This, then, is hardly a paradise, and indeed the novel's title doesn't refer to an ideal or heavenly place, but rather to the paradise trees that fill the city and strew it with their 'poison beads', toxic little fruits that come in through the windows and for which the antidote is the bark of the same plant. 'The antidote alongside the poison, that sounds reasonable,' reflects the narrator, although it is also a problematic and confusing state of affairs, that the source of harm and its cure be found in such close proximity.

Those tensions and uncertainties are at the heart of *Paradises*, which sets the fugue-like state of its narrator against a phantasmagorical backdrop, one seething with snakes and monsters and terrors. Once again, Havilio asks us to suspend judgement on what is materially real and what is a projection of some variety of inner turmoil or distress; to consider whether desire can ever be straightforwardly itself or whether it is always the displacement of another, less approachable appetite; to ponder on what, ultimately, constitutes freedom. These existential questions, impossible to answer, find their unsettling expression in Havilio's shifting, undefinable exploration of alienation and its surprising consequences.

Alex Clark
London, March 2013

PARADISES

ONE

Jaime died at the start of spring. Someone who didn't see him, or who caught sight just too late to swerve and avoid him, ran him down as he was changing a tyre at the side of the road. From the skid marks, it was thought to have been a lorry, but it could have been a bus or one of those big four-by-fours. And he was left there, lying between the tarmac and the verge for several hours, until around midnight, when a family collecting cardboard to make a few pesos discovered him and notified the police. And even though I saw him in the coffin just the other day, I have a clear picture in my mind that he was found on his back, eyes wide open, looking more drunk than dead.

I didn't have to take care of anything. Héctor, Jaime's brother, dealt with it all. He went to the morgue to identify the body, dropped in to the police station, took care of all the formalities for the insurance, arranged the wake and transport of the body with the funeral parlour. All very swiftly, as if it had been planned. First, a policeman who had known Jaime since childhood notified Héctor, who in turn called me at dawn, the time of day when this type of news tends to arrive. It's terrible, he said, I can't believe it. I didn't know how to reply, having forgotten about the possibility of death. Not Jaime's death or mine, or that of anyone in particular, but Death as a whole. Hello, hello, Héctor repeated and then I let out a Yes, it's terrible, my eyes on Simón as he slept sprawled out in Jaime's place. Then I kept still, as still as a person can be, looking without seeing, at the furniture, the high ceiling, the spiderwebs, getting nowhere with the questions about life that were filling my head.

The night of the accident, it didn't strike me as strange that Jaime didn't come home to eat, but for the fact that he didn't let me know. Recently he had become addicted to his mobile phone; he used it all the time, under any pretext, to ask me whether I'd had lunch, pretending he'd forgotten something, to let me know a storm was approaching, always needlessly. In fact, on the phone he seemed like someone else – expressive, self-assured, almost a modern man. I went to bed convinced that inebriation had caught him early. An inoffensive habit that he indulged once or twice a week. At best, he would stagger home, his breath rancid, effing and blinding to no one in particular, and disappear into the woods to vomit. Other times, he would find some open piece of ground and lie back in the front seat of his pickup until he was less plastered. That's how he described it, plastered. Once, a breakdown truck had to drag him out of a ditch. I remember the expression on his face when he got out to open the gate, equal parts shame and mud. I also remember the breakdown guys brazenly making fun of the old man.

The wake started just after eight, the day after the accident. The funeral home was just a few blocks from the Basilica of Luján, three floors of granite facade with long balconies and tinted glass. At half seven a taxi ordered by Héctor came to get us. A white car, shining white, with black lights inside and a mini-bar that seemed nothing more than a prop, not at all like a funeral car. Five minutes into the journey, Simón was asleep. It wasn't surprising; he had skipped his siesta, running around all day with unusual energy. I made him comfortable on the seat, curled up with his head in my lap, and I abandoned myself to the scenery.

I had made this trip so many times with Jaime, coming and going, to the vet, to the shopping centre, to the railway station. The very road where the accident had taken place, more or less halfway between Open Door and Luján. By the Camel sign, Héctor had told me on the phone. And although I was looking carefully, forehead pinned to the glass, I couldn't see anything, no marks, no bloodstains, nor the pickup, which must have already been towed away. Too late: when we were almost on top of it, I recognised the giant, muscular camel posing with a cigarette in its mouth.

At some point in the journey, I wondered whether the taxi driver, a very young, dark-haired lad, knew about us, that we were in mourning, about the tragedy. Whether he knew he had gone to pick up the wife and child of someone who had just died, that this wasn't just any old trip. I'll never know; we didn't exchange a single word and the tuneful FM station he was playing at a very discreet volume allowed for either possibility.

We had to go round the houses to get there. A spring rock concert had been organised in front of the cathedral. The event was announced with overhead banners every two or three blocks: 21st September 5pm 21 Bands. We went round the perimeter of the plaza along side streets, held up in a bottleneck that was unusual for a place like this. The driver, one hand on the wheel, the other arm hanging out of the window, sighed several times in protest. The third time, he caught my eye in the rear-view mirror in search of complicity, a comment, or perhaps not, perhaps just apologising. I didn't know what to say so I ignored him and kept my eyes fixed on the cars around us. A twenty-minute delay. In the background, the high and low notes of guitars and basses competed with car horns.

At the door of the funeral parlour, I could make out Jaime's twin nephews from afar. Like two soldiers, more twin-like than ever, as if the occasion of their uncle's death had forced them to emphasise their natural similarity: both dressed in grey suits, almost certainly school uniform, the same hair and fringe, truly identical. I hadn't seen them for a long time, which must have been why they greeted me distantly, raising their hands rather than moving to kiss my cheek. Or perhaps because the situation made them uncomfortable and they hoped to go unnoticed. Too many changes of position forced Simón awake and there in front of them he opened his eyes, teary but not actually crying, looking for something around him.

That was when it first occurred to me that sooner or later I should try to find some way of telling him what had happened. I had spent the entire day attempting to organise a whole series of thoughts, past and future, relating to Jaime, to me, to the house, to life in Open Door and at no point had it entered my head that I needed to talk to Simón; the more distant and distracted he was the better. Now it was late, I had to surrender to what was coming, I would think about it tomorrow. Anyway, time and Jaime's absence would take care of explaining better than me.

After greeting the twins, I don't know why, perhaps intimidated by their rigid posture, I avoided the main door and entered through the garage. I moved forward with Simón in my arms, in near darkness, between a small ambulance, a quad bike and a barbecue that still contained ashes from lunchtime. Instead of retreating, which would have been the sensible thing to do, I grasped the handle of a panel door and surprised two girls painting their toenails in front of a giant television. Sorry, I began to say, and vaguely waved a finger in the air. Not so much unwilling as in a state of absolute sloth, one of the girls, shaven-headed and wearing a sleeveless top, stood on her heels and gestured to another door, next to a string of garlic bulbs hanging from a hook. Go through there and climb the stairs.

We enter another room, not as dark as the first but definitely much more frightening, with a row of coffins standing on end, leaning against the walls like resting totems. Show coffins, waiting for their time. I follow a light and we finally come out in the foyer of the funeral parlour. We appear at the foot of a wide staircase, once again face to face with the twins, who have abandoned the door and are now guarding their father, eyes swollen with exhaustion.

The sight of us unleashes Héctor's tears. Lots of tiny tears. He embraces me, I'd like to cry too but I can't. I'm sad, inside myself as well as by contagion, but more than that, I'm stunned. For the few seconds the embrace lasts I can smell a strong odour of mothballs. Images of Jaime and Héctor run through my head, not as I knew them, already old, but at the start of everything, when they were really brothers, five and seven years old, chasing each other, playing, fighting, the countryside always there in the background, snapshots of a childhood I imagine to have been happy.

Héctor dries his face with his cuff, recomposing himself quickly. He tells me that the wake will be on the second floor, that he's just come from the police station, that no witnesses have come forward as yet, other than the cardboard-collecting family who found him, and that the room will be ready in fifteen minutes. He provides this information without making eye contact. Héctor's wife, Marta, also takes part in this little conclave, and another man I've never seen before, white haired and smooth cheeked, who doesn't stop nodding. The man asks how it was, what happened, and Héctor goes over the little he knows out loud, as he will continue to do for the rest of the evening. He says that the man who ran him over didn't stop to help, that it's hard to believe he didn't see him, that he must have felt the impact, although perhaps he thought he had hit an animal. Marta sighs, silently indignant. He'll go on to tell how a lawyer approached him in the police station. An arsehole, Héctor calls him, who accompanied him to the scene of the accident to take photos before they took the pickup away. What we know for sure, he concludes, is that Jaime didn't put out the markers when he changed the tyre and that he was parked very close to the road.

The wait seems long, we're squeezed in under the landing. As people arrive, they look at me from a distance, measuring me up, observing Simón; they must know the story, they will have heard of us, of Jaime's new life. They'll know that in some way I was his wife for the last four years, that the child in my arms is our son. They don't approach, just in case. I think about Boca, the ranch hand and companion who spent so much time with Jaime. I say to myself that someone should have told him, I'm about to ask Héctor but I hold my tongue, he's already got enough on his plate.

A boy with a piggy nose announces that the room is ready. We climb the stairs in a slow procession. The layout and wallpaper make it feel like an old house. First, a room with mirrors positioned opposite each other, to multiply the number of people, to make you feel less alone. Before it was converted into what it is now, this must have been the living and dining room. A bit further along, on either side of a wide corridor, are the bathroom and kitchen. At the back, a closed door and the room where the coffin lies.

I let Héctor and the twins approach Jaime before me. The truth is I don't really know how to behave. I suppose I'm something like a widow and yet I'm not. When Héctor withdrew, I asked Marta to hold Simón so that I could go up. As I stepped forward, I realised I was less frightened by the idea of seeing Jaime dead than of seeing him disfigured. Héctor had given me no indication of the state in which the body had been found and I hadn't asked. I slowed down for the last few steps, so that I would see Jaime's body appear gradually and so lessen the shock. Not as pale as I would have expected, hands interlaced over his chest with a rosary between his fingers, jaw held up by a white handkerchief knotted round the neck, Jaime seemed, as they say, to be at peace. And for me, seeing him, no longer imagining him, had a calming effect.

I touch his forehead with the back of my hand, as if checking for fever, then his chest, and I rest my clenched fists on the cold handles of the coffin. After the initial shock, I take a step back, running my eyes over the objects decorating the room – the wreath of flowers, a standing crucifix, more flowers, in vases, bunches, some loose, two chairs made of dark wood – and I go back to observing Jaime, more carefully this time. Then I notice something perturbing.

In this new Jaime, the final Jaime, who I'll only see this once, in addition to his stillness, the smell of alcohol, or formaldehyde, I'm not sure, I suddenly discover an oddity that bears little relation to death. Instead of his lips being sealed, as was his habit, somewhere between resignation and embarrassment, I catch sight of a small opening at the right-hand corner of his mouth, a sarcastic, sly smile, as if death had caught Jaime mocking something.

I must have been standing alone by the coffin for five minutes. From what I heard in passing, Héctor had paid extra to have a slightly superior coffin to the standard model provided by the insurance. Polished and varnished, with a bronze-plated cross. Appealing to look at and to touch. Gradually, other people began to approach, relatives, friends of the family, all unknown to me. A tiny old lady with platinum hair and sagging cheeks, a younger woman of around fifty with acne pockmarks, and two very circumspect shaven-headed men. Whether deliberately or in imitation, the four of them positioned themselves on the other side of the coffin, leaving me without protection. For a while I could feel their eyes wandering from the dead man to fix on me out of poorly disguised curiosity.

Pushing my introspection to its limit, at some point I can't bear any more and raise my head suddenly, to greet, to make myself known, and I meet those four pairs of eyes directed at me, which look away slowly but simultaneously. I thought I felt marked out before, but this is worse. To my relief, a man in suit and tie appears and causes them to forget about me. At first he is disconcerting but he soon reveals himself to be part of the ceremony. He walks around the coffin, straightens a badly folded cloth, retreats a few steps, adjusts the stand where the wreath is and finally approaches the candelabras. He removes a spoon-like tool from his pocket and collects the wax accumulating at the base of each candle so that it doesn't spill. He does this with great care, taking pride in his work. I suppose a candle with spilled wax would give the wrong impression, somewhere between sloppiness and indifference.

I need air, so I disappear. To reach the street, I have to go via the first floor. Unlike Jaime's, which is more intimate, the wake on this floor is brimming. So much so that, timidly at first, gradually with more confidence, the attendees will invade our territory throughout the night, using the toilet, stealing chairs, helping themselves to coffee. They also take ownership of the staircase to sit and chat.

Out on the pavement, the night is lively. I notice many passers-by crossing the road a few metres before the funeral home. People prefer to avoid death. A blonde girl with no superstitions, ice cream in hand, comes towards me pushing a pram. She comes so close that I'm convinced she's going to speak to me, but no, she carries on unhurriedly. I sneak a glance into the pram: she's carrying supermarket bags. The fake baby reminds me of Simón, who I left in Marta's care. I go back inside and no one notices my distraction; they must think I went to the toilet to cry in private. Marta and Simón are in the kitchen making little boats and planes out of paper napkins. Thanks, I say, and she replies: He's an angel.

By one o'clock, there's hardly anyone left. Simón is sleeping on the floor like a puppy, between a couple of women wearing too much make-up. Marta approaches Héctor, who is sitting three chairs from me. The boys are hungry, she says. Héctor springs up: Let's go. And to me: Will you come for something to eat? First, he breaks away towards Jaime, takes a look at him and returns. I follow suit, without wanting to; I feel I've already said goodbye, but it's the done thing. He's the same as before, slightly less alive, with that stony smile that will stay with me for ever. At the very last second, there's time for a fleeting memory of that rough man I fell in love with unintentionally and with whom I fell out of love without realising it. I can still feel him jerking about on top of me, like an animal, impotent at times, insatiable at others. A memory that belongs to me and me only, I think as I turn my back and move away.

Héctor and Marta walk in single file to the stairs; one of the twins, I'll never be able to remember their names, turns his head before disappearing to check whether I'm following them, looking slightly put out, who knows why. I pick up Simón, who doesn't wake in spite of all the commotion, the conversations flying around him and the noise from the floor below, which by now sounds more like a party than a wake. On the way out, I discover a little pile of ashes and cigarette stubs, swept into a corner but not yet thrown out.

When we reach the street, Héctor gestures to say he's forgotten something. I'll just be a minute, he says, pushing back through the tinted glass door. As they wait, the twins start to argue. One wants a hamburger, the other pasta. Honestly, boys, Marta says indignantly. An ambulance identical to the one I saw in the garage arrives at full speed and brakes sharply in front of us. From the driver's side, a short man with a beard gets out, in a nurse's uniform, and runs into the funeral home. I wonder whether those girls are still painting their toe-nails. Héctor reappears and says in a low voice to Marta and me: I went to ask them to close the coffin so that he doesn't spend all night on show.

In a daze, or perhaps not, perhaps just to take our minds off things, Héctor chooses a pizzeria half a block from the basilica. It couldn't have been noisier. Stragglers from the rock festival move around us: gangs of boys and girls, singing, trucks with equipment, lots of mess. The next room has table tennis and pool tables. At the back, a row of bowling lanes separated from the dining room by a transparent screen that doesn't quite reach the roof.

Initially we sit there feeling rather uncomfortable. In fact, before we are served, Marta will suggest to Héctor more than once that we look for somewhere else. Yes, he'll say, I didn't realise but we're here now. Marta shakes her head but doesn't back down. She just protests: Honestly, Héctor.

As the minutes pass, it feels as though all the various sounds in the place are helping us fill the void. Random shouts of triumph; cursing; the sound of balls hitting the wooden floor and skittles toppling, sometimes all at once, sometimes out of time; the waiters' orders as they pass in front of the till with loaded trays, never stopping; and snippets of conversation from the tables around us.

Héctor and the twins devour the pizza without chewing, at record speed. Marta gestures with her hand for them to slow down, but they take no notice. I'm given two slices of napolitana and one of *fainá* flatbread. I eat with no appetite, out of habit. The pizza is topped with mashed hard-boiled egg, which makes it difficult to chew. More than once I have to hold down a retch.

Are you still hungry? Héctor asks, standing up. He goes out to smoke, the twins go to the toilet together and take half an hour to return. I'm left alone with Marta. She stretches out her arm and offers me her palm. I hesitate, I'm not in the mood, but it would be much more difficult to refuse, so I copy her movement and put my hand in hers, which she immediately covers with her free hand. It's as though we're going to make a promise to each other. She looks me in the eye silently and finally says: You have so much yet to live.

Héctor returns, orders another beer and we start chatting. In reality, they talk and I listen, occasionally emitting a Yes. The topic of conversation is roads, accidents, the brutality of lorry drivers and Jaime's carelessness. Why on earth did he stop there? protests Héctor. If he'd just pushed the truck a few metres further in, he'd still be with us. What a man, he keeps saying, and Marta pacifies him by squeezing his wrist. I come out in his defence: But he was always so careful. They look at me in unison, reprovingly, as if I spoke unknowingly, as if I'd never met the real Jaime, and once more I feel like a perfect intruder. Luckily, Simón wakes up and his ill humour makes us forget everything for a while.

In a daze, understanding little of anything, Simón puts pieces of pizza in his mouth and magically wakes up. More beer and Héctor starts ranting about the folk from the other wake. How disrespectful. Back and forth, making a terrible mess, as if they were at a football match. Marta says that everyone says goodbye to their loved ones as they see fit. The discussion grows heated, I follow fragments of it, busy ensuring that Simón doesn't stray too far. Not so much out of fear as to keep Marta quiet, because she keeps throwing out warnings: Oh, I'm terrified he's going to head over there, watch one of those balls doesn't escape, she says pointing at the pool tables.

On the return journey it wants to rain but doesn't. Just a few insignificant drops land on the umbrella, you could count them if you wanted. Not even a drizzle. Instead, the night is cooling quickly, winter's last effort. I sit behind the twins, who are entertaining themselves with a hand game. As soon as the car pulls out, Simón falls asleep for the third time since we left home. Neither Héctor nor Marta speaks to me for the entire journey. Nor do they say much to each other, just a few short phrases; they can't agree whether the boys should go to school the next day. Two or three times, Marta will point out the fuel needle, already in the red. There's more than enough, Héctor will reply.

We leave the Camel sign behind; no one says anything. As if we had come to a mutual agreement, out of respect for Jaime and for fate. We take the dirt track towards the farm in the deepest darkness. Several winds get up at once, whirling the air in all directions. The car's headlights form a long cone of light full of milling dust. I'm not wearing a jacket, nor is Simón; I never thought the cold would return.

When we finally arrive, Marta caresses my cheek over the back of the seat, one of the twins says Bye, the other stays silent. I carry Simón, who is lying almost crossways, like a pennant. I'm shivering. Héctor waits by the gate with his hand on the latch until we get out of the car. He hurries us a bit. It's ridiculous for him to drop us so far from the house, he doesn't even suggest the possibility of taking us right up. Nor does he justify himself. He doesn't want to come in, to see what his dead brother left, he prefers the distance. In a sense I understand him. With one foot in the car and the other on the ground, before he gets in and shuts the door, Héctor grabs me by the arm, drawing me towards him, and says, very close to my face, his breath smelling unmistakeably of pizza and beer: You have to be strong, things will sort themselves out, you'll see.

TWO

I had to imagine Jaime's burial. It rained all night and the taxi wasn't able to pick us up. Héctor phoned to let me know: The man says the road is impossible. Anyway, he added after a silence, a bit of interference or a drag on a cigarette: Why such a long send-off? Héctor sounded annoyed, angry, a far cry from the friendly, affectionate tone of the previous day. It must have been lack of sleep and the certainty that death, after the initial novelty, brought nothing but complications and desolation.

I imagined a small, hurried burial, the duty priest going through the motions of a quick prayer, not wanting to get wet. I imagined a sober tombstone, no epitaph. I imagined Jaime, his mouth stuck in that sarcastic smile for all eternity. I thought about all those things his eyes suggested when we were face to face, things that came out suddenly, all at once, not in words but in grunts or kicks, always clumsy. I also imagined that if he woke up, which they say happens once in a million burials, because he'd been taken for dead when he was just unconscious, Jaime wouldn't go crazy, beating the coffin lid for someone to open it. Instead, he would calmly consume the air he had left, guessing at the grain of the wood in the darkness.

Earlier, in the middle of the night, I had nightmares, shivers and something that felt like fever but wasn't. My stomach spasmed too, driving me blindly to the bathroom. I vomited three times in a row, everything I had eaten and more. Red, tomato-tinged vomit. As it was happening, I had the impossible feeling that I was bringing up small triangles, like mini portions of pizza that my intestines had taken the trouble to reshape before sending back to the surface.

Around midday, after spending all morning watching television – two news broadcasts, *El Zorro*, a cookery competition – I got out of bed when hunger started to make Simón grumpy. Aching bones, in my face and limbs, as if I had been stretched on the rack in my sleep. Leaving the room brought confirmation that it had been raining: pools of water in the corners and a small lake in the middle of the house. I put a pan of stew on to heat, left over in the fridge from two nights ago, Jaime's last supper, and I picked up a tea towel to mop the floor.

At the end of the winter, Jaime had experienced a surge of uncharacteristic enthusiasm, finally ready to devote himself to a bit of home maintenance. After a great struggle, he had managed to retire, and now that he had he felt diminished. Fed up of doing odd jobs in faraway houses, repairing roofs, stopping drips, unblocking drains, he never took the step of fixing the leaks in our own home, although they multiplied after every rainfall, especially above the fireplace. He limited himself to putting out tubs, buckets or rags in the corners to catch the water. Until one cold morning he took out the big stepladder, the one for important jobs, and started cleaning out the gutters. He took out the earth, the dry leaves, all the accumulated mulch, and the task clearly spurred him on because that same night he announced: I'm going to raise the roof.

First he spent some time studying how to do it, whether to replace the broken tiles, remove the rotten struts or change a central, worm-ridden joist. He decided to go for a mixed approach: one part of the house, the kitchen, the bedrooms and the bathroom, would keep its original roof, and he would put corrugated iron over the other part. That's what he said: I'll rip off all this shit and put down corrugated iron. The job was half done: he had replaced the broken tiles with new ones and raised the roof, which he had covered with plastic sheeting, but the corrugated iron never arrived. On the night of the accident he was on his way to or back from buying it, I'll never know which.

Clutching the tea towel, I stood distractedly for a while, my eyes fixed on that provisional, half-naked roof. When I had finished with the cloth, I leant into the bedroom to tell Simón the food was ready. I sat down and once again fixated on all the ornaments, lamps and old-fashioned junk that perhaps the time had come to start recycling. I realised that, somehow, this house belonged to me now, or at least it had ended up in my charge.

I pondered all this as Simón ate, playing at trying to squeeze his tiny elbows through the tines of the fork. I raised my eyes and fixed them on that plate hanging on the wall, with a blue border depicting a hunting scene.

A plate Jaime had rescued not long ago, a reminder of his mother or grandmother that he had hung next to the window, the only decorative gesture I'd ever known him to make. In the middle, it read in cursive, sprawling writing:

> *Make a bigger door, Pa,*
> *For I no longer fit,*
> *You built it for the children;*
> *I've grown, to my regret.*

I realised that Simón was staring at me as intently as I was at the plate. The spoon, suspended dripping in the air, demanded my attention. When our eyes met, he smiled. An ambiguous smile, ironic yet kind, testing me, an adult smile, lips nearly sealed, identical to Jaime's smirk in the coffin. I was about to say something to him, in fact I mentally rehearsed several phrases, but I failed in the attempt and kept quiet.

We had lived in this house for the last four years, moving less and less, going out only when necessary. No sudden shocks, obligations or big adventures. In fact, we had formed something that wasn't far off a family. A family that was harmonious in its own way. We shared breakfasts, lunches and dinners. A frictionless family, each of us in our own little world. Now things had to change and my role was still to be determined.

We went out to the veranda. Simón started playing with some broken tiles, while I moved a few metres away from the house, my espadrilles sinking into the mud. I thought about the roof again. Corrugated iron, I thought, and said out loud: Corrugated iron. I couldn't think of anyone who might take care of it. I remembered an old tarpaulin folded up under the mill. I set myself a challenge.

Manoeuvring the roll of canvas wasn't easy. I dragged it as if it were a corpse, pulling it by the feet. Unbelievably, it was just about the right size. I climbed the ladder and lifted it, secured by a rope. I stretched out the plastic Jaime had put down and spread the canvas on top, nice and tight, pinning it in place at the edges with branches and stones, along the line of the crossbeams. I was exhausted and sweating heavily, a smell of burnt caramel rising from my armpits. It wasn't the ideal solution but it would buy us some time.

The first week passed as if Jaime was still there. Prowling. Leaving at dawn and returning when we were already in bed. His presence was evident in every corner. In the dirty boots at the foot of the bed, in his clothes hanging in the wardrobe, in the shovel and the rake, covered in soil and dried grass. In the smells, too, in the room, the bed, the shed, the constant sweat, the dampness of the walls and that spicy tang impregnated in the sheets, which wasn't exactly Jaime but which I always associated with him.

Naturally, Simón came to sleep with me, usurping the side made free by Jaime. The cot, which was actually getting too small for him, started to fill up with clothes, boxes and papers. Simón didn't seem particularly bothered by his father's absence. He didn't look sad or quiet. Quite the opposite in fact; shedding his usual calm demeanour, he developed a series of skills, as if he were undergoing a sudden growth spurt: the tricycle he had previously used as a handcart or a seat from which to contemplate the horizon was now used for getting around. He was so excited by this novelty that he didn't stop cycling back and forth from one end of the veranda to the other, pedalling as if possessed. Only once did he ask for Jaime, and after pausing for a long time to find a gentle but effective formula, I ended up saying: He had an accident, I don't think he'll be coming back. That's how I put it: I don't think. Simón listened to me with his brows furrowed, he stayed silent, sighed deeply as if commenting on the situation like an old village gossip, then returned to his pedalling. And that was it.

I, on the other hand, began to feel his absence more keenly as the days passed. I needed his hands to yank the water pump, to battle the rats and also, although he had barely done so recently, to touch me. It had been a long year since we had last made love, not even caresses; physical contact had been reduced to accidental brushes in bed, in the bathroom, going through a door. Now that he wasn't here, it gripped me like a new kind of fever. A heat I could only calm with a lot of masturbation, every night, two or three times. Almost always thinking about the last Jaime, the one in the coffin; other times it was abstractions that turned me on in the darkness. Nervous rubbing, full of fury. Then it passed and I forgot about sex again, as before.

Without the pickup, we were more isolated than ever. Twice in one month we walked into Open Door, loaded up a taxi at the supermarket and came home. We hardly had any neighbours left. The few remaining shacks had disappeared the previous summer. Eloísa's house too, the store-shed and the shop. We had witnessed machines razing the lot. I'd stopped seeing Eloísa before the demolitions. She'd moved to the capital and very occasionally came back to visit her parents. Only once did she approach the gate, and we had a short, awkward conversation, which Simón took it upon himself to interrupt with a tantrum. She hated Jaime, the baby; she liked me but not my life.

It was said that the Dutch people who had bought the club with the polo fields and stables were offering a lot of money for the surrounding land. The idea was to put together an immense country club with a golf course in the middle, right where we were. Everything together in one single complex, almost as big as the adjoining psychiatric hospital, but not quite. Jaime had laughed when he remarked on it: They're going to end up throwing the loonies out in the dirt. But he never said anything about selling the farm, didn't even mention it, he seemed determined to resist.

Six weeks after the burial, just when I was starting to wonder how long I could take care of the house alone, lacking the will to cut the grass, with the scrub growing and advancing, but above all unable to imagine a way to make money to pay the bills, a very tall man appeared, claiming to be a representative of the firm. He dragged us from sleep one heavy morning, the sky covered in storm clouds. Beeping his horn. First it woke Simón, who began to whimper and kick me. I opened the shutters slightly and peered through the slits, taking care not to be seen. On the far side of the gate, perpendicular to the track, a red car was parked. I spent a while trying to guess who it could be, I didn't recognise the car or the man standing next to it, and all the hypotheses that occurred to me were discouraging. I left it for a while in the hope that he would get tired and go away. But the guy seemed determined, or else he knew we were there, because he persisted, blasting the horn ceaselessly. I got dressed in the first thing I found, a raincoat of Jaime's, and went outside with Simón protesting in my arms. Inevitably, I kept guessing all the way to the gate. The man, sunglasses, lots of grey hair, formal but clearly a country type, reached into the car to take out a briefcase when he saw me approach. We made our greetings across the wire fence, not touching, with a nod of the head. Sorry to call so early, but I had to catch you at home, that was how he began. Then he shot out: Do you know who owns this land? Satisfied by my silence, the man started talking again: That was what we assumed, you have no idea about anything, do you? So much the better, why would you want to complicate things with other people's stories, he said and handed me his card: *Agent*. While the man flicked through a sheaf of papers in the briefcase he had opened on the bonnet, I wondered what those stories might be and who these other people were. This is what it's all about, he said, proffering a printed sheet that I took a few seconds to accept from him, Simón's weight making it impossible for me to move my arm.

I tilt my neck to read the heading: *Eviction Agreement*. I raise my eyes in search of answers and the man rotates his finger for me to keep reading. I scan the text from top to bottom, right to left, and random words leap out at me: *OPEN DOOR, The Occupier, The Owner, Camino de la Legua, cancellation, debt, reinstate, farm, single instalment*. Several spelling or typing errors also catch my eye: *peanal* for penal, *retension* for retention, *divergense* for divergence. The man is clearly impatient because he takes the sheet from my hands and puts on a pair of magnetic self-assembling glasses: It says here thirty days, but we can talk about that, it could be forty-five, even sixty, and in respect of the rent owed, taxes, rates, etcetera, you'll see that we're offering you total debt relief. Look, he said, I suggest you get this sorted quickly, I'm saying that from my heart. It's best for you; sign on time and don't complicate things. If you make a decision, then we'll get the parties together and talk money. I can assure you they'll offer you a tidy sum. I thought about saying: There must be some mix-up, or even, Are you sure it's this land, this house? I thought that someone else in my place would have told him where to go, would have screwed up the paper and thrown it in his face. Before taking his leave, he suddenly became very familiar with me, saying in a low voice, as if someone could hear us in the middle of the countryside: A word of friendly advice, think of something that makes you happy – here's the means to do it. The guy got into the car, reversed and drove off, raising a cloud of dust.

That night, after giving the matter a lot of thought, I called Jaime's brother. I told him about the agent, the eviction agreement, I mentioned the money. He wasn't surprised. He sighed heavily. I warned him about this, he said, and launched into a monologue that sounded overacted to me, full of clichés and formulas that gave me the feeling that it was directed not just at me but also at whoever was standing near him: That's life, sometimes nothing, then everything happens at once. It's the same old rotten story, I wouldn't get involved if I were you, and another thing, sooner or later they'll make you crack. A pause and he continues: Things aren't going that well for us either, it's an uphill struggle. What do you want me to tell you? that's what he says and I stay silent, with a But on my lips and the telephone in my hand. It was the last I heard of Héctor.

Several days passed with no sign of the agent and I began to think they'd been mistaken or moved to pity. Perhaps it was just to size me up, a test. Of course they'd found out about Jaime's death and believed they could catch me with my guard down, an estate agent's strategy. But no, the man returned during the week with two blond men, I could have sworn they were father and son. These gentlemen have to take some measurements, said the tall man, and I opened the gate in no mood to resist. The agent settled himself in the kitchen. As he spoke, I could see the other two entering and exiting my field of vision through the window. They took photos and notes, they joked. Have you given it any thought? I shrug. He writes on a bar napkin that he removes from his trouser pocket and shows me: *5,000*. How about that? He raises his eyebrows and on top of the five he now firmly marks a six. I don't know what to say. The blond guys enter and the man scrunches up the paper and hides it in his clenched fist.

The agent almost lost his composure, his eyes narrowed with childlike annoyance and he was, it seemed to me, on the verge of hitting the table. But he contained the violence with three short breaths and a thought seemed to strike him. He switched tension for threat. I'll leave you my number, think about it, look, time's running out and later on things may take a slightly more, let's say, drastic course. Take it as a piece of friendly advice. He insisted on being my friend.

After that second visit, things started to precipitate, by coincidence or necessity. An accumulation of episodes that weren't so much serious as significant ended up driving us out. First it was the water pump, which I forgot to turn off, causing it to burst and spark. From that point on, I had to go back and forth to the stream or the pond filling buckets. And then water complicated our lives in another way, this time from above. A strong wind, the kind they call gale force on the radio, made the canvas and plastic take flight as if they were paper. The following morning we woke up to a space of open sky in the middle of the house, between the bedroom, bathroom and kitchen, a patio complete with armchair and fireplace. I no longer had the strength to climb a ladder in search of a solution. To tell the truth, the thought didn't even cross my mind. For a few weeks, the final weeks, we shut ourselves in the bedroom, sleeping, eating, watching television. I only crossed the strange furnished garden to go for a pee or to boil some noodles in the kitchen.

Ultimately, it was the dogs. Packs of hounds we heard at night-time that brought us close to terror. Unhinged, barking and getting into interminable fights. They were nothing like those more or less inoffensive prowling dogs to which we occasionally threw scraps, bones or rice. This was something else, wolf howls that kept us from sleep.

Without a phone, which had been cut off by a fallen pole or lack of payment, I never knew which, the biggest effort was gathering the momentum to call the agent. One horrible morning, when everything seemed to be falling irreversibly apart, I got myself together and we went to the entrance to the hospital, where I remembered there being a phone box. Half an hour's walk, only part of which Simón did on foot. He travelled on my shoulders for the longest stretch. The booth was there, but not the phone. It was removed a while ago, one of the guards informed me. And he risked adding: Nowadays no one uses public phones, what with mobiles and everything. He also pointed out a phone box at the service station.

The agent's voice sounded like someone shouting from one riverbank to another. Hello, hello, I hear in the distance. I leave it a few minutes, assuming that he's busy or unable to speak, and I dial again. Ah, it's you, he says. Yes, yes, good, you're doing the right thing calling me, he continues, and adds: The thing is that it's a bit late now, I did warn you. I wanted to interrupt but the guy was in full flow: I made it quite clear, these people don't mess around, it's just like I told you. A pause, a bit of interference and he continues: All the same, I'll see what I can do. Shall I arrange a hired van for you? What for, I manage to ask. For the move. No, no, I say, nothing in the house is mine. It's just the two of us and a couple of bags. A taxi, then. What day is it today, he asks and answers himself: Tuesday the thirteenth, well, it would be within a fortnight. I'll be calling you, but I have to go now, he says and leaves me thinking about Tuesday the thirteenth, I would never have known.

The eviction order arrived, but there was no eviction. Very early on 30th November, a white car was waiting for us on the other side of the gate, very similar to the one that had taken us to Jaime's wake. Guarding it on either side, in a V formation, there were two other cars, the agent's and a four-by-four. When everything is stowed in the boot of the taxi, the tall man approaches me, leans down and says softly: It's a shame things had to be this way. I did my part, he says, and puts an envelope in my hand: Don't mention this to anyone, take it as a gift. On the way to Luján, I tear open the envelope and count 1,500 pesos. Enough to survive for a month or two.

THREE

We arrived in the city along with the floods. We got out in Pacífico at around midday. A short while earlier, we had heard the barrage of hail on the roof of the bus and the complete darkness passing by the window. In fact, it was only me who heard it, as Simón was still sleeping unawares. The deluge must have lasted half an hour, long enough to turn avenues into rivers and streets into streams. We got out at a bus stop in the centre of a labyrinth of cars pointing in all directions. Car horns managed to do what the hail hadn't: they woke Simón, who opened his eyes in the midst of all the chaos but didn't cry; the noise was bigger than him, as was the atmosphere of uncertainty. We walked a few blocks along the middle of the street, the only island of tarmac in the stream of waves lapping over the drains. To cross the road we followed a line of people guided by a rope tied from one pavement to the other. Further along, some men in fluorescent jackets were using a boat to rescue an elderly lady and her dog.

Without much choice in the matter, we took refuge in a bar crammed full of people. Squeezed in at the

counter, we shared a ham and cheese sandwich and a
7UP. As Simón chewed, he swivelled his gaze from side
to side like a mechanical doll, from the madness in the
street to a giant television screen replaying footage of
the old lady navigating between cars with her dog. He
observed the panorama without astonishment, the way
you accept dreams.

We must have stayed there a good hour, until the
situation outside seemed to calm down slightly. We
moved away from that rehearsal of apocalypse, hugging
the side of a walled enclosure that hid the gardens of an
endless building. Two blocks further on, water up to our
ankles, we came across a hotel. With no time to hesitate,
I rang the bell. But the Hotel Lyon, as it was called, didn't
allow children or pets. We were attended by a woman in
a hairnet, her legs swollen with fat varicose veins, who
was quite friendly despite the restrictions. As she spoke,
she was holding her sandals in one hand and a hairdryer
in the other. You've got another one on the far side of
the avenue. It's not that expensive and it isn't bad either,
she said. What I can't tell you is whether they'll have
room. She saw us off, raising the hairdryer as if it were
an extension of her arm.

I walked a few blocks along the pavement with Simón
in my arms and the bag over my shoulder, my trousers
quickly succumbing to the soaking. It was quite an effort
to find the Hotel Fénix, in fact I walked past it twice
without realising. It was a three-storey house, the front
covered in graffiti, slogans and remnants of posters. The
name was etched on a bronze plaque, the kind used by
dentists and notaries in small towns.

Another bell, another woman opens the door to us, wringing out water. But this one is smoking. She has a wrinkled face and a button nose, and she looks us up and down distrustfully. I ask for a room. I've only got one left, without bathroom, she says in a very marked Spanish accent, the kind you hear in films, and adds: Payment up-front. She lets us in. We follow her down a long, dark corridor that leads out to a flooded courtyard. Barred windows, lumpy walls and a statue of the Virgin Mary built into an artificial cave. In the centre, there's a cement drum, a cistern that's half buried or was never finished. All around, ferns. Hanging, on the tables, in pots, climbing the cables. The place is reasonably well cared for and yet exudes a feeling of irredeemable sadness. The woman disappears and returns shortly with a bunch of keys. She shows us our room, long and narrow like a coach: two beds, a bedside table in between and a wooden wardrobe that takes up half the space. Here's the kitchen, she signals to me and explains: You use it, you wash up and you clean it. To get to the bathroom you have to cross the courtyard, she tells me. We're used to that, the last month at Jaime's was the same. She raises her chin to ask whether I like it, whether we'll stay. It's fine, I say, and pay for a week. I feel extremely relieved.

The room has a window that takes some effort to open, with its old, iron latticework. When I finally manage, it isn't really worth it – more floods and flowerpots. In addition to the ferns, I discover a bed of thistles.

No sooner have we arrived than we meet the first challenge. In a moment of distraction, Simón, who hasn't lost that intrepid attitude he's adopted since Jaime's death, climbs up onto the fake cistern and jumps. The Spaniard, which as I'll discover later is what everyone calls her, sticks her head out of a window identical to ours on the other side of the courtyard and gives two violent tsks, as if shooing away a cat. Simón pays no attention and the woman seeks me out with her gaze and purses her lips, reproaching my lack of care. Get out of there, I say, and Simón does as I tell him.

In the afternoon, as the water level drops, but with the flood still making itself felt in the whirr of sirens and the traffic jam in the background, we go for a stroll around the neighbourhood. The hotel is on a street with no traffic lights, which is impossible to cross because of the speed of the passing cars. On the same block as the Fénix there is a row of old town houses, small mansions from another era, some of them camouflaging their abandonment behind clusters of bougainvillea and climbing figs that don't understand the concept of dividing walls, others laying bare their decay. Opposite, across the lanes of traffic, a construction site split by two jibs pointing in opposite directions. At the foot of the embankment, a few shacks are holding their ground: corrugated-iron roofs, walls made of canvas and cardboard. Without crossing the street, there's also a mechanic's workshop, a warehouse and, half a block down, in premises that still have a sign saying *Grills to Go*, an Evangelical temple.

CHURCH OF THE KING OF KINGS
The Helmet of Salvation

I take a flyer without stopping. Meeting timetable: Tuesday, Thursday and Friday, from 5pm to 9pm. Wednesdays, 9.30am: path to the sacrament of confirmation. On the way back to the hotel, we stop at a kiosk. Actually, it's Simón who stops, captivated by a window at ground level, his eyes glued to a plastic cat on a motorbike complete with sidecar, somewhere between a piece of junk and an antique. I decide that all this upheaval deserves some kind of reward, so I knock on the window and a man with nicotine-stained teeth and several days' growth of white stubble pulls back the window reluctantly. A cold, dry wind hits my face; the man prefers his air conditioning to making contact with the outside world. How much is it? I ask, pointing at the cat. The old man deflects my question with his eyebrows, as if I had said something absurd. I insist: The price. He still doesn't respond, he shuts himself back into his winter, examines the toy all over in search of a label and shakes his head. He opens the window again. I don't know, and he says to Simón: Do you like it? Simón grabs on to my leg, embarrassed, but still nodding firmly and clearly to say yes. Take it, the man says to me, give me whatever you think, and he extends his trembling arm with the motorcyclist cat, which could end up on the floor at any moment. For that reason, to prevent it from falling, even though I'm not sure about having to decide the price myself, I take it. From my pocket, I remove a five-peso note, screwed into a ball, reshape it and venture: Is that all right? From the expression on his face, it would appear the old man had something else in mind; to make up for it, I buy a packet of coconut biscuits. Back at the hotel, I throw myself face-down on the bed. Almost a siesta. Simón entertains himself playing with the motorcycling cat, along my legs, my back, my head, as if they were mountain paths. My body feels large, aching and damp, nails scratching at my skin, my neck stiff, my arse wet. I stay like that for a good while, abandoned, until Simón falls asleep at my feet. I turn over and prolong the lethargy imagining countries in the cracks on the ceiling.

It's still daylight when I go out into the courtyard. The kitchen clock is showing half eight. At first glance: pots, pans and dishes hanging up and a series of pizza trays and cake tins balanced on a low unit with a worktop and loose doors. In the fridge, everything is identified with tape, names written in thick marker pen, coloured plastic containers. Matilde, it says on a pat of butter, some eggs and a plastic bag containing minced meat or lentils, something dark and small. There's also a packet of gnocchi, a sachet of tomato sauce and a bottle of tonic water labelled Raúl. The red containers have a '2' or a 'z' in black on the front and on the lid. The doors of the cupboard are covered with mosquito nets, like in the country. There's enough food to cope with a siege: lots of packets of noodles, polenta and flour, several piles of tins.

Halfway through my inspection a man walks in – he is heavyset and stooped, not from age but from chronic bad posture, perhaps a labourer or docker – and greets me with a polite and friendly hello. He opens the fridge, takes out a bottle of tonic water and I realise that he is Raúl, unless someone else shares his things. I sit down at the table and think about some food for the evening. Voices, growing as they approach and weakening as they move away, and a baby's cries create a din I'm unaccustomed to. Everything went so fast, when barely anything happened for so long.

Suddenly, the Spaniard's voice erupts like a whirlwind: The little boy's crying, she says in a reproachful tone as if I had hidden something from her when I arrived. I hold my hands out in front of me, excusing myself, get up and walk the ten steps separating me from the courtyard where Simón is, barefoot, with a dizzy expression. I walk over to him, hug him and realise the woman has followed me and is now observing me from the door, contorting her mouth, eyes like eggs, waiting for an explanation I'm not about to give. It's all fine, I say in Simón's ear. In the room I ask him whether he had a bad dream. He shakes his head. Pee, he says, and it doesn't take me long to realise that his trousers and back are wet with urine. After changing him, we stay in the room for a long time, me, stroking his back, him, gradually calming down after his fright. I wonder whether he's got it into his head I might abandon him.

Later, in the kitchen, as I'm preparing some rice I brought from the house, I meet a Romanian woman of around my age, with very blue, alarmed-looking eyes, a broad back, from rowing or swimming, a violently uneven fringe. Initially she doesn't speak, she does everything stealthily, ignoring me, unfriendly, or maybe just shy. She lights a ring on the hob, fills a pan with water and leaves.

When she reappears, I tell her I lowered the heat because the water was boiling. Ah, she says, and throws in the two sausages remaining in the pack. She looks at me suspiciously, side-on, almost with contempt, wrinkling her nostrils as if I smell bad or she's about to attack me. She gives the impression she doesn't want anything to do with anyone. Just in case, I venture no further than hello. In a while, it's she who looks for an excuse to move closer and strike up a conversation. Have you got the time? is the first thing she asks. I'm about to guess at nine o'clock, but I raise my eyes and gesture at the clock over the fridge: quarter to ten. And then: Mayonnaise? I don't have any, I apologise with a tight smile. We only arrived a few hours ago. Where from, she wants to know. The country, I say, and she nods mutely, several times, as if the word country inspired respect or solved some mystery. And you, I ask. She says she's from a small village. Transylvania, her voice darkens, she grits her teeth, pulling a monster face, suddenly funny. Returning to her own voice, she tells me that it must be two years already since she arrived in this country. It's good here, she concludes with a shrug. She asks me whether I work, I tell her not yet, that I'm going to start looking. She stays quiet, her mouth slightly open, as if about to blow out a candle, which only reinforces that air of permanent surprise in her eyes, somewhere between fright and fascination. She says she spent about a year selling coffee on the street from a little cart that she still has in her room – they never came to claim it back. And she can't remember the location of the warehouse to return it herself. She explains how the business works, she talks about rents and percentages. Because she struggled with the language at first, she operated with gestures and photos stuck to the cart: coffee, croissants, sandwiches, even soup. It's good work, she says. No boss and out in the fresh air.

We eat our rice. She munches standing up, with a sour expression, eyes on the pan. I invite her to sit at the table. She doesn't hesitate. She pricks her remaining sausage with a fork and approaches. She tells me her story in snippets, getting tied in knots by her tongue and the past. Her mother died in childbirth, or shortly after she was born, I'm not sure which, her father left her in her grandmother's care until the age of twelve, after which he took her to live with him in Bucharest. At school she met Draco, her boyfriend, who convinced her to come here. They lived in guesthouses for a year. In several neighbourhoods, she says. He got involved in a business with an uncle who already lived in Buenos Aires, importing tyres from India, but it failed, they never got the money, and she had to work the taxi ranks with her cart. Yuri, Draco's uncle, lives with his wife in a hotel full of transvestites in Constitución, she says, and purses all her features as if there were a rotten smell. At the racecourse, Draco met a guy who tricked him into buying half a horse that didn't exist. Very bad, she says. They split up. He decided to go to the south to try his luck: He likes mountains. She preferred to stay: I was already too cold.

And now I'm here, she says. In June she managed to get a visa with a work permit and started working at the zoo. Thinking that she's got the wrong word, I make her repeat it twice. She insists and explains: In the subtropical rainforest. I smile, laughing at the joke, but she looks at me seriously, almost offended, it's no joke. She tries to explain what it's all about but it gets complicated. I understand that it's something along the lines of a roofed jungle with tropical plants, hanging bridges, some real animals, tarantulas and snakes behind glass, and others fake. Fake? Yes, made of rubber. She works on the door, checking tickets, she says it's good work, although she doesn't earn much. She says it with an expression of disgust. Because of the animals, because of the money.

She suddenly falls silent and turns her head to one side, avoiding my eye, as if she had spoken against her will. My plate is still almost full; I quickly swallow three spoonfuls to meet the requirements of nourishment. She stands up, lights the hob again and puts on a kettle full of water. Now she faces away from me, turns on the tap and rinses the fork and the pan she used to boil the sausages. What did I do in the country? I took care of horses, I say. For a while, neither of us utters another word, all that can be heard is the crackle of the flames under the kettle, the stream of running water, my jaws grinding a biscuit and the collisions Simón causes with his little cars at the other end of the kitchen. Before we say goodbye, the girl speaks again to tell me her name: I'm Iris.

In the dark, in this strange, damp bed, I spend several hours trying to find a position that will allow me to sleep. In my half-awake state, I can't help thinking about the house in Open Door, which I imagine covered in water. Submerged, or floating away. I also think about Jaime, who must be freezing his arse off underground.

FOUR

Three days later I'm at the entrance to the zoo asking for the office and a girl dressed as an explorer points out a row of windows. Iris and Simón wait outside. I walk up, only to be sent in another direction: Human resources is the second door. I knock. A boy with freckles appears and tells me I have to go to the website and upload my CV. That's what he says, your CV. Without really saying goodbye, he sees me off with a quick smile as he glances back into his office, beyond my line of vision. He gives the impression that something's burning.

On the way out, a cross between Charlie Chaplin and a mime artist insists on giving Simón a balloon. Iris moves away, she doesn't want to get involved. Assuming that he doesn't talk, I explain with gestures that I have no money and he, exaggerating a tic at the corner of his mouth, and also in his eye, which keeps winking as if there's a fly in it, says that it doesn't matter. Thanks, I say, silently looking at the strongly outlined eyes. I can't work out whether it's a man or a woman. Iris becomes serious, frowning, and wants to know how I got on. I tell her what they told me and she touches her forehead. Ah, yes, she says, apologising for not having remembered. We say goodbye, she goes into work, we don't really know where to go.

We make a bad job of crossing the road, too far from the pedestrian crossing, and walk into a fenced-off plaza of red stone chippings and squat bushes. I sit down on a stone bench. Nearby, two teenagers are kissing like amoebas. He is leaning over, embracing her, simultaneously taking care not to spill a tall bottle of Coca-Cola. Laughter and more kisses. Opposite, on either side, all around, is a vast scale model of the city. This landscape that is still incredible to me. I struggle to conceive of so many people, so many cars, so much everything. And yet, quickly, very quickly, I allow myself to surrender to the evidence.

Now, in front of me, a sequence of events brings me back to earth: Simón, running with the balloon, lets go of it and, wanting to get it back, trips and falls flat on his face in the shards of stone. First he looks at me, then he cries. I don't go to his aid. He stands up by himself and comes towards me covered entirely in orange. He touches his knee, it hurts. A long scratch, superficial but long. The kind that looks impressive. And it's impossible to tell where it ends because the red of the skinned knee mingles with the colour of the clay. I spit on my palm and pass it over the wound. Ow, ow, he jumps, it stings. It's nothing, I say, and he curls up at my feet drawing in his legs like a wet dog.

At the bottom of the sky, or what appears to be the bottom of the sky, two flat, thin clouds are racing like greyhounds. The one on top is a few body-lengths ahead of the other, which is advancing fast and, because of the madness of the winds, in less than a minute gathers enough speed to overtake. I straighten my neck and am met with the figure of a horseman on a pedestal in the centre of the plaza. Hat and sword, galloping, a hero's pose. But who? Belgrano, Urquiza, Güemes, San Martín run through my head, but no, this man doesn't fit with any of the Argentinian greats of my memory, this one definitely escapes me. Impelled by intrigue, I walk the ten steps to a plaque that will enlighten me: Giuseppe Garibaldi (1807–1882). Another inscription engraved on bronze helps me picture him better:

COMBATTEREMO PER L'INDEPENDENZA,
LA PACE E LA LIBERTÀ DEI POPOLI.

Simón forgets his injury and is now entertaining himself throwing stones at the pigeons. From despair to euphoria, with nothing in between. A plaza warden, sitting on a plastic stool next to her cabin, watches us but can't decide whether to intervene. Perhaps she's tired and hopes I'll do something instead of her. I don't see the danger: the pigeons take flight and save themselves, the projectiles are landing a long way from anyone else. In the distance, the statue gives such a sense of propulsion that it seems about to gallop off into the air at any moment. Hard and flying. A song enters my head, first as a hum, then with lyrics and everything, I have no idea where it comes from.

> *Who ever said Garibaldi was dead?*
> *Poom Garibaldi Poom Garibaldi*
> *Who ever said Garibaldi was dead?*
> *Poom Garibaldi ha ha ha*

On the way back to the guesthouse we stop at an internet cafe with swing doors like a saloon from a cowboy film. The boy behind the counter, a chubby lad who looks like he's never seen the sun, is speaking into a mobile phone and doesn't raise his eyes immediately. Computer? Yes, I say, and he points at the first one against the window. But I don't move, I need something else, he realises this and hangs up ill-humouredly. I have to do a CV, I say. He bites his lips, not concealing his annoyance, but his altruistic side wins over. You have to pay for CVs, he says, remember that for next time. I'll give you one I did for a girl yesterday, use it as a template and change the details. I thank him with my best smile. With a magician's touch, the boy moves his fingers over the keyboard, he opens and closes screens and programs, he mutters, in a trance, until he suddenly interrupts himself. That's it, now you can enter what you want. Before turning my full attention to the computer, I pause and follow the retreating footsteps of this fat boy in his Anthrax World Tour T-shirt. I manage to read: Melbourne, Liverpool, Dublin, Barcelona. And Simón? Hidden beneath one of the tables, curled into a ball.

The CV belongs to a Nora, ten years younger than me. She has worked as an assistant in various clothes shops, in a supermarket, also as a waitress in El Caracol and as a publicist for Océano publishing house. Her hobbeys, that's how she spells it: dancing and running. I start with the easy part. I replace Nora's forename and surname with my own, as well as my ID number and date of birth. I put Iris's telephone number, which I have written on a piece of paper, and the address of the Fénix. University studies, incomplete, computing and languages, blank. Under work experience I leave the bit about Océano publishing, it sounds good and seems unverifiable. There's a spell of around three or four years when I did nothing, I didn't work, study or anything. I invent a rural veterinary hospital in Open Door and give myself the position of assistant for a year and five months.

When I'm almost done, I shake the mouse but the arrow stays still. I ask the chubby boy, who comes back around the counter again. If I may, he says, then types and types but nothing happens. It's crashed, he tells me, you opened too many windows at once. They opened themselves, I defend myself, and he looks like he doesn't believe me. And because Simón is impatient, but mainly because the idea of starting from scratch drives me mad, I give up. I'll come back later, I say out loud. Ok, he says, I'll try and save it. We eat on the street on the way back to the guesthouse, pork in bread rolls sold to us by a woman sweaty from the grill of her tiny stall under the bridge. Going through my head for the rest of the day: Garibaldi poom, Garibaldi poom.

In the evening, Iris forces me out again. She says I have to hurry and send my CV because there are public holidays coming up that will complicate things. Because Simón is sleeping, she'll wait for me in the courtyard in case he wakes. I retrace that morning's steps and reach the cyber cafe. The entrance is now lit by a neon arrow. I'm served by the same boy in the same T-shirt, but he doesn't recognise me, I have to remind him. The CV, I say. Ah, yes, I managed to save it but I don't have any machines free up here, I'll send you down to number thirty-three. So I go downstairs, where a never-ending basement opens out with fifty-odd compartments separated by curtains. I get settled and in the centre of the screen an icon called CV is flashing. Magic.

After a while I realise that I'm caught in crossfire. They're playing to the death. Initially it sounds as though there are two of them, one on either side of me, but as the minutes pass, the war cries multiply. Occasionally, because they're wearing earphones, someone will let out an ill-tempered, uncontrolled cry, which makes me shudder. What are you doing, you bastard, you shot me in the back. Stick your machine gun up your arse, dickhead. I go to the zoo's website and have to upload my CV three times before it's accepted. I don't want to go back too soon, so I start browsing. I scroll through an online newspaper. I find out about the death of a singer I've never heard of, goals, a multiple collision on the coast road and an archaeological discovery in Palestine that could change the history of Christianity. An advert appears for a car that operates without fuel. I close everything and a page pops up with women in bikinis or underwear, framed by endless little windows. They show their tits, their arses, they blow kisses. Some reveal their faces, others have their eyes pixellated. The crème de la crème, says the slogan. Astrid, Marina, Perla, Natalí, Kiara, Casandra and many more, each with a telephone number below their picture. I click on Mona, facing the camera, posing on all fours, enormous tits, erect, like foam rubber, and nipples like corks, with some kind of Hindu decoration in the background. I watch her for a while, my gaze distant, resting on the furthest point, trying to guess where this girl came from, where she's going, why her and not me.

Sunday morning. The songs, hallelujahs and applause from the Evangelical church drive me out of bed. I'm beginning to suspect that it shares a wall with my room, I should go up to the hotel roof to find out. Up too early, in order to prevent Simón from waking the rest of the guesthouse with the tears of boredom I can see coming, we go to the plaza. A local plaza that takes up a whole block, surrounded by bars, ice-cream parlours and clothes shops; there are early risers like us and others who are still resisting the idea of going to bed.

We install ourselves in the sandpit. As I push Simón on the swing from the other side of the railings, I see a blond coffee seller, Russian or Romanian like Iris, surrounded by a group of taxi drivers, some in uniform, even wearing ties, others more informal. The guy serves coffee and hands out croissants with the gravity of a civil servant, without raising his eyes, meticulous and slow. During the lulls, he changes round the flasks, the silver for the red one, the red for the green, a mysterious operation. Trade secrets, superstition, who knows. Despite the seriousness, it looks fun. He doesn't take part in the conversation, as if he only understands the language of requests, which he interprets with emphatic blinks and fulfils with an ostentatious nod. Almost reverential. Nor is he affected by the peals of laughter, not even when two customers have a play fight very close to him. I lift

Simón down from the swing so that he can keep playing in the sand with an empty plastic bottle. Without saying anything, I leave, I turn round and approach the coffee seller. I wait my turn and ask for a black coffee. Hearing my voice, the man is surprised, he's used to dealing with a different clientele, but he hides it by interchanging the flasks and serves me the coffee in a polystyrene cup. Before he hands it to me, he shows me a lid and mimes covering it. No, no, it's fine like this. It strikes me that this man could be doing anything else, anywhere, but no, he's here, unhurriedly serving coffee. I move away a few steps and put myself in his place, a coffee girl like Iris, why not. I'd have to find another plaza, another corner. A freelance job where I could bring Simón along without having to ask anyone's permission. Iris's cart is still in her room. Although I'm not sure whether she still has the flasks. Coffee, pastries, sandwiches, fruit salad. I talk myself into it.

Back at the hotel, I spot Iris from the corridor, sun-bathing in a corner of the courtyard, the only wedge of light that isn't blocked by the surrounding buildings. I never would have imagined that she was into tanning. I'm about to say: Do you still have the cart? And the flasks? Because I was thinking . . . But as soon as she opens her eyes and sees us, she waves and gets in ahead of me: I was looking for you for ages, she says. Her expression is radiant, she builds the suspense, she has some news for me. I think about Draco, her boyfriend, who must have returned from Patagonia. I could swear that's it. No. She says that on Friday the people at the zoo left me a message on her mobile asking me to go in on Monday. I just heard it yesterday, Iris apologises and starts pressing her phone. Aren't you happy? Yes, I say, and swallow my other idea.

Five minutes before twelve on Monday, the sun as hot as it could be, I knock on the human resources door again. Yes, they're expecting me but I have to wait for forty minutes in a tiny reception in front of a gigantic map of the zoo's attractions. A last-minute meeting, the freckly boy explains. Iris has the day off, so she's stayed with Simón in the hotel. I make the most of the time to familiarise myself with the place a bit, the layout of the cages, the food stands, the toilets. If it occurs to the person conducting the interview to test me, ask me for example what was behind the Hindu temple where the elephants live, I would be able to answer: The Bengal tiger.

When the door finally opens, the person inside, still invisible, says: Come in. I enter a small room with an oblong window close to the ceiling, just like a doctor's surgery. My first feeling is of having opened a fridge, and it will stay that way the whole time I'm there. A dry, artificial winter. The man is dark, thirty-something, with leathery, porous skin, his hair spiked up with gel like a porcupine. He has a little gold chain round his neck, a cross with no Christ figure, camouflaged against his chest hair. As the minutes pass, I come to realise that his hairstyle is a perfect reduction of the other parts of his body: his small, nervous mouth; fidgety hands, which cross and uncross at least a hundred times during our meeting; strong shoulders, as if he lifts weights between sentences. I'm listening, he begins. I open my mouth without much conviction and say the little I have to say. Nothing spontaneous, I recite with middling fluency what I wrote a couple of days ago on my CV, in more or less the same order. When I mention my years of studying veterinary medicine, he interrupts me, waving his hand in the air like a traffic policeman. We have more than enough vets here, he says.

I list my jobs, real and invented. Yes, yes, he cuts me off again, I've already read all that, he says and points at some printed sheets. Tell me something new, something I don't know about you. I stare at him and try to think of an answer that will satisfy him. Something about me? I repeat. The spiky-haired guy screws up his eyes, lustful or conceited, as if I've insulted him, he starts fanning himself with a leaflet and says: Something, anything you like doing. I don't know, I say quite honestly, and suddenly it comes to me: Dancing and running.

Good, good, he says, letting a smile escape, and he doesn't know where to put his hands. As if they were superfluous. From then on he strikes me as a strange creature, one that inspires sympathy. I can't look him in the eye any longer. On the desk is a frame with a family photo: him, the wife and three kids forming a human pyramid on the beach. And a magnetised desk-tidy full of paperclips and a little acrobat.

The thing is that there are two vacancies, one in the reptile house, the other in the children's play area, he reveals quickly, as if trying to wrap things up. Any preference? I shrug. Well, if you haven't heard within a week that you've definitely been picked, I'd advise you to keeping looking elsewhere. He says all this as he stands up, in a tone that makes no effort to disguise the fact that I have very little chance of being hired. He grips the handle and opens the door before I've even got to my feet. He doesn't say goodbye so much as expel me. At the end of the corridor, before stepping outside, I think I hear a Good luck, very quiet, aborted by the sound of my footsteps; I add the final syllable myself.

The light of the sun at its zenith multiplies everything, endlessly. The asphalt steams; you can smell the soft tar. I cross the avenue and slip down a side street sheltered by enormous banana trees that manage to provide proper shade, a heat repellent. Halfway along the block, flanked by a series of narrow buildings, there's an Adventist church. Three identical arches, a pretentious tower and a hand-painted sign.

ALCOHOLICS ANONYMOUS
TODAY ONLY

I turn my head and look the other way. Next to the kerb there's a skip full of debris and rubbish. Shoe soles, springs, computer carcasses and books. Volumes of encyclopaedias, historical journals, leather spines and marbled bindings, most of them rotted away by humidity. A waste. I grab one at random: *The Decameron*. Underneath it, a picture of snakes is revealed. The words reptile house, spoken by the greasy man I've just seen, echo in my head. The coincidence prompts a quick, self-conspiratorial smile, as if I were standing with my double. A sign of destiny, an oversight of chance, it could be either.

It's a heavy book, bound in hessian, difficult to handle. In a corner of the second page there's an embossed stamp: Eduardo Ladislao Holmberg Library, it says in relief, framed by a plume and a knotted ribbon at the bottom. At the foot of the page, in black ink and italics, it says: *NAT 351/II*. I flick through the pages: snakes, lizards, tortoises, some rare plants and many other creatures. I think about Simón. I hesitate, I picture myself carrying this monster of a book the eight or nine blocks between here and the Fénix. I take it, in spite of its size, the fungus and fate.

FIVE

Today I returned to work after four years. A bit more, a bit less, it doesn't matter, just to make it a round number. All that time I had no serious, formal occupation, or even an informal one, no boss, no rotas, no wage. Without fully realising or feeling guilty about it, allowing the days and the countryside to lead me. There, people work without appearing to, either because they do nothing else or because they do nothing, quite the opposite of the city. I go back to work and in some part of me, through contagion, through defiance, I feel as stupid as I do proud, depending on the moment, generally more the former than the latter.

Despite the interview with the human resources man, I received another call from the zoo. This time it was to take psycho-physical tests. First they sent me to a clinic where they measured and weighed me, took a blood sample and an electrocardiogram. A few days later they summoned me to some offices in the centre of town. There, I was met by a girl quite a bit younger than me, probably a psychology student, who interviewed me for twenty minutes, subjecting me to questionnaires, illustrations and logic puzzles. She handed me a test with a hundred questions, beginning with: *Do you feel that there aren't enough hours in the day for all the things you need to do?* I answer no to all of them and suspect that something must be wrong. There has to be a trick question somewhere. The girl flicks through it, nods in silence, exposing her lower lip, and says something she immediately regrets: Perfect score. She's blabbed, rookie mistake. Instructions then follow to draw a house, a tree, a woman and a man, separately, on four blank sheets, and all together on a piece of blue card. Finally, a set of exercises with numbers and geometric shapes that make my eyes ache.

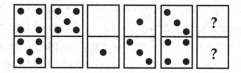

Now that I'm walking along beside the zoo railings, more than once I almost turn back, convinced this isn't for me, things will sort themselves out, someone will provide for us. But I carry on, to everyone else's rhythm; this is seemingly what I have to do. I try to picture what it will be like, the greetings, the introductions, the assignment of tasks. I'm out of the habit of dealing with other people, I imagine myself to be awkward, shy. A bit primitive.

I meet Iris at the main door first, for a relay operation. I go in, she comes out, Simón changes hands. The deal is that she's going to take care of him while I'm working and in return I'll cook for her at night. She doesn't want anything else, don't even mention money. I think about giving her some pointers but as soon as I open my mouth Iris frowns, annoyed in advance; she doesn't like being told what to do. Simón eases the situation, I move away a few steps and he offers her his hand in a gesture of trust. Sometimes I feel I underestimate him, it must be because of his size, his laconic manner, everything that makes me believe he thinks less than he does. I'm mistaken. After saying goodbye, I spy on them over my shoulder. From a distance, despite the fact that they're nothing like each other, not in their features or their gestures, even less in the colour of their hair, it would be perfectly natural to think they were mother and son. Iris's ill-humoured face, her congenital bitterness, the kind that's not so much an expression of something as a birthmark, anyone would associate with the tedium that some mothers feel no compulsion to conceal when taking their kids for a walk.

I present myself at the booth on República de la India ten minutes before the recommended time, as was suggested to me the last time I spoke to them. Staff entrance. I'm new, I'm starting today, I say. The security man shows his head at the window and for a moment I only have eyes for the fat, soft wart that lengthens his lip like a sleepy, sprawling beetle. The man comes out of his booth to better inspect me, a bloated guy, face like a boxer, with his golden canvas insignias on his shoulders and a badge that says *Fortalezza*, like that, with a double 'z' level with his right nipple. He communicates through his walkie-talkie with someone who speaks back in a broken, short-circuited robot voice. I can't explain how, but the man understands everything that's said and conveys the instructions to me. You have to pop into the human resources office to sign the contract, you know how to get there? I nod and give a quick Thanks. I'm welcomed by three camels living amid ruins. On the way to the administration building, I get a bit lost, twice I come out behind the toucan cage until finally I recognise a bower, the bridge and the lake.

In human resources, there's no sign of the man with spiky hair who interviewed me nor of the boy with freckles. I'm received by a mature woman of about fifty, very polite, who, although she takes a few minutes to work out who I am, becomes enthusiastic as soon as she does, as if she had a real interest in my debut. Take a seat, she says twice, and I decline both times. I have to find you on here, she explains, and draws her face right up to the computer screen, moving the mouse painstakingly, by the millimetre, as if it were a scalpel. There you are, I'll print it out and that's it. First she has to fight with the printer, which swallows the pages, crushing them as if rebelling against having to carry out the same task continually. She finally succeeds and hands me the three pages of the contract, which I glance over briefly; I know I'm going to sign it anyway. In a while, after finding me a uniform in my size, she accompanies me to my work post. At the entrance to the reptile house, she introduces me to Yessica, my colleague. That's what she calls her, your colleague, and adds: I'm leaving you in good hands.

For what's left of the day, Yessica will make no effort to ease things or help me integrate. Quite the reverse, she's going to devote herself to making me feel like a nuisance at every opportunity. She has no intention of teaching me anything, she just points out what I'm doing wrong, what I'm not doing, complaining, smacking her lips in a most unpleasant way, like an alien. As if to say: It's useless, not worth trying, poor little human. As soon as someone else appears, another colleague, one of the security guards, the girl from the bar, not only does she not bother to introduce me but she breaks off whatever she's saying to me as if I didn't exist and starts speaking to the person in front of her, throwing out comments that are unsubtly directed at me: What a day or What have I done to deserve this.

Unwillingly, presumably because she doesn't want any complaints later on and because it's her job to intro-duce newcomers to the working environment, Yessica eventually gives me a tour of the reptile house. She lists the names of the animals with an exaggerated lack of enthusiasm as we are already passing them: The boas, the pythons, the caiman, the lizards and further over, the tortoises. But don't ask me anything, she says as we turn back, I have no idea.

Then, instead of following her, I rebel and return to the start to recommence the visit at a more leisurely pace. I say: I'm going to keep familiarising myself with the terrain. She shrugs, head tilting and eyes bulging, indignant: Who do you think you are, it would seem she's going to say to me, but no, she keeps quiet. Some animals, because of their name, size or position, intrigue me more than others, they force me to stop walking and approach the glass that separates us. Above each species there's a lit panel with information detailing dietary habits, behaviour, method of reproduction and habitat zones coloured in on a world map. There are hidden snakes that don't show their faces, camouflaged behind the artificial trunks that make up their micro-world, others aren't visible at all, very few of them moving, only one is looking out, the royal python. I read the sheet with the intention of memorising it: nocturnal habits, mostly land-based, areas of undergrowth, tall forest grasses, excellent swimmers. They hunt by lying in wait on the ground or in trees. Oviparous and carnivorous. They feed on small mammals, especially rodents. Also known as the ball python, their colouration varies from browns to ochres and golds. Average lifespan: twenty to twenty-five years. Location: west coast of Africa, from Angola to Senegal, also Zaire, Uganda and Sudan.

I also study the boa constrictor and the rainbow boa, neither of which is venomous; like the royal python they kill their prey by coiling round it until it suffocates. The rainbow boa is found in arid zones. Pastures in Central and South America. The constrictor has a very wide-ranging habitat, from high summits to sea level. It can be found not far from here, in Córdoba, Mendoza and San Luis.

Further along are the green iguana, the broad-snouted caiman and the American alligator. I leave them for another day. Something about the gloomy light, the smell of enclosure, the watchfulness of the snakes in captivity, produces a hole in my stomach, an anguish that forces me to increase my pace. I skirt the large tank of water turtles, ignore the lizards, walk past a door saying nursery and go outside.

A corridor of reeds, and I come out behind the polar bear's pool. The keeper, I assume he's their keeper, throws me a friendly smile: Are you lost or trying to escape? I like him. He's a good-looking boy, with a man's face, very hairy. On his arms and chest, as well as his hands, forehead and cheeks. He shows me the way back but he's clearly keen because he stops what he's doing, resting a long stick with a kind of rubber handle at the end against the railing, and approaches, coming to stand next to me: I'll go with you. When did you start? he asks, and my response: Today, an hour ago. He laughs and I join in. I point at the reptile house like a little girl who's relieved to recognise her own house after an excursion that took her too far. I raise my hand to thank him, but he insists on accompanying me. Seeing us arrive, Yessica gets down from her stool and opens her eyes wide. The boy says: We got lost. Yessica lets out a harsh laugh, exaggerated and porcine, and I begin to feel the irritation growing inside me.

The rest of the afternoon goes by with no major incidents. I pick up in passing from conversations between Yessica and another employee who stops off on his way to the office that the school holidays begin on Friday, and from Saturday on, this place will be mental with little brats. That's what I hear: mental with little brats.

We get a twenty-minute break every shift to go to the toilet, smoke, do whatever you want, Yessica explains to me without taking her eyes off her mobile phone – she's reading a message, searching for a number, playing solitaire, I don't know. She raises her head and says: I'll go first and when I come back you can go for a bit, ok? Yes, I say with a smile that doesn't quite manage to be ironic. For the first time that day I sit on her stool ready to check tickets. I don't see much action, only a pair of tiny pensioners. I pass the time watching what's going on at the food stand opposite, painted with the colours and logo of Coca-Cola and surrounded by ducks. The girl working at the bar doesn't have many clients either; she entertains herself moving a cloth over the counter, arranging the plastic cups, restocking the drink and popcorn machines. After a while she takes a break, leaning on her elbows next to the till, chin on her closed fist, and she looks in my direction. There we are, eyeing each other up until the sunlight forces us to squint. Not so much out of embarrassment but so as not to make her feel uncomfortable, I take advantage of a shout and avert my gaze: Look, Daddy, a peacock. Indeed it is, unfurling itself between the small canal and the red Coca-Cola chairs. A peacock.

Now you can go, Yessica tells me, and I obey even though I don't really know where to go. I take ten steps and stop short. Disconcerted, I look in both directions and Yessica, who hasn't stopped watching me, points out a circular construction surrounded by very tall pines before the feline cage. On the way, I come across a guy with a large broom who looks at me for so long that I end up greeting him. He introduces himself: Canetti, with a double t, head janitor. The dark shadows on his face make him look as though he has two black eyes. He's lame and cross-eyed, obliquely: he drags his left leg and his right eye looks up to the corner. His lip trembles as if he's received a low-intensity electric shock. He's worked in the zoo for seven years. Seven years, he repeats, do you realise? I go into the toilet, I sit down to pee but don't do anything, I splash my face with water and in the mirror I see myself dressed as an explorer for the first time. Another me. When I come out the guy is still there. He accompanies me to the reptile house, describing the terrain with a cigarette in his mouth. You'll find everything here, he says and stresses, separating the syllables: Ev-ry-thing. He speaks well of some colleagues but slags most of them off. We say goodbye with a friendly handshake.

At around six, nearly closing time, Esteban appears, the vet in charge of the reptiles. A skinny, bald guy. Yessica introduces us. My first impression is pleasant: frank eyes and babyish skin. During the short time he spends coming and going along the aisles giving instructions to a boy who I suppose must do the dirty work – clean the cages, feed the animals, wash them – I think about approaching Esteban but I don't know how to. I'd like to tell him, he has no reason to know, that I was going to be a vet too. As if I need to make it clear that I'm not here by chance, like in a kiosk or tollbooth. Luckily, I never find the right moment.

At the end of the shift – working days aren't days, they're shifts – in the changing room, as I swap my uniform for my street clothes, I feel as though I'm in a film. Yessica undresses at my side, she walks around in bra and pants as if unintentionally, her body firm, plastic, bulky. Without looking at me, she chats to another girl about a cream for varicose veins.

When I arrive at the Fénix, Iris and Simón are watching television in the kitchen, a programme with water games. How was it? Fine, strange, I almost got bitten by a viper, I say. Iris acknowledges my joke by spitting out one of her Slavic sniggers. Simón is on good form, even better than when he's with me. We go to the shop, I buy tomatoes, a bag of rice and two tins of tuna.

During the night, an unexpected wind gets up which brings us some relief. In the courtyard, with a slowly warming beer, Iris tells me stories about snakes. Her aunt Lena became rich all of a sudden, thanks to perestroika, when her husband started to dance in petrol, that's what Iris says and I can't help imagining them dripping in black goo in the middle of a nightclub dance floor. Her aunt, who had always been a worker, didn't know what to do with the money. She got bored. First she became obsessed with tattoos and had about a hundred done. Everywhere, arms, legs, back. Even on her arse, she says and laughs loudly. Then she began to collect pets, from the conventional – chihuahuas, Siamese cats, hamsters – to the exotic – tarantulas, frogs and pythons. Pythons? Yes, yes. Once Iris accompanied her aunt to a fair on the outskirts of Moscow, a neighbourhood for the poor, she calls it, to buy mice. Three or four, depending on the size, which she, Aunt Lena, tied head to tail with thread so that the python wouldn't get in a muddle when the time came to eat them. As he grew, the beast became voracious. So, not to save money but for the sake of convenience, Aunt Lena chose to set up a rat nursery in the laundry of the apartment, one of the most luxurious in Moscow. Listening to Iris makes me think of Esteban and I decide that next time I see him I'm going to mention it. I find it hard to believe that the zoo would feed animals with rats. But it could be true.

   With her anecdote about Aunt Lena pursuing the snake down the stairs of the apartment block, Iris reveals a side of herself I never suspected, she's quite the dramatic raconteur. It would seem that through a maid's negligence, the python escaped from the apartment. That Aunt Lena went round knocking on all the neighbours' doors, floor by floor, all of them rich like her, businessmen, artists, mafiosi, diplomats, and when she got to the ground floor, she found it writhing in a corner of the staircase about to be attacked by the caretaker with an axe. That Lena pushed the man away and embraced her pet, sheltering it under her silk pyjamas and that a woman fainted right there. Lena apologised and got into the lift. *Izviní, izviní,* repeats Iris, imitating her aunt, and runs out to the corridor leading to the patio with a tea towel under her blouse like an imaginary serpent. She comes back in shaking her head and rounds off the story with a snotty guffaw, just like the roar of a bear.

SIX

Sleep is impossible. The bed is beginning to sink in the middle from so much tossing and turning and I'm going with it. The hours pass, the fatigue grows, as does my state of awareness. The only parts that manage to drift off, very much in spite of me, are my arms and legs, in turn, left arm right leg, right arm left leg. In search of sleep, I masturbate. Gentle strokes, lethargic, more consolation than masturbation. Nothing, the insomnia remains unscathed. I sit up in bed, my feet dangling, invisible in the darkness, I count to ten and feel my way out of the room to entertain my wakefulness.

I go into the kitchen without turning on the light. I get myself a glass of cold water, then another, and a third. In the half-light, I distinguish the outline of the furniture, still strange to me. When I'm about to leave, I see a pack of cigarettes on top of the fridge and I grab it without hesitating. It's a box of Jockey Lights with a small lighter held in place by the cellophane. It occurs to me to try smoking, just to see. In passing, I notice the wall clock with its aged phosphorescent hands: three twenty.

In the courtyard, I sit on the bench under our bedroom window. I remove a cigarette, sniff it, bring it to my lips and light it. I take one, two, three drags but it sickens me immediately, a rancid taste invades my mouth, followed by nausea. I can see that once you lose the habit, you lose the taste for it. I stub out the cigarette in the dry soil of the flower bed next to me and look at the scant piece of sky cut out between the buildings, a geometric, pathetic sky. Not a single star. Suddenly, a movement between the leaves. From the creeper at the back, a swift mouse climbs to the gutter. I can see it clearly because, once it has stumbled through the foliage and attracted my attention with the noise, it passes through a stretch of yellow light. Country rats are definitely much fatter and more ungainly. Finally I fall asleep. I have a very strange dream about Iris, gnomes and pianos.

I wake to Simón beating at my knee as if it were my front door. I open my eyes and we exchange bemusement; he won't understand what I'm doing outside, sleeping sitting up, and I can't explain how he has managed to get up, leave the room and find me without causing a scene. It's starting to get light, I reckon it must be between five and six. Simón offers me his hand, it takes me a few moments to accept it, and I let him lead me towards bed, his bed, which we're going to share for a few more hours. First, without entering the kitchen, I lob the pack of Jockeys I'm still clutching. I make the shot and the cigarettes land on top of the fridge, not far from their original position.

A hot morning follows, although not quite as bad as the last few days. A tumultuous breakfast: shouts, arguments about a bar of soap, a chorus of sirens passing at top speed and a whistling kettle that no one silences. We take Simón to the little plaza round the corner from the hotel. A small island of cobblestones and palm trees contained between two streets. On one of the benches, a drunk with flowers. He is wrapped up to his nose as he sleeps, a real drifter. At his feet, a mattress of long-stemmed roses in full bloom with loosening petals. Florists' rejects or stolen from the market. There are also carnations, chrysanthemums and several others I can't identify. It's as though the previous night, before his latest inebriation set in – two wine crates remain as proof – the man had arranged his own homage, a foretaste of his funeral. Simón watches him too, we share the interest and intrigue.

We take refuge in a small children's play park with a sandpit, a slide and a tubular frame. There's an inescapable smell of urine. In the corners, on the cement, on the railings too, I can see traces of piss, its ochre stamp. Simón pulls a disgusted face but doesn't complain so I resign myself, thinking that it will be fifteen, twenty minutes at most, and that it's just a matter of getting used to it. In a while, another boy arrives with an arsenal of outdoor toys, different types of spades, rakes, moulds and three different sizes of bucket. He is accompanied by a lady wearing a lot of make-up, hair the colour of fire; I assume she's his grandmother. The boy lays out all his tools and starts digging a well. Simón prowls around him, not daring to make friends until the other boy throws him a spade, which almost catches him in the eye, a form of invitation. The exchange doesn't last long. Not two minutes pass before the woman, who had been hovering at the sidelines smoking a long, thin cigarette, bursts into the play area and starts gathering up all the toys, complaining about the smell. This is a sewer, she says, throwing me a glance over her shoulder, I'm not sure whether seeking assent, so that we too will withdraw, or blaming us, as if we were the ones that had peed everywhere.

We have hard-boiled eggs and rice with peas for lunch. Simón eats the whites, I always preferred the yolks. There is a lot of traffic in the kitchen this lunchtime, like breakfast but even busier. A never-ending rotation of people, noises and smells. In addition to the Spaniard, who comes in and out all the time, very nervous, a notebook in one hand and her mobile in the other, people I've never seen parade past: one opens the fridge, another turns on the grill for a steak, a third sits at the table to do sums on a calculator with giant buttons. The radio is constantly on in the background. The news of the day is that a helicopter went off-course near Magdalena and has now disappeared off the radar. At one o'clock we go out and at half one I meet Iris at the entrance to the zoo to swap over. Next to the photographer with the pony, as always, as if we had agreed on it. Simón doesn't complain, he appears to have adapted quickly to the new routine.

The worst is about to come, prepare yourself, Yessica tells me in lieu of a greeting. And I don't need to ask her why, she immediately points towards the entrance, sweeping the terrace with her index finger in the air. It's the start of the holidays. But despite Yessica's foreboding, the constant mechanical activity, the hundreds of tickets

I check and the many faces I see without really looking at any of them all distract me. You hear the children, but after a while you tune them out and their shouts seem natural.

So far, in the week and a bit I've been working, I haven't had any major difficulties. Only small issues. It's been hard to familiarise myself with the walkie-talkie system: when someone speaks to me I can't hear it, and when I manage to respond, they're looking for someone else. The only incident takes place with a group of corpulent Brazilians who don't want to understand that the ticket they bought doesn't include entry to the reptile house. I point out a hut where they can buy the supplementary ticket but as they move on, their hand gestures tell me to go to hell. Yessica shows solidarity, she hates foreigners. They really rile me, that's what she says.

It becomes a habit to take my break with Canetti. An enforced habit, the guy comes looking for me, he latches on to me and I can't avoid it, I'm a new arrival. He's a strange man, with many problems. As well as his limp and his lazy eye, from time to time, without warning, maybe because of nerves, maybe it's the heat, he is gripped by a trembling in his fingers that prevents him from holding his broom. He has to wait for it to pass, then he shakes out his hands, rubs them against the grass or the bark of a tree. Localised epilepsy. After-effects, he tells me on one of the first days; I am intrigued. An accident, a brain haemorrhage, the war? I don't know, it could be any of them, I can't work it out. We usually sit on a bench behind the photographers' booth. He smokes a cigarette, sometimes two, and I listen to him in silence, looking straight ahead towards the lake. Some days the jets of water are turned on, other days they aren't, it depends. I don't understand the logic behind it.

One afternoon Canetti tells me his story with a bag of crisps in his hand, which he offers me every so often and which I refuse every time. He says he shouldn't be working any more, he retired nine years ago but he doesn't get a peso. Canetti was a treasurer in an important bank, he stresses the word important with a raised eyebrow. Twenty-eight years grafting in the same office, from the age of nineteen. I was office junior, clerk, account executive, then cashier and finally head of the treasurer's office. He had his own property, which he had bought with a special credit for bank employees, quite a nice little flat in the city centre with a balcony and garage, occasionally he got away to the seaside or into the hills with his wife, he couldn't complain. Cinema, theatre, restaurants, always some little outing on a Friday night. Until his mother died and he was overcome by terrible depression. My world came tumbling down, I wasn't ready for anyone to die, especially not Mum. Listening to him, I don't understand why he's telling me all this, given that we barely know each other, but I can't stop him, he's getting sentimental. The thing is that he started to drink, boozing he says, he went to bed late, missed work, didn't wash. Really bad, basically. So, wanting to help him, his wife put him in touch with a psychologist she knew from school. The guy sees him a couple of times in his office and suggests that it's not his mother he's stressed about but his job. Even though he wasn't entirely convinced, it was clear to Canetti that taking a holiday would be good for him in his condition and he went along with it. But they became bolder and what was initially going to be a request for stress-related leave eventually resulted in an application for early retirement due to psychological incapacity. The man told him treasurers are under a lot of pressure because they deal with such large quantities of money and he reckoned Canetti could claim a decent amount of compensation to cover the costs of treatment and retirement. The arrangement was that he would give a percentage to the psychologist as his fee. Despite his state, but also largely infected by his wife's enthusiasm, Canetti allowed himself to be led. Worst mistake of my life, he says, lighting a fresh cigarette, but the move had already been played. So the preparations began for him to pass the medical exams. I had to arrive at the interviews in the most broken state possible for them to believe me. He spent six months barely working, devoted to turning to shit, that's what he says. He barely slept, he was mixing drugs, tranquillisers, cocaine, alcohol, he slashed his face, he burnt his palms with lighters. He shows me some scars. This was all part of the plan to convince the psychiatrists from the insurance company. And in spite of his doubts, it all went quite well. He even managed to get admitted to a clinic for a couple of weeks, to make the situation more believable. He appeared before the various insurance committees without raising suspicion. One of those sleepless nights after going too far, I slipped in the shower, I damaged myself permanently, he says, showing me the leg that drags when he walks. The fact is that after a multitude of tests, sessions, clinical analyses and about twenty doctors along the way, his incapacity was certified.

Everything went ok, I received the first two instalments, I paid the guy his share, I even took a trip to the coast, but in two weeks I was sent a registered letter, an official one. The lawyer from the insurance company had discovered that the psychologist was involved in a lawsuit for having given a false diagnosis. Confronted with the evidence, Canetti confessed, accusing the man of having incited him to commit the crime, but they had no sympathy. That's what he says, his mouth full of smoke: They had no sympathy. They threw me out of the bank without paying me a single peso and started criminal proceedings for fraud, which are still going on. When she found out, my wife wanted nothing to do with it and I didn't have the will to keep fighting. And the worst thing is that, I don't know how he managed it, but the guy went and moved to Brazil. I was fucked, truly fucked, he says. As Canetti falls silent and I look into his eyes, sad, broken eyes like an orphaned, tortured cat's, I don't know what to say to him, I'm left hanging on the last word he said, that Brazil that echoes through me, carrying distant memories. I sympathise in silence, with my eyebrows, all the words of consolation that occur to me turn out to be impossible to articulate. He realises this and must feel a bit disappointed.

Suddenly, because it's a certain time, or in order to receive the last wave of visitors, or because whoever operates them happens to be in the mood, the jets of water in the centre of the lake are turned on, more powerful than ever. Flicking it hard with his index finger, Canetti throws down the stub of his cigarette, which lies smoking in the grass. Annoyed, he stands up and limps to the ember, which he stamps on, twisting his shoe. Then he turns round and says to me: Do you know how to give injections? I shrug, believing that I know, or rather that I would be able to do it. He insists: But you've done it before? I answer Yes, assuming that he's talking about animals: dogs, cats, horses. Even a hamster. Well, says Canetti, it must be the same, flesh and bone, yeah? He explains two drags of a cigarette later. Where he lives, a building some ten blocks from the zoo, there's a lady, the building manager or something along those lines, a very ill old lady who needs two injections a day. Are you up for it? Canetti presses me: It could be a few extra bob. If you like, we'll go there together tomorrow afternoon and I'll introduce you, then it's between the two of you. Somehow I accept, I can't see why not. On the way to the reptile house, I glance at him. He moves away, dragging the broom towards the bower. He whistles and limps in a regular counterpoint; in fact, everything about him is harmoniously disjointed. When he's not talking, I'm starting to realise, Canetti is smoking or whistling. I struggle to imagine him in his former life, in the bank, counting notes, married, with his wife, armchair and holidays. Even harder to imagine all the effort he put into passing as insane.

In the evening, in the dark of the room, I trip over the huge tome with the reptile engravings. Simón, behind me, pauses in the threshold, alert to the fall that never happens. We settle down together in my bed, the ceiling fan on full, and start flicking through the engravings.

LOCUPLETISSIMI
RERUM
NATURALIUM
THESAURI

As I read I try to decipher a long list of Latin words on what must have been the original cover of the book, which dates from 1735. Simón is eager and I'm forced to turn the page. There's Albertus Seba, author of the catalogue: curly wig, purple robe in a fabric with many folds which I suppose is silk, and a handkerchief knotted round his neck. He poses with a commanding air, gazing straight ahead, tense, not particularly convinced by the setting chosen for his portrait. As if he were doubtful of the painter's skill. The man is in his study in front of a shelf filled with glass bottles: insects, corals, fossils. He is holding a jar containing a foetus in formaldehyde. With his free hand he is pointing to a notebook with illustrations of apes and trees, as well as a collection of molluscs displayed on a green cloth. In imitation of Seba, Simón stretches out his arm and points his finger at something in between the monkeys and the shells, several centuries later, but with the same intention.

The volume consists mainly of illustrations of reptiles, amphibians and plants. Snakes of all colours and sizes, fat, stripy, hunting and hunted. Also some frogs, lizards and an inexplicable swan that is completely out of proportion. I turn the pages and realise that the animals have very human shapes. There are lizards with the features and posture of a man, snakes with women's faces. Sometimes slightly android. Somewhere between scientific and grotesque. Simón observes them with interest but in general he hurries me to turn the page, he wants to see what comes next. A boa scoffing a rat will keep him absorbed for longer. I think about Iris and the story about her aunt Lena and the python. The most striking thing about the picture isn't the hunt so much as the fluidity of the action.

As I progress through the pages, I can't help noticing the pattern of fungus fattening out the book. Like a mountain chain in profile. Simón falls asleep; tiredness still hasn't touched me. I go back over some of the figures and discover others that passed me by in the first flick-through. This one, for example, of a ferret sitting on its hind legs biting a pear, or the dissection of a toad with its veins on show and its parts numbered.

I return to the start and find the embossed stamp of the Ladislao Holmberg Library: Buenos Aires, 1899. I wonder who he was. I run the tip of my thumb over the protuberances of the paper, it's a nice sensation, almost tickly.

SEVEN

Canetti comes with me the first night. He picks me up at the hotel after ten, when I have no energy left for anything. I feel absolutely shattered: Simón, hours on my feet, sleeping badly, this new life I didn't expect and which began so suddenly, without warning. I don't know why I don't change my mind while I still can, in fact I mentally rehearse excuses not to go: my son has a fever, I'd prefer not to leave him alone; I'm feeling unwell, vomiting, the best thing to do would be to look for someone else, there must be loads of nurses in the neighbourhood. But when Canetti turns up smiling, freshly showered, in a check shirt that must be about as old as me, convinced he's doing us a good turn, I swallow my words and allow things to happen. Simón has just fallen asleep, Iris will be in the kitchen, or in her room but with the door open so as to hear him. If it's something to do with work, she'll always be willing to help out. I don't think he'll wake up, I say, just to say something. It's not like he'll die if he does, she says, with her own particular brand of humour, and sends me packing, swatting the air with the back of her hand. Like someone trying to scare a fly. Let's go, I say to Canetti, who is waiting for me in the hotel corridor, keeping a wary eye out for the Spaniard. Walking along the pavement, I realise I'm wearing boots. It's ridiculous, it's not raining nor is it going to rain, it's as if I can't get rid of some of my country habits. I can't be bothered going back to swap them for more urban footwear.

First we skirt a very long block, which must actually be four or five together, against the shell of a ruined building, old warehouses that advertisements promise to convert into something stunning and futuristic. We cross to the other side of the railway tracks, take a leafy gated passageway between the barbed wire and a series of buildings with visible brickwork, another street, two more blocks, then we turn left and cross the avenue next to a very organised camp of cardboard collectors.

On the way, Canetti returns to his story, about his sham illness, how he tried to pass as insane and leave work. Increasingly, as he adds details, contradictory at times, it strikes me that he must be exaggerating his tale. The limp is real, his past as a bank worker is also plausible, but the whole business of drunkenly beating the bathroom tiles so he could go to the psychiatrists' interviews with fresh wounds, that's what he says, fresh wounds, that really stretches the limits of credibility. He keeps his mouth closed for a few minutes, as if recalling it all. I glance at him, his face hardened with scars, the tortured eyes, and my doubts vanish, I believe it all. There was a point, he says suddenly, eyes on the ground, waiting for the traffic lights to change so we can cross, when I felt like a hero.

After he has whistled for an entire block, we come to the foot of a high-rise that anyone would think was abandoned, unfinished or under construction, if it weren't for the clothes hanging over balconies, the lights flickering on and off, and a rickety armchair on the pavement. Without further ado, Canetti announces: We're here. The front door is made of corrugated iron. Black and reinforced, with three numbers painted in aerosol: 975. That's when I realise that this building is a squat. Relax, we're safe here. Two sharp knocks on the sheet metal and a voice asks from the other side: Who is it? Canetti says his name and adds: From fourteen. The door opens and a flat face in a hood peers out, like a caricature of a guard dog that's scary all the same. Follow me, says Canetti quietly, and we walk along a dark, narrow corridor with puddles I step in without seeing. We stop at the foot of a staircase lit by a neon tube hanging directly from the cables. Further along is the shaft for a non-existent lift.

Canetti knocks at another door, three gentle knocks this time, like a child asking permission to enter his parents' room. The response takes a while. It's me, he says. We're welcomed by a head that seems the size of two and a grave hello, distorted as though a recording is doing the speaking. We enter an atmosphere that's fuzzy round the edges and, despite the weak light, I can see him a bit better now. He's an enormous boy, handicapped, of uncertain age, somewhere between adolescence and forty, deformed. In the centre of the room, sprawled in a red armchair, is a very wide woman surrounded by cushions, more than just fat, she's inflated, pure volume. I can also make out an iron bedstead, a lamp with rings on it, a small shrine and a desk on castors, covered with untidy papers which, on seeing me, the woman pushes to one side with her foot. Canetti introduces me to Tosca and the rather deformed boy, Benito, who stays standing the whole time, watching a television that's as bulky as he is. I'll wait outside, says Canetti, and Tosca repeats the last word but in the tone of an order. Outside, she spits, and as soon as Canetti leaves she says to me: He's a worm.

Come here, girl, closer, I won't bite. I obey. As I approach, I take in the true proportions of this immense woman, wrapped up in spite of the heat. I find it hard to imagine how she gets out of her chair, to eat, to sleep, not to mention to go out anywhere. Sit here, she points to the bed. She's about to say something else, but instead pulls a face. Ow, she complains and squeezes that limitless belly. Holding on to the arm of the chair for propulsion, she stands up. I make as if to offer her a hand but she scares me away with a sharp gesture of contempt. Incredibly, she manages by herself.

Tosca goes to the bathroom, she walks leaning on a stick. For a while I'm left sitting by the boy with the Cyclops head, index finger in his nostril. Benito is wearing blue overalls, like a mechanic or a painter, too tight for him. On the muted television, lottery numbers are filling up an electronic scoreboard. Next to me, on the bedside table, is a colourful bust of Jesus and a bronze cross, two compartmentalised pillboxes, precariously balanced piles of medicine boxes and an old mobile phone with a broken screen. Above that, an image of a Virgin Mary with a burning heart in the middle of her chest. I stretch my neck to better see that symmetrical red organ connected to the body by an artery that perforates the skin. A fantasy heart, but one with vital functions.

> *Sweet Virgin of Syracuse,*
> *wipe away the tears caused by*
> *hate and violence*
> *in so many regions of the World,*
> *in particular the Middle East*
> *and the continent of Africa.*

Still just a shadow, Tosca releases a Tsssk, and although I'm not sure whether it was directed at me, I straighten up quickly. At the same time, accepting responsibility for the scolding, Benito removes his finger, still digging, from his nose. The woman advances very slowly, like a sea lion out of water, tongue slack, rocking. At the foot of the armchair, she collapses. Thirty-six with the head of a nine-year-old, she says, presumably referring to Benito.

So, girl, you know how to give injections. Yes, I say. I need two a day, when I get up and before I go to bed. All right? Before I can reply, she asks again. It wasn't Mercedes who sent you? I shake my head and show by my expression that I don't know any Mercedes. Look, I have to take these, she says and shows me some long, amber-coloured glass phials: Morphine 10mg. The pain keeps on hurting, I just use it so I can forget for a while, so that it hurts somewhere else, she says. I nod in silence, with a minimal smile, and since I don't ask, she becomes impatient and explains: A tumour, girl, here, at the back, she says, indicating the nape of her neck with her thumb over her shoulder. A peach of a tumour. She coughs, laughs, both at the same time. But don't worry, it's nice and tame, if you behave yourself, I'll introduce you one day. Are you sure you know how to do this? Beni, come here, orders the woman and the huge boy obeys. She looks me in the eye: Let's see, inject this into his arm. She gives me a syringe and a bag of saline solution. I hesitate, but she encourages me with her hands. I fill half the tube, I ask for his arm, I feel it, I look for the vein, I press down and prick. Uh, protests the boy and the woman asks him: Did it hurt? No, he replies, a bit. Ok, continues Tosca, someone's coming today, but not tomorrow, so I'll expect you at eight, or better, seven thirty. Agreed? Yes. When I'm already on my way out she wants to know how much I'll charge. I shrug, I haven't thought about it. Well, tell me later, but don't go crazy.

Outside, Canetti comes towards me, emerging from the gloom. He guides me towards the door with his arm extended. And? Fine, I say, she seems like a good woman. Yes, fierce but good, he replies contentedly, almost proudly, as if speaking about himself. We go out to the street and it looks like he's planning to see me home. Let's go, he says, and I leap in first: You don't need to come with me, I can find the way myself, I lie. But he insists on taking me the block and a half that separate us from the main avenue. Then I understand, the check shirt, the combed hair, the clean-shaven face, it wasn't altruism, he's expecting something in return for finding me this little job, as he called it this morning. It's not clear. I glance at him for a good few seconds, trying to guess his intentions: will he want to invite me for coffee to continue telling me his woes, or will he expect me to ask him to my hotel room. Just in case, and to prevent a return journey filled with tedious questions, I only take drastic action when we reach the corner: I'd prefer to go back alone, thanks for everything. Canetti stays silent, with a disappointed expression, as if I'd tricked him, and I hurry to cross before it occurs to him to follow me.

Venturing down new streets on the way back to the hotel, I immediately forget about Canetti. In my mind, he becomes less and less offensive, just a man with real, incurable loneliness. Instead, Tosca occupies all my thoughts, that impossible woman. I think about the Virgin Mary in her shrine, about the macrocephalic son, about the silent television, the piles of medicine boxes, about her swaddled cancer, but also about Jaime, the truck that ran him over, the driver who carried on pretending not to have noticed, how could he not have seen? I'll never know.

Illnesses, accidents, pills, gunshots, the sea. I make a mental list of all the ways of dying that occur to me at that moment. I wonder which will be destined for me.

EIGHT

Hotter and hotter: enveloping, sticky, like a distant relative, invisible and giant, the kind that bears down and
won't stop hugging you. After injecting Tosca's morning
dose, I return to the hotel and spend the morning watching Simón make a thousand attempts to climb the cistern
that never was. The Spaniard has resigned herself and
no longer reprimands him. The rest of the day unfolds
in more or less the same way as the previous day: at two,
handover with Iris at the entrance to the zoo, that world
of children and reptiles until half six, when I return to the
guesthouse, prepare some food, put Simón to bed before
ten, back to Tosca's and a night-time walk in solitude. By
virtue of repetition, all the things that just a few weeks
ago seemed absurd now feel completely normal to me.

Yessica treats me better now, there are even days
when she speaks to me as an equal. Over the course of an
afternoon, she often asks me to take her place so she can
escape to the toilet. Cover for me a while, that's what she
tells me. She doesn't say as much but I know she's going
to retouch her make-up, which has melted in the heat,
exaggerating her features. She comes back looking like

new, healthy, her cheeks red with a double flush, from the powder and the temperature. Sometimes she slips off when her mobile rings too. She has lots of boyfriends, or none, I haven't worked it out yet.

Today she confesses. A different, almost tender Yessica is looking me in the eye: I've been out with guys, she says, waving her phone, but this is different, he's not just anyone. I'm totally hooked, just imagine if I fall in love. And what do you like about him, I ask just for the sake of it, to sound friendly. Everything, the way he is.

Apart from her and Canetti, I often run into the boy who takes care of the polar bear, I don't know his name, to me he'll always be the boy who takes care of the polar bear. He's a friendly guy, who stares at me intensely, to see if I notice.

When it's quiet, I make the most of the time to study the plaques above the animals. Sometimes I question Esteban, who always answers hurriedly, as if he doesn't believe I'm really interested. Yesterday, for example, seeing that the Indian python was unusually active, coiling and uncoiling itself around the petrified trunk, I remembered the artificial mouse nursery Iris's aunt had set up in her Moscow apartment and I asked him what the snakes ate. Without stopping, eyebrows arched, surprised by my curiosity, my ignorance, he said twice: Rabbits, rabbits. He enunciated clearly, almost soundlessly, as if it were a secret, or just obvious. Assuming they eat them live, I would have liked to ask him what he knew about the technique of tying mice up by the tail to make them easier to eat, whether the same was done with rabbits, but he'd already moved away.

Now, for the last few days, I've been studying the crocodilians. I already know them more or less by heart. Alligators, whether Chinese or North American, are less aggressive than crocodiles, they only attack for food. They eat fish, small mammals, birds, tortoises and, in some cases, carrion. They are also distinguished from crocodiles by their lower jaw, which wedges right against the upper, hiding the fourth tooth. The adults are dark green and the young, black. Like cats and dogs they have a third eyelid, that white membrane that slides over the eye making them look like extraterrestrials. Among the Yacare caimans, the male and the female share their tasks equally: they build the nest together, they care for the eggs and protect their young. Their diet varies as they grow and depending on the season. Newborns feed on insects, amphibians and snails. This is the most southerly of the caiman family.

After eight days and fifteen injections, Tosca proposes a deal. First, without my asking, because she must have seen me looking at the picture on the first day and she's beginning to like me, she tells me the story of the Virgin of Tears. She thinks it was in 1953, but it could have been '52 or '54, she can't remember any more, she had just turned fourteen, she's sure about that. So it had to be '53; I was born in '39, the day war began. Tosca, her father and her sister Violeta – her mother had died of tuberculosis the previous winter – travelled to Syracuse on a pilgrimage when talk of the miracle began to circulate. A humble woman from a family called Fangasso had suddenly gone blind during pregnancy. But the blindness lasted less than a week. On the seventh day, she recovered her sight. And the first thing she saw when she woke up was the plaster Virgin she had been given for her wedding with tears falling down its cheeks. One just like this, Tosca tells me in a fit of enthusiasm, pointing at the image hanging on the wall. The miracle lasted a month, many people had the opportunity to see it for themselves: the Fangasso family, pilgrims, priests from neighbouring parishes, even an investigating commission sent by the Vatican to accredit the miracle. The Virgin cried ceaselessly. *Lagrimi humani*, says Tosca, who was a witness.

She finishes her story, we go through the morphine ceremony and, five minutes later, revived from the initial effects, she speaks again: There's an empty flat on the third floor. And she stops there, she closes her eyes as if to sleep and leave me guessing. But no, she half opens them, rather sleepily: If you want you can stay there in exchange for continuing with the injections. As long as you keep it between us, because if the other nobodies find out they'll all come crying to me. The only thing you'll have to pay is your share of the electricity and the gas, and sort out the water with Benito. Thanks, I say although I'm not sure. You can stay here tonight after seeing me, you think about it. I nod. Benito accompanies me to the door and I'm about to ask him if he'll take me to the third floor, if he'll show me the apartment so I can get an idea of it before I decide, before I move in, but I can't find the right words, he moves behind me like a giant shadow, unapproachable.

When I get back from the zoo, I tell Iris about Tosca's proposal in the kitchen of the Fénix. Free accommodation, I say briefly. I tell her what I've been mulling over all afternoon. Anticipating her ill humour, I extend my hand and ask her to give me a moment. She purses her lips and raises her eyebrows, smelling betrayal. I tell her about Canetti, yes, she knows him well, and in fact she finds him disagreeable, I don't like him, she says, and about Tosca, the old woman I've been giving injections to for a week, I say the old woman contemptuously, as if wanting in some way to soften the decision to leave. I also mention the building, a squat but not dangerous. Iris shrugs, as if she doesn't care, with that mixture of annoyance and indifference that is so like her. A pause and the challenge: Why not come with us? I was thinking that if I tell Tosca she'll surely agree to there being three of us. It's all the same to her, I add, wanting to convince Iris. She looks at me perplexed, as if I'd invited her to a session of masochism.

During the time I spend packing my bag, Iris disappears. Offended or sad, she hides in her room. Night falls, Simón runs around the patio, twice I have to lean out of the window and shout at him to stop trying to climb the dividing wall. Now the question of tomorrow and the day after is circling round my head, I didn't stop to think what I'm going to do with Simón when I go to work, who will look after him, because I don't suppose Iris will do it once we've gone. I think that perhaps I was too hasty, I don't even know what kind of place we're going to end up in.

The Spaniard claims for one more night and we spend a while complicating things with the calendar until she's convinced I've paid up until the following day. I don't, however, manage to get her to return the hundred pesos I left as a deposit for the keys because she says the ones for the wardrobe are missing. Not that I insist. Iris shows her face again at the last minute, as if she's been spying on us. She raises a hand from the end of the corridor and says, as if it were any old leave-taking: Tomorrow.

NINE

As well as being called the tower, the building is known to the locals as 'el Buti' because of someone who lived there and died resisting an eviction attempt ten years earlier, at the start of the occupation. A lad, they tell me, who went by that name. Sprayed on the staircase walls at the bottom of the lift shaft in really large red letters, carved on unpainted iron railings, over the rust, on the ceilings, on the doors, as well as the outside walls, even on the muck-covered pipes:

EL BUTI LIVES AND RESISTS

Until the night of the move, all I know of the place can be reduced to Tosca, the *señora,* as almost everyone calls her, and her world. That multi-use area of hers: bedroom, dining room and kitchen. The taxi drops us half a block away, the driver decides without asking that it's better for us to get out there because otherwise he'll have to go all the way round. I can't work out whether he does it out of concern for my pocket, laziness or fear of attack. What's clear is that I have to lug the suitcase and Simón, as well as a selection of bags that we have accumulated since we arrived in the city: tins of pâté, a packet of powdered milk, an extra towel that Iris lent me and insisted we take with us, damp clothes, my zoo uniform and the Albertus Seba book. At the door I say the same thing I do every day: I'm here to see the *señora*. I'm still no one, I don't even have a number. The hooded boy, who sees me come in and out every night, who never says hi or bye, because that's the way he is, not much of a talker, protecting himself with the loud music pumping through his earphones, this time he can't help making a gesture of surprise, seeing me appear with another person and all my stuff. In fact he gets slightly worried and, instead of staying at his post as usual, he follows me. As if he wants to help me, or not, perhaps quite the opposite, to check that the *señora* is aware of my intentions.

I push on and knock at Tosca's door. It doesn't open for a while. I have to shout my name three times before I'm recognised. Come in, I finally hear. I push timidly; the bags and Simón remain in the doorway, distant but on view. You're early, girl, Tosca tells me and I'm scared she's forgotten her offer, that it's all been a big mistake.

I've surprised them in the middle of a meal, stuffed flank steak with potato salad. Tosca and Benito never cook. They order from the deli: omelettes, chicken and chips, spring rolls. When it's time for the injections, the little plastic trays holding leftover mash, the colourful smears of a Swiss roll, the empty pizza boxes or picked bones remain on the table and the quiet storm cloud of fried oil in the air can still be inhaled, even seen. Benito doesn't register my presence, he chews standing up, spellbound in front of the television, squeezed into those overalls he never takes off, two or three sizes too small, as if he needs constant reassurance that he hasn't grown. After a bite, perhaps because she has a suspicion, perhaps because she can see something in spite of the half-light, Tosca waves a hand for me to approach her. Her full mouth, false teeth flecked with egg, pork and carrot, is still able to say: You didn't tell me you had a boy. My son, I say, pointing rather stupidly at Simón, as if I too had only just realised he was with me.

Simón takes a step forward and Benito greets him by inclining his heavy head. Surreptitiously, firmly but without causing a flap, surprised by the ogre boy's features which from his perspective must seem even more giant and deformed than they are, he grabs on to my leg and hides. If I were someone else, if I believed in signs, in children's intuition, I would think it a bad omen, that this move isn't a good idea. It's fine, but keep an eye on him, I'm fed up with the little shits, one day I'm going to tell them all to bugger off, says Tosca. She chews and adds: Beni, take them up to seven.

We follow the hulking mass up the stairs and on the third floor he guides us along the corridor to a flat with just one room, almost bare. Two rolled-up foam mattresses and a wardrobe that looks too important for so few square metres. A bulb with no shade does too good a job of illuminating everything. On an old sewing-machine table there's a portable stove connected to a cylinder by a rubber hose. For water, says Benito in his friendly monster's voice, use the bucket, and he points to a paint-stained one under the bathroom basin.

The first night I barely sleep. Or not at all, I can't be sure. I stay awake with my eyes closed, simulating sleep. On the alert. Getting accustomed to the noises that lead me towards dawn: shouts, screeches, slamming, fights, telephones that no one answers. I can hear the rumble of several superimposed conversations, real, televised, barely discernible. And suddenly, a voice that detaches itself from the rest: *shit, whore, honey, c'mon, Beto*. The murmur quickly returns to the level of a muffled but permanent presence. The outside world also makes itself heard: brakes, engines, footsteps, explosions and sirens.

But the thing that keeps me from sleep more than anything, adding to the insomnia of recent days, is not the noise from the street or the music or the conversations, but those strange murmurs produced in the bowels of the building and which at times I think might be in my head. Metallic sounds, wind-like, flushes, hums, sputters, like the secretions of a decomposing organism. And although I could guess at the origin, broken pipes, perforated vents, dying electrical appliances, the fact is that all together they compose a striking, overwhelming echo that's impossible to ignore.

And yet, despite the filth, the heat, those intestinal noises, and the smell of shit that rises in waves, at some point in the early hours Canetti's words from the first time he brought me here come to mind: We're safe here. I even babble them to myself, to confirm it. And so I relax and rest a bit, although still without sleeping. On the third day I cover the windows with black bin bags to prolong the night.

It takes me a while to understand this strange community, to get used to certain codes, at least the most basic ones. There's a system of hierarchy that I'm picking up through observations and comments. Within the group, some top dogs quickly come to the fore, privileged folk who delegate routine tasks to others. Among the most famous are Perico, el Buti's younger brother, who does what he wants: Whatever the hell he feels like, says Canetti; the famous Mercedes, a man feared by everyone; Tosca, of course; and a transvestite called Eva who lives alone on the top floor.

There is a series of guidelines for coexistence that, over the first few days, Canetti and Benito will take it upon themselves to reveal to me. The former, too longwinded, his friendliness always ambiguous, the other quite the opposite, rustic, almost caveman-like. In el Buti the rules are meant to impose order, but in many cases they are also linked to resistance. One mistake could end it all, Canetti explains to me, and adds: Eviction is just round the corner. Those guys are a bunch of shysters, Tosca tells me one night when I'm trying to elicit a bit of history from her, but she leaves me hanging. She mentions her father, some wasteland, the construction company, a rogue engineer and a bankruptcy request. I also find out that there's a judicial order that has been pending for something like ten years but that no one wants to carry out a violent eviction. You have to ask permission to bring people from the outside, give some notice. Not just anyone comes in here, girl, you have to keep an eye out, and to keep an eye out, you have to know, Tosca tells me, slashing the air with her index finger to leave me in no doubt. Entries and exits are certainly monitored. Just in case, Canetti clarifies.

Tosca takes care of the electricity. Before, everyone worked it out for themselves, they hooked up to the building on the corner, the Chinese supermarket or the convent school that occupies half the block. But inspections began to take place much more often and things got complicated, so Tosca managed to place a meter on each floor and she divides it up at the end of the month. She collects the money and pays the bills.

Since no one ever came to install the pumps, the daily rhythm is marked by the issue of water. One day is enough to get the idea. Some flats still have taps; others, like mine, don't. The water is raised up the lift shaft by a system of buckets, ropes and pulleys. On each floor, someone takes care of transferring it to other containers. To take advantage of this, I need to make arrangements with Benito, who organises the turns. At best, the pressure from the street during the night allows the water to reach the first floor. The only ones who don't have to worry are Tosca and Benito. Or rather they do, because if there are any leaks their flat will be flooded straight away, which would cause a short circuit that would leave the whole building without electricity.

Most people make do with gas cylinders for cooking, some with electric heaters. It depends. The problem is transportation: the higher up they live, the harder it is to carry things. We need to take a cylinder up to the seventh, Canetti tells me, shaking out a hand. It's still a long way off, so I don't even want to guess what winter will be like.

A week passes without me realising and it's as if we've always lived this way. Iris continues taking care of Simón while I work but now, since I don't cook for her and although she resists, I've started paying her, not with money, which she would never accept, but with chocolates, tins of sardines and jars of black olives.

TEN

As I'm leaving the zoo one very sunny afternoon, a red car pulls up suddenly a few metres ahead of me. Someone sticks an arm out of the window, waving in my direction. I look both ways, no one's paying any attention, but whoever it is persists. They must have confused me with someone else, that's the first thing that occurs to me, so I don't respond, I look away so that they will quickly realise their mistake and carry on their way. But now they aren't just beckoning me, they add festive blasts of the horn, pestering me to the point of embarrassment. I cross the street and increase my pace to escape the error as soon as possible, but curiosity or instinct forces me to turn my head again and I find it hard to believe what I'm seeing. It's Eloísa, different, changed, but Eloísa. She shouts my name as she leans out of the car window. I stay where I am, head spinning, paralysed, between discomfort and amazement; it's been at least two years since I last saw her face. Amazed, because I wasn't expecting this at all, discomforted when I realise that today, exceptionally, because I didn't want to hang around in the changing room listening to Yessica repeating her banalities, I've gone out onto the street without getting changed, still dressed as an explorer.

When I don't respond, Eloísa gets out of the car and comes bounding towards me, flapping like a butterfly in a fix. She seems shorter, or could it be the distance. As she approaches, she makes signs to whoever is at the wheel to wait for her a minute, she'll be right back. Eloísa. We embrace, she doesn't let me go. She grasps me firmly by the shoulder blades, her face buried in the hollow of my neck, as if not wanting to see, out of love, rancour, I don't know, until finally she releases me and we look into each other's eyes. Yes, she's changed, her features are more adult, she's slim and blonde. A messy blonde, with dark streaks here and there which give her a wild look. She also has a tattoo climbing her arm, a honeysuckle that turns into a long hand that squeezes her neck as if strangling her. And one more novelty: a silvery pearl at the tip of her tongue that she continually reveals and hides.

What are you doing, you maniac? is the first thing she says and she points at the khaki shirt, tapping the zoo badge with her index finger. I laugh, because she called me a maniac, because if I put myself in her place and see me like this it must be funny, but also because I don't really know how to act, what to say, how to explain everything. I'd have to tell her about Jaime, that we came to the city because apparently the farm didn't actually belong to him, it was on loan, he was taking care of it, and that the owner decided to sell the land to the country club. I would tell her we arrived the day of the floods, Simón and I, that we stayed in a little hotel near here, the Fénix, where I met a Romanian called Iris who works in the zoo and well, here I am. I'd tell her about Canetti, Tosca and el Buti another day.

But I say nothing. I stand there like an idiot, introspective, making a visor with my hand so the sun doesn't get in my eyes. And she says: Where are you living? I'm about to lie, tell her anything, invent an address, but I come out with a vague remark. In a building ten blocks that way, I say, stretching my arm out in front of me, and retort: And you, what are you doing here? She shrugs. Life, she replies. And adds, as if she needed to: It's been so long. Well, I have to run, she says, gesturing towards the red car with her chin. Do you have a moby? I shake my head, smiling at moby. Here, take a note of my number, she says, and she pulls a pen from her pocket and writes it on my palm. We have to meet up, man. You have to call me, no questions, it's an order.

The encounter, so unexpected, and at the same time so right, leaves me feeling distracted. Instead of carrying on, I seek refuge in the botanic gardens. I pick the first free bench I come across, next to a fountain of greenish water and floating plants, a mixture of water lilies and rottenness. I quickly try to recover Eloísa's face before it's erased from my mind, her new face, from today: more drawn than before, her mouth small, that little fringe covering her forehead, the pronounced bags under her eyes, a combination of excess and maturity, the same gaze as ever, innocent despite everything. And the red coupé with tinted windows and the guy driving it, hurried and mysterious. A boyfriend with money, it occurs to me. Perhaps she thinks I'm still with Jaime, that I brought the old man to the city. She didn't ask me about Simón either, it's highly probable that she's forgotten him. There are things, people, you should never see again. Why would you? There should be some mechanism to prevent situations from the past repeating themselves, like in a board game, from the start to the end square without turning back.

A very tall man sits down next to me. A few minutes of silence, then he turns his head without twisting his torso, like a marionette of a big ugly bird, and says to me: I'm a poet. Skinny cheeks, his lips pursed as if he were smoking an invisible and eternal cigarette. Coughing between drags. He offers me one of his books, I thank him, I say perhaps some other time. Rather than giving up, he gets exasperated. I agree to let him read me one of his poems.

> *All our selves*
> *will make universal a feeling,*
> *and the curtain will fall*
> *never again to be a colony.*

He finishes with a long, aspirated Ah, as if in need of air, staring straight at me with enormous, unfathomable, animal eyes, waiting for my approval. I smile and he insists I take his book, he wants to give it to me: Don't pay me a thing, he says. On the cover there's a picture of a man bent over himself in a painful-looking foetal position. It's signed: Marco Abel Muscolino. I wonder whether that's his real name or an artistic pseudonym. I return the book to him: Next time, I say, next time I'll buy it from you, and I stand up, taking my leave with a quick, quiet bye before he tries to keep me there.

I cross the road badly, a taxi scrapes past me, I circle the plaza three times and linger for a few seconds at the foot of the Garibaldi monument without looking up at it. Poom. The same route as ever. By the skips from which I rescued the snake book, a small dog comes out of nowhere and barks at me, irritated, like a large rat, running after me for a few metres and threatening to bite. The barks force me to jog to the corner, something I don't decide for myself; my body is in command. As I run, I throw a kick in the air to get him off me but instead of scaring him away, because I gave him a fright, he takes a leap and a bite. He only manages to wet my ankle with his muzzle.

Later, saying goodbye at the door of the guesthouse, Iris reminds me: It's Christmas Eve on Thursday. She pins me down with her eyes waiting for my reaction, which doesn't arrive, not so much because I have nothing to say but because I feel put out. Christmas Eve, I repeat with a smile, as if it makes me happy. For no apparent reason, the idea brings back the image of Jaime in his coffin, still too fresh, as if he were suddenly in front of me. Why don't we go to the all-you-can-eat buffet next to the church? There's a special promotion on, three eat for the price of two, she says, raising her eyebrows as if it were a serious matter. She adds that the menu includes a glass of champagne for the toast; I can't work out whether she's saying it ironically or to convince me. I'm about to say: In our case, given the amount Simón eats, it would be better if two and a quarter could eat for the price of two. But I restrain myself, I'm in no mood to make her laugh, even less of a mood to laugh myself. Sounds good, I say quite sincerely; the truth is I can't think of a better option.

ELEVEN

On the twenty-fourth, with the sun still a long way from disappearing, we go to the hotel to pick up Iris. First, I inject Tosca with an especially strong dose; I feel better that way, she says. Drop in when you come back, you can give me another if I need it. Iris suggested walking for a while to work up an appetite and get our money's worth out of the food. That's how she put it, she let out a cackle and I thought it a good idea. Simón walks on the way out; on the way back we take turns carrying him on our shoulders. We go to the large plaza, we pass the corner where el Buti stands, I point out our window, we stop at a kiosk to buy 7UP, we go into a shop filled with Chinese merchandise, miniatures, plastic flowers, handheld fans; Simón is fascinated by a miniature samurai sword. When we start to feel our legs, we head for the restaurant.

In the little square that smells of urine, we join the sparse audience watching a live nativity scene. I'm not sure, but I get the impression the event is organised by the evangelical church next to the Fénix. Around a shack improvised loosely from cardboard boxes and canes, a series of sinister characters is parading, trying to pervert a naive young girl. It's actually a woman who's well into her thirties wearing a school uniform, white blouse and kilt, which detracts a fair bit from the credibility of her role. Among the demons hounding her, there's a man dressed in leather trying to seduce her with a bunch of flowers, and when he doesn't succeed, he pounces, groping her, just like a monkey. Now another man appears, bald with bulging eyes and a revolver tucked in his waistband, who flings a shower of banknotes at her. He is followed by a rather primitive-looking woman who tempts her with a piece of raw meat. Finally, she is approached by a punk swaying with a bottle of beer in his hand. Besieged by all the sins surrounding her and forming a kind of tribal dance, the girl is about to kill herself when out of the shack emerges a strange Jesus wrapped down to his feet in a tunic, no crown of thorns or beard, who throws himself on top of her to protect her from the vices, which flee from his presence in terror. Iris gives in to temptation and runs off laughing into her hand; Simón can't believe his eyes.

We get to the buffet restaurant at around half nine. The place is already full. Two or three large families, several couples alone and a group of young boys whose features, gestures and tans betray them as foreigners – Australians or North Americans. They are the quietest at the start of the night, the most uninhibited by the end. We sit by the window, a bit of a squeeze, but it's fine. The tables are decorated with streamers, paper serviettes with Christmas motifs, rubber mistletoe and a tiny tree that keeps falling over. For the duration of the meal, Iris or I will keep trying to stabilise the little tree by propping it up in every way possible, using breadcrumbs as a base, spearing it to the tablecloth with toothpicks, wedging it between two glasses. Later on, as the alcohol takes effect, the toppling or perhaps just twisted pine becomes a source of amusement rather than annoyance. We see who can keep it standing for longest until Iris comes up with the ultimate solution: sticking it to the table with a bit of gum which she chews rapidly between courses.

The food is arranged in two large display counters facing each other. On one side, all the hot food, on the other, the cold cuts and salads and, a bit further along, the desserts. The abundance, the shape of certain items and the colour of some of the sauces is amazing at times, even repulsive. There's lamb, rabbit's foot, frogs, squid rings, octopus tentacles, all kinds of schnitzels, an obscene amount of chips. I wonder where they got the frogs, whether they have a breeding tank out back. I eat with relish, like never before. Steaks, a colourful cabbage salad, whitebait and a cheese roulade, palm hearts and olives. I help myself to seconds as if I had been fasting for a week. Iris is more daring: without hesitating she fills her plate with half a dozen frogs, piled in a pyramid. Simón, on the other hand, doesn't want to experiment at all, he limits himself to some cheese and ham *empanadas* and, three times, makes me bring him a stainless steel dish of red jelly cubes. We drink white wine; Iris takes it upon herself to order one bottle after another.

Without saying much, we devote ourselves to chewing, to joking about the decorations, laughing at people, that's how our Christmas Eve unfolds. When we can't go on, Iris releases a burp which Simón laughs at and attempts to imitate. A very young waitress in leggings that reveal the line of her arse and the folds of a camel-toe – May as well be naked, Iris says – collects our empty dishes, a mountain of bones and cartilage.

We start chatting about people from the zoo. We criticise almost everyone, we share gossip, we list physical defects, as work colleagues tend to do when others aren't there. I talk about the few I know, Yessica, Esteban, the polar-bear keeper, the old woman in the office and the guy from human resources. He's a troglodyte, says Iris and I can't believe she uses the word troglodyte, I don't know where she can have learnt it and even less how she manages to pronounce it. We also mention Canetti, she gets to her feet to imitate him, lame and stooped, mouth twisted, just like Quasimodo.

Iris is out of control, almost euphoric. She takes a breath and hurries to empty her glass; she has another anecdote, something she's never told me. On her second day of work she almost died. That's what she says: I almost died. It seems that a woman, a fat lady, she explains and mimics her by spreading out her arms, got her footing wrong as she was crossing the hanging walkway in the subtropical rainforest; she broke a plank in two and got her leg stuck between the wires. In mid-air, she says, and continues describing the scene, which provokes one of her distinctive cackles, shaking the table and beyond. Iris recomposes herself and tells me how she almost had a fit, the plump lady swearing from on high and herself unable to move for laughing. I thought they'd throw me out right then and there, she says. I've never been in the famous rainforest, I've only seen the building from a distance, so I have to imagine the situation from Iris's descriptions. The vines, the tarantulas, the recorded monkey shrieks and a woman trapped in the middle of this artificial jungle. And of course, I can't help laughing along with her. Apparently, because of the risk of the bridge collapsing, they had to bring in a stepladder to rescue her. When they finally got her down, Iris disappeared, she hid in the bathroom until everyone left.

Midnight arrives. The countdown begins at the tables to either side, there are arguments over who has the exact time, one taps the glass of his wristwatch with an index finger, another shakes his mobile as if it were a rattle. The waiters, some Chinese, some of Hispanic descent, hand out plastic flutes among the tables. You can see the chips in them; they aren't new, they've been used for some other celebration, last Christmas or a birthday party. We make a toast. Iris and I with our extremely light glasses, Simón with his fist clenched. But I can't drink much, the champagne is acidic, like old-fashioned cough syrup. Either it's really bad or I'm just not used to drinking and it's a matter of taste.

Surprise, says Iris and takes a bag containing two packages out from beneath her chair. One long and curved, for Simón, the other small and narrow, for me. We unwrap them at the same time: for me, a fan with dragons on it, for Simón, amazed, the samurai sword from the Chinese shop. Thanks, I say, and it's inevitable that I feel inadequate. It didn't occur to me to buy any presents, not that anyone is going to reproach me for it.

After the toast, there's a commotion. People are abandoning their tables and congregating by the entrance, some out of anxiety, others just following the crowd. The door becomes a bottleneck. Although my plan is to stay where I am and watch through the window, Iris and Simón force me to get up. The fireworks, Iris chides me. Sure enough, the restaurant staff have prepared a small fireworks display that puts a silly smile on every face.

Once the excitement is over, after the arsenal of rockets brought out by one of the Chinese men, the eldest, who spent all night behind the till, everyone apart from the teenagers and the foreigners sits down again. Simón stays outside, on the window sill, back leaning against the glass, legs dangling. Another bottle of white wine and I'm not sure whether it's the second or the third. In her drunkenness, Iris passes from euphoria to melancholy in minutes. First she tells me she met a man online. A systems analyst. A strange guy, solitary type, with a moustache. They saw each other once, they went to the cinema, then to a motel, says Iris and in her mouth the word *motel* sounds deep and serious, like a mythological character. When they were in the room she asked him to take a shower and the guy slipped getting out of the bath and split his septum on the towel rail. He spent the rest of the night with a piece of toilet paper stuck in his nose to stop it bleeding. They slept together that once and never called each other again. Then her tone changes and she returns to telling me more details about the story I heard the first day, how she met Draco, what a great time they had over there in spite of everything, how he convinced her to come here, how difficult it was at the start, the uncle and the tyre business, the way he was gripped by racehorse madness, the fights and the separation. The whole time, it looks as though she's going to cry but she never cries, it's deeper than that; at times the sadness turns to hate and she looks like she's on the verge of throwing a chair across the room. Until the calm arrives and it's all held back in her watery eyes.

Ok, I say before she loses it, it's an old story, it's in the past. My words must have some effect because she proposes another toast. We drink. Iris is pensive, gazing outside, with the whistle of the last rockets in the background. And what about you, she throws at me suddenly, coming off her cloud, do you fancy anyone? I shake my head and smile; she does too, as if saying she doesn't believe me at all.

On the way out of the restaurant, Iris wants to walk me to my building. I pick Simón up when he starts dozing off after ten steps. We take it in turns to carry him, one block each. On the way, at corners, in front of bars, in the square where the nativity scene was, people are getting together, beeping horns, two men are shouting from one car to another, their heads sticking out. Come here and say that to my face, arsehole, shouts one who is driving in a Father Christmas costume. The other replies by threatening him with a fist. The light turns to green and they both shoot off at the same time. I can't work out whether they were genuine insults.

Three blocks further on we cross the avenue and turn down a passageway the celebrations haven't reached. No noise, no shouts, no firecrackers. Because Iris can barely stand, it's me who ends up carrying Simón most of the way, and if at first it feels like he'll break my back, I adapt as we go and that annoying kick between the ribs becomes just another part of my body. Like everything, once the novelty has passed, things stop hurting or making you happy.

At one point, Iris stops short, using a tree trunk to prop herself up, she doubles over, mouth open, as if she's going to vomit but she doesn't. She takes a deep breath, rearranges herself and as she starts walking says: She won't be able to look after him any more. She says it like that, in the third person, as if she were talking about someone else. Five disconcerting seconds before she explains. She's been offered shifts at the zoo, manning the cash desk for the sea-lion show in the afternoons. I won't be able to look after the boy any more, she says and stumbles on a broken paving stone. She looks at me askance, gauging my reaction. She's going to work ten- or eleven-hour shifts, depending on the day. It seems like a lot to me, but I say nothing, all the same she justifies herself. She says she wants to buy a plane ticket so her father can come and visit her. She makes some calculations, babbling figures: in five months she'll have enough to pay for the trip. I tell her I think it's really great, not to worry. The thing is that from the second of January, I won't be able to count on her any more. I'm sorry, she says, and starts crying all of a sudden, like a child, not because of this, of course, but because of so many other things I couldn't even begin to suspect. With Simón on my back, I can't hug her as I would have liked to. I pat her on the back, she leans her head against my free shoulder and the tears fall harder.

The building's entrance is occupied by merrymakers. Iris stays at the fringes, she wants nothing to do with it. I tell her to wait for me a moment, I'll take Simón to bed and walk with her for a few blocks. She shakes her head: No, no, no, she says, I'm fine. I insist: I'll be back in a minute. Entering el Buti, there's a commotion in the corridor, I push my way through carrying Simón. Tosca's door is open, I try to pass undetected but if she can't see me, she can smell me. Come in, girl, she murmurs. I'm about to feign deafness but somehow I can't and I go back. I lean in, wave with my free hand and show her Simón sleeping on my back. Put him to bed here, come and drink a toast, girl, she insists. Later, later, I promise. On the staircase I bump into some familiar faces, we exchange silent greetings, without stopping. Canetti too, who invites me into his flat for a drink. I've got chilled cider, he says quietly, so as not to wake Simón. I tell him maybe later.

When I finally put Simón to bed and open the window to let in a little air, I remember Iris. I go downstairs quickly, dodging bodies. I walk to the corner, nothing, not a trace. I wait for a while in case she comes back, unable to decide whether to follow her steps back to the Fénix. In the end, neither happens. Back in el Buti, I linger at Tosca's; she's very animated, with a bottle of spumante on the desk. She pours me some, we clink glasses: You think I'll make it to the end of the year, girl? Let's bet on it. And Benito? I ask. He's with his father's family, that's how it is every Christmas. It's going to be a struggle to get out of here, she doesn't want to be left alone. To keep me there she constantly refills my glass with that delicious wine. A touch more? And she talks ceaselessly. She also sings opera arias, a trio of tarantellas and the Italian national anthem.

I won't be able to sleep with the unstoppable racket in and outside the building, the *cumbia* music, the shouts, the explosions. I think about Iris, about her extremely pale face like an old-fashioned porcelain doll's, about her eyes always full of amazement, about her fortitude and fragility, about how if Jaime hadn't died, if what happened with the house hadn't happened, if we hadn't arrived on the day of the floods, if we'd been accepted at the first hotel we tried, I would never have met her – it makes no sense. The idea saddens me. The alcohol is getting the better of me too. If it hadn't been for Simón in my arms, instead of consoling Iris with those cold pats on the back, I'd have given her a real embrace. And a kiss. It would have been the most natural thing to do.

TWELVE

The twenty-fifth dawns with a tremendous hangover. The stairs of el Buti smell of vomit and urine or, at best, of spilt alcohol. The events of the previous night flood back to me with the rhythm of an unpleasant reflux, a mixture of food, white wine and that bad champagne. And with each retch, as if I were also bringing up leftovers of memory dissolved in the body, Iris's face appears to me, her sudden mood swings, from ecstasy to tears and back to her cackle, her stories, the parade of dishes I'd like to erase from my mind, the fried frogs, the roulades, the cubes of jelly that wouldn't stop wobbling, as well as the party on the street – these were all the images that had stolen into my dreams.

My head hurts so much that my only relief comes from complete immobility; I barely change position, even millimetres make it explode. I stay like that, face up, watching a corner of the ceiling where there's a bend in the pipe that leads nowhere. It takes me a few minutes to make out two large beetles camouflaged by the grease covering this iron elbow, one on either side of it. They must be between four and five centimetres long. They are so still that anyone would think they were drawn on. It's a strategy, as if they are studying their next step. Just as I'm starting to think they're not going to move at all, at least not until I stop watching them, one of the two, male, female, impossible to tell, takes the initiative and begins to turn in circles like a dog chasing its tail. But it goes beyond that, it makes a decision and flies over the pipe to join its lookalike, as if to surprise it. But no, it was waiting. Each knew about the other, they scented each other, one supposes. They play, hyperkinetically, their legs clash until they freeze once more, this time both on the same side but facing in opposite directions. I can no longer tell which is the adventurer. All I know is that while one keeps moving its antennae, the other plays dead. Simón sleeps until half eleven.

My nursing duties aren't suspended in spite of the holiday, but the timing is a bit more relaxed today. Tosca is in a bad mood, she regrets having had a drink. I'm stupid, she says but she doesn't look that bad, she just likes complaining. She offers me a piece of sweet bread that falls apart on the way to my mouth. As I prepare the syringe, Benito, standing in front of the television, releases a seguidilla of farts. It's not the first time he's done it, nor does it particularly annoy me, but today, because it's just occurred to him, or could it be that he's beginning to trust me, instead of hiding them as he usually does, he amplifies them, duplicating them with his mouth in a counterpoint that's as funny as it is repugnant. At the third or fourth fart, which is actually between six and eight, if you count the echo,

Tosca, who didn't even appear to notice, lets out a shout that makes everything shake: Benitoooo! But he pays no attention, and she doesn't seem too bothered, it was just a shout, the necessary closure for the series of double farts.

Now that Tosca is beginning to feel the effect of the morphine, I avert my gaze and concentrate on Benito, who has taken refuge in a corner of the room. A dark, stooped mass, will he cry? Benito is one of those people who have such an impact at first sight, inspiring such intrigue as well as repulsion, that the natural instinct is to leave him alone. The idiot boy, cow-head. People aren't keen to confront him, not so much because of what he might do to them, more because they don't know how to treat him.

Apart from Tosca, who calls him by his name, everyone else in the building calls him Bear. Some, behind his back, call him She-Bear. His only formal occupation consists of managing the buckets of water that are hauled up the rope to the various floors of el Buti. Kind of like a water-boy. He is also in charge of putting the rubbish into giant sacks and taking them out to the pavement. Other than that, he devotes himself to watching television, eating and taking devices apart. A heap of junk, says Tosca, nodding towards Benito's corner. Mobile phones, radios, speakers, printers, whatever he finds. He only breaks them apart, he doesn't fix them or resell them. The pieces accumulate on a magnetic board, forming a mountain of screws, circuits, microprocessors, it's impossible to distinguish the origin of any of it. The result, he'll show me some time later, is some strange baroque sculptures suggesting torture, darkness and pain. Among his creations is a tower, at least a metre high, permanently oscillating.

On Saturday I go back to work. On the way to the zoo, something I can't put my finger on is nagging at me, something outstanding, unresolved. I see Iris in the distance and everything becomes clear. I remember that she's going to start working double shifts so she can buy her father a plane ticket, that she won't be able to look after Simón any more. I have a week to find a solution.

I'm withdrawn all afternoon, half listening to Yessica's Christmas stories. At two in the morning she went to a disco in the arse end of nowhere, so she says, out in the country, a party with some friends of her boyfriend, who never showed up. A complete downer. The worst thing was that the boyfriend didn't answer his phone the whole night and only sent her a text message at three the following afternoon. If I see him I'll kill him. She also tells me about a fight during the meal at her house, between aunts, uncles and in-laws, but I pay no attention.

I bump into Canetti and he reproaches me for not having gone up to drink a toast with him. I was worn out, I say, and he frowns to show that he's upset. Annoyance makes him laconic, which saves me from his interminable chatter for once. The rest of the day passes without note. The threat of a storm that never breaks means fewer people come.

At times my mind returns to the matter of Iris and Simón but I get nowhere. The time of year complicates things. I rule out a nursery, deciding that, if I have to pay someone, I'd be better off not working at all. In fact, I seriously consider the possibility of resigning and looking for something on the injection side of things. I'd often heard talk of the lack of nurses. I could even take Simón with me, I don't think anyone would mind. But I get swamped by the idea, I end up in a muddle, I'm not used to thinking so much. To forget, I rest my eyes on a fixed point, a goose, a Coca-Cola sunshade, the sun broken up by starchy clouds.

I leave the zoo, avoiding the photographer with the pony; I cross the avenue, join the labyrinth of long queues at the bus stop and get off at the paved plaza full of bookstalls. I look around me and wonder how long it would take for everyone in my range of sight right now, pedestrians, drivers, people in cafes, those queuing to enter the chemist, cyclists, those hidden away in apartments, everyone, me included, to disappear.

I walk all the way round and pause at the last stall. The books are on shelves, in boxes, organised by genre, author and various labels: *Bestsellers, Crime, Vampire, Self-Help, Borges and Sabato, Historical Novels, One4Five, Three4Twelve*. The vendor, younger than thirty with thick, rather forced sideburns, like a caudillo or an Elvis impersonator, is talking on a mobile phone connected to earphones, slanting his chin slightly so as to speak into the mic. He looks straight ahead as if at me, but no, he's looking beyond me, at the short horizon of traffic on the avenue. It really pissed me off, he says, falls silent and in a second adds: Yeah, he's a fucking bastard, he just doesn't give a shit. I stay there for a while flicking through the books with no real interest, more intrigued by this guy who is now laughing and spitting. In the *Science Fiction* section I come across *The Marvellous Journey of Mr Nic-Nac to the Planet Mars* by Eduardo L Holmberg.

On the flap, the author's biography: A writer and naturalist, he was the first director of the Buenos Aires Zoological Garden between 1888 and 1904. In addition to his extensive scientific work, he wrote, among other books, *Hoffman's Pipe*, *The Bag of Bones*, *Insomnia* and *The Diabolical House*. Eduardo Ladislao Holmberg, the very same man mentioned on the stamp of the bestiary I found in the skip in front of the Adventist church. Another coincidence, too much. Making timid signs so as not to disturb him too much, I ask the boy the price, he doesn't stop talking and answers by showing two open hands. Ten pesos, I understand, but I don't have enough. Another day, I say circling my index finger in the air. Before returning the book to its place, I read the first few lines, murmuring out loud: *There is nothing more admirable than the perfect mechanism of the skies. Nothing is more pitiful than human ignorance.*

In the evening, Tosca asks me to inject her with an extra phial of morphine. I'm not sleeping at all, she says. Two or three hours at most, it's less every day. I'd like to think I sleep but I don't at all. I close my eyes, that's it. At the start, she doesn't exactly feel pain so much as the shadow of pain approaching. It grows gradually, like a snowball, but when it grabs you it won't let you go. Sometimes it makes her want to shout for me to come down and inject her again in the middle of the night. She feels like two big hands are squeezing the back of her neck, the scruff as she likes to call it, strangling her almost to the point of asphyxiation. A perverse game, sometimes unbearable. She pauses, coughs and continues. The worst thing is the lack of sleep, those long-nailed hands squeezing her neck become so real that she can't help thinking that they belong to someone, that somewhere beyond there must be a body, a pair of arms and a head, someone contriving to fold away behind the headboard. And that mystery is precisely the thing that's hardest to tolerate, even more than the pain. She'd like to be able to turn round and discover who he, she, it is, the one who shelters in the darkness to wring her neck.

Torture, she concludes and gives a long sigh that's only interrupted by the agitation the tale has caused her. I agree to inject her with another dose. The same ceremony every day: I take the top off a phial, load the syringe, look for the vein, right arm in the morning, left arm now. Then Tosca, as if she didn't think I was entirely convinced, or just to impress me, says what she's never said before: Give me your hand, come here, touch it, it won't do anything to you. I've already seen it, the first day, I studied it from a distance under the fabric of her nightdress, but I don't know whether I want to touch it. What for?

It's the size of a lemon, a tennis ball, a bull's testicle, rough, ever so slightly more hairy than the skin surrounding it, definitely much purpler. The spud, she calls it. First I press it carefully, as if it were a delicate creature, the back of my hand on the ball of flesh, fat, tissue, that knot of cells that are quicker than the others. I barely graze it, just in case, to see her reaction. Tosca's words resound in my head: It's another being that lives with me, inside me. I continue, growing more confident, I become bold and press it without hesitating, covering it, my hand wide open, then cupping it. A curved, prominent nerve splits it down the middle, like a swollen vein, strange to touch. The most powerful, most terrible, most evident thing is its strong, regular heartbeats, not Tosca's, which beat elsewhere, but those of this small, raw being. Gentle, she says to me, be gentle. We don't want to disturb it so much that it wakes up. As she speaks I think how stupid I am, that I know nothing of pain.

At least you can see this one, touch it, says Tosca. My sister's was much worse, a horror, it was right inside her like a poisonous gas, like a ghost. First in the uterus, then the lungs, blood, bones, everywhere. Metastasis, she says loudly as if she'd said Magnificent. She really had a bad time of it, and the treatment was even worse. It left her bald, shrunken, wrinkled, like a raisin. One day I'll tell you all about it, she says and concludes: Violet was killed by the medicine.

I become engrossed staring at the ochre phial of morphine, thinking about illness, about matters of the body and about decomposition, the time it takes for flesh to disintegrate. A matter of days or months, depending on the climatic conditions, I studied it a while ago. I wonder what Jaime looks like by this stage. It also occurs to me that one day I'll tell Simón, assuming that he'll be the one taking care of it, that when the time comes I want to be burnt to ashes.

Tosca brings me back to earth with her hoarse voice: Get me some water, girl, I'm dying of thirst, she says, and after three gulps she spits on the floor. The sight reminds me of Iris, the vomit that never came on Christmas Eve, her features drawn, as if halted by reins pulling at her jaw to stop her from bolting. The difference with Tosca is that her reins are inside, rolled up under her skin, in the form of cancer.

Before injecting her, I ask whether she knows anyone who could take care of Simón in the afternoons. I don't call him Simón but the boy, like she would say. I explain that my friend isn't able to do it any longer. A long silence and she calls Benito over. Go and find Sonia, she says. Benito leaves and I inject the morphine. Tosca tilts her head, inflates her chest and slackens. I stay, watching her false teeth submerged in a glass. She now removes them before every injection because her mouth goes to sleep and she hurts herself on them.

Instinctively, like a child left home alone who takes advantage of the occasion to search his parents' room, I stand up and head for Benito's hideaway. I snoop around his things, the junkyard. An extraordinary world, jam-packed with everything, which in some way explains the size of his head. The bed is too short, he must sleep with his legs hanging out. I take another three paces and decide to step through to the other side of a glass-bead curtain. A dark tunnel, access to the basement, the entrance to a garage that never was, an inexplicable space. In some strange effect of angles and refractions, the scant light illuminates from the waist up, as if the scene were submerged in muddy water. In front of me, a door invites me to spy. I lean into a windowless bathroom, brought in from somewhere else: a bathtub with feet, a tank with a chain and a chequerboard floor. Remote in space and time.

A snap of fingers summons me and I jump back into the room. Tosca has returned from her trance. Where did you get to, girl? I thought you'd split. I gesture to the curtain and Tosca nods, understanding what I'm saying, my curiosity. A pause and I clear my throat: Between you and me, when you want, you can take a bath. I thank her with a smile. Sitting on the edge of the bed again, something comes out of my mouth which I regret as soon as I utter it, convinced I've said something really stupid: Better? She shrugs, deflecting the question back to me with her chin raised. And suddenly she lets her arms fall, as well as her head, she relaxes her facial muscles, unlocking her jaw in slow motion, like a rehearsal for death. And what seemed like sarcasm or a challenge before becomes serenity and candour. She says: Much better, yes.

I think about the delayed effect of the drug. As I'm beginning to see, after the injection, after the narcotic peak produced by the fluid entering her body, the balsam, the nothing, the dreams, when she opens her eyes there is a vertiginous comedown, as violent as the ascent, during which she doubtless recovers awareness of her surroundings, what is real, what the senses detect, colours, light, the aftertaste of bile, the roughness of the hands, and the presence of the tumour and all that it is. But fortunately that ends too. Accustomed to the comings and goings, it would seem that, in desperation, the mind comes back to offer a helping hand to what remains of the morphine in the blood and constructs a plateau of well-being, the true effect, the good, long-lasting one, but one that also finishes, gradually abating towards morning.

That's where Tosca is, entering the field of relief, when Sonia appears. For a moment, no one speaks. Not the woman who's just entered, nor the giant escorting her, nor the woman lying back in bed, even less me, observing them all as I bite my lips. But the reasons for the silence are different, particular to each of us, timidity, mental retardation, expectation, torpor. It's Tosca who's directing the scene, taking all the time her body requires to intervene. But when she does, it's without words, a repeated, sluggish gesture, like a drowsy traffic cop, tracing an imaginary line with her index finger joining me to Sonia. I take a while to interpret it, which exasperates her slightly, even though she lacks the strength. She wants me to talk. Sonia listens to me with a concerned expression. She's a slim woman, more than that, skinny, with fine features, hair to her waist, men's clothing. In order to think, Sonia opens her deep black eyes wide and looks at me, but not exactly at me, more at the portrait of the Virgin of Syracuse hanging a few centimetres above my head. She stays like that for a good couple of minutes, more gone than concentrating, as if she's forgotten the question and doesn't know how to get out of the situation, what to invent. Until she wakes up, gives a slight jump and addresses Tosca as if she were the only valid interlocutor. She says: Herbert, it could be Herbert. Tosca, still silent in her cushioned morphine cloud, gives two eternal nods.

THIRTEEN

I dream about snakes. There are hundreds of them, thousands, very fast, fleeing from the reptile house en masse, as if surging from a spring.

Herbert, I should have guessed, is an eleven-year-old boy. He comes at quarter past twelve, fifteen minutes earlier than we agreed with Sonia. I hide my surprise and ask him whether he fancies keeping an eye on Simón. Yes, miss, he says. You know it's for the whole afternoon. He raises his eyebrows and asks: Can I take him to my house?

I introduce the two of them and move away. Herbert and Simón immediately click, they soon start operating under their own codes. In a corner of the room, I pretend I'm tidying so I can watch them. Herbert is taking his job seriously, he tries to work out how to entertain Simón. He chats to him, asks about his toys, and the other boy responds silently, pointing out the shoebox where his little cars are kept. I get distracted for a moment leaning out of the window, a grey, heavy day, and when I look back, they're already mid-game. Sitting cross-legged on the floor, Simón is holding a hook-shaped piece of black plastic, somewhere between a C and an L. It looks like the elbow of a pipe, the piece that drains a washing machine, a reject from something broken. On his feet, Herbert issues instructions for him to hold it in a certain position, the base parallel to the floor, the short arm perpendicular. Herbert corrects him several times, Simón does as he's told but he keeps turning his hand a little more or a little less until finally the other boy tells him, in a voice approaching a shout: There, leave it there, don't move. Then Herbert, two or three metres away, launches the little cars which, if they pass the test, ascend the ramp and go flying through the air. Not at all easy. They switch positions, but Simón gets bored and rebels. He throws the cars everywhere. Then Herbert, who knows I'm watching, twists his head, stretching the corner of his mouth as if to say: Poor thing, he doesn't get it.

I go into the bathroom and brush my teeth for the second time that day to see if I can get rid of the bitter taste that every so often makes me produce involuntary clicks with my tongue, and it occurs to me that it's crazy to leave one child in the care of another.

Now they have made a bridge with the piece of plastic. Every time Simón manages to get a car or the cat and sidecar underneath it, Herbert celebrates as if it were a goal. Great, he says loudly with one arm raised, perfect. But Simón doesn't return his enthusiasm, he limits himself to passionlessly repeating the game. He lets himself be led by the other boy's suggestions and at times he gets lost, his gaze fixed somewhere else, an expression that someone who didn't know better might associate with sorrow. An attitude in which I can't help but see myself. So obviously and to such an extent that I wonder at one point whether he's doing it on purpose, to show me up, even to blame me. Yet this likeness to me, which I can now see in him as never before, could just as well be inherited from his father's personality: that passive air, the moroseness, the stomach out. Watching him interact with Herbert, I can't help thinking about him as an adult, my age, or fifty-something. I can imagine his face, the build of his body, his gaze, but I can't decide on his circumstances. I don't know where to locate him, whether in the country, in the city, neither of the two, whether he's with a woman, or a man, alone, a nomad, sedentary, a warrior or subordinate, I can't even be sure whether he'll be near me or far away.

Herbert, I say, and he comes up to me smiling like a model employee. I ask him about his days, what he does. He tells me his routine: he gets up at six and goes to training until half eight. Training? Yes, football. He wants to be a professional footballer, he's a defender. The last man, as he says. From the club he goes to school and comes home for lunch. Then he's free until seven, he goes back to training at quarter to eight. Half nine he eats and he goes to bed at ten. He says the trainer tells him to get a good rest. Some nights, he goes out for a drive with his father.

I prepare some noodles which the three of us eat quickly and in silence. I explain to Simón that he'll be staying with Herbert until I come back, he looks at me as if to say he already knows. He makes me feel entirely dispensable. Before I leave, I ask Herbert how much he wants paying. He exposes his lower lip, I offer him thirty pesos for the six hours. That's fine, he says biting his lips, I can't tell whether it's a smile of approval or discontent.

On my way out, I come across two boys loitering outside the building: ripped jeans, white T-shirts and black sunglasses. They're looking for the Chemist. I don't know him, I shake my head. I'm new.

Six hours at work and I walk home with Canetti. There are days when his company doesn't annoy me at all, it's almost pleasant. His philosophies are childlike, generally predictable and occasionally wise. He's full of surprises, which you would guess he was making up, but he isn't. After walking a couple of blocks in silence, he gestures with his arm extended upwards and starts praising the rosewood trees, noble and indigenous like few others, he says. From one side of the avenue to the other, a multitude of rosewoods. I raise my eyes: extremely tall, sturdy trees adorning the city with their drooping limbs, enormous but tame. We cross. On the street with the Adventist church, Canetti swaps praise for protest in front of a row of banana trees: A pestilential blight.

He explains. Before starting work at the zoo, he spent six months tramping round the city. A tree census. It was his first job after the debacle, as he calls it. Kind of a resurrection. He took some photocopies with him so he could recognise the different species and he made notes of his findings. Just think, I couldn't even tell the difference between a silk floss tree and a palm. He did the even sides first, following the route on a map he was given, and then he returned to do the opposite sides. Even odd, even odd, coming and going all day. He says the job changed his way of thinking. You always walk along looking right in front of you and all of a sudden I had to cast my eyes upwards.

Let's go down here, he says, a detour, I know, but I let myself be led. Just for today. This is one of the most varied streets I've come across. No two trees are the same. He lists them as we advance: An acacia, an orange tree, a jacaranda, the true national flower. He falls silent and, pleased at my interest, feeling obliged to proffer a conclusion, he says: They piss themselves laughing at us. I assume he means the trees. Canetti points out a trunk chopped almost to ground level because it was destroying the surrounding paving stones. A walnut tree. At the end of the block, the dense tangle of a mulberry: the glory of rats.

All the way back to el Buti, Canetti fills my head with names, characteristics, fruits, flowerings, he pulls off some leaves so I can distinguish one tree from another. He makes me smell and suck them. When he's not talking, he's whistling. A funny melody that repeats endlessly, circus-like. As we arrive, he describes the trees from the corner. All ash, except for this one, he says, steadying himself against the fat trunk in front of the building, whose branches, I notice as I raise my head, collide against the windows of our flat. The only paradise tree on the block.

Benito gives me some old camouflaged walkie-talkies he found on the street so that I can monitor Simón whenever

I come downstairs. He doesn't use those words, he makes himself understood in his own way. Guttural. They work, he says gravely, with a touch of indignation, anticipating my mistrust. And he shows me how, with a matchstick, I can keep the button pressed down and hear what's happening at the other end all the time. I thank him with a pat on the back. Sincerely.

Tosca tells me about Mercedes, Herbert's father, Sonia's husband. The dealer of the building. I learn that as well as providing Tosca with her morphine and Canetti with his sedatives, he sells drugs to Perico and his gang. Everyone hates him but no one dares say a word. Only Sonia calls him by his name, those inside call him Paraguay, those outside, his clients, call him the Chemist. Ah, I say, remembering the tanned faces of the two little chancers who approached me at the entrance to the building. You have to take care, Tosca adds, he's a sly one.

FOURTEEN

Eloísa reappears one night, without warning, when I've already started to erase her from my mind again. Determined to get Simón, who's annoyed at everything, to go to sleep, I ignore the first knocks at the door. Their persistence eventually distracts me and forces me to my feet. Who is it, I ask, exaggerating my reluctance, certain that it's Canetti with his melancholy vibe. It's me, I hear that unmistakeable voice, echoing as if in a cave. I open the door and Benito's huge head fills my entire field of vision. A long silence and finally: Someone's looking for you. He stands watching me and says: People.

I go downstairs with Simón. The hooded boy who used to guard the entrance hasn't been there for a few days. Change of habit. Nose to the door, I peek through the crack between the sheet metal and the wall. It's Eloísa and seeing her again is no surprise. To some extent I was expecting her. Her cheeks are puffy, red, as if she's been running. Also, I realise when I greet her, she smells of a fresh joint, recently smoked, her eyes narrowed and sickly. Behind her is the same car she got out of the other day when we met by chance on the corner by the zoo. The full-on glare of the streetlights makes the chassis shine. You didn't call me, bitch, that's the first thing she says, with the deepest frown she can muster, like a mask. I'm about to tell her the sweat rubbed her number off my hand, but there's no point, what for? She gets there first anyway: Let's go for a drink? I'm with Simón, I say. Eloísa raises and drops her shoulders, as if she couldn't see anything inconvenient about that until I clarify: My son. I open the door slightly further so she can see him sitting at the bottom of the stairs, a little ball of annoyance. Ah, says Eloísa, suddenly remembering what she had buried completely. That's a bugger. Can't you leave him with someone? I smile to say no. Come on, she says, let's go out for a bit, my friend will take us in the car. The proof of Eloísa's return is that she makes me hesitate. I don't think so, I'm going to stay here, I say and close the door.

I drag Simón by the arm and almost crash into Benito, who has been lurking in the shadows, a sentry. With each flight of stairs, I nearly stop, play for time, turn back and come up with a quick lie, say that the person who might have taken care of him went out, she's sick, or asleep, that next week we'll definitely meet up. But the impulse to retreat clashes with a mysterious and tenacious force that makes me carry on climbing and so we arrive at the third floor and Simón turns into the corridor towards the flat and kicks the door. The heat, the humidity, something deeper I can't fathom has disagreed with him. I give in.

Come on, I tell Simón, who doesn't protest, sure that he has won the battle. We go up to the fifth and ring Herbert's doorbell, he sticks his head out rather disconcertedly. Is your mum there, I ask. Herbert glances behind him and lets us in. Sonia and Mercedes are sitting at the table, they've just finished eating, lethargic, their eyes duplicating the television screen. Nothing, no hello, not even indifference. The first impression I have of Mercedes confirms all the stories I've heard about him. He's a sitting bull. The naked torso, the square head, bushy eyebrows and a mass of tangled hair that couldn't be blacker. He really is frightening. For a moment, I'm invisible, just long enough for a recce of the territory. It's an ambiguous setting: unplastered walls, pipes exposed, as are the cables and the bare concrete floors. There are numerous cardboard boxes piled up on one side and a series of very new appliances: stainless-steel kitchen, a fridge big enough for a whole community, an ultramodern washing machine. Excuse me, I say, wishing I hadn't come. I'm about to ad-lib: I have to buy something from the Chemist. Or no, better tell the truth: A friend I haven't seen for ages came by. In the end, it's neither of the two, I don't explain a thing, I'm direct: Could Simón stay for a while, I have to go out. Like dominoes toppling, Herbert and Sonia transfer my question with a turn of the head until it reaches Mercedes, who takes a while to react. He's devoting all his attention to tearing the last bits of flesh from a chicken leg. With the bone in his hand like a pointer, he raises his brows, directs a stiff smile at me, shakes himself like a mime artist and nods with his whole body. It's a yes, I take it as a yes, but I still can't tell whether he's making fun of me slightly, whether he's suggesting that in some way I'm going to have to pay, perhaps it's just an odd way of saying yes, of course. You stay with me, says Herbert, and Simón immediately perks up. He doesn't even wave goodbye.

I close the door and realise how much time must have elapsed; Eloísa has probably already left. So, with that outcome in mind, once again feeling disconcerted by the contradictory forces of a moment ago, instead of hurrying I move with increasing slowness over the distance separating me from the ground floor. I count to three before I take the next step. All the same, I think, if I go back to get Simón now they'll think I'm mad. The best plan is to go around the block a couple of times, take about twenty minutes at least. On the pavement, I realise the red car is no longer there and that the heat is more or less the same inside and out.

I begin to walk towards the corner and two short blasts of a horn stop me by the supermarket. They're on the other side of the street, facing the wrong way against the traffic, lying in wait. Eloísa calls me over, waving her arm through the window. Let's go, she says, get in. Something quick nearby. Good, I say, nearby, I can't be long.

I get in the back, the upholstery smells new. Eloísa is in the passenger seat. She twists round, hugging the backrest, and introduces me to Axel, who's driving, the same guy as last time, I assume. Axel greets me through the rear-view mirror. For a while, until we get out and I can see him face-on, his figure is reduced to a hunched back and portions of face that enter and exit the frame: an eye, the tip of the nose, pieces of ear and cheek. Where are we going? Axel asks. Surprise us, replies Eloísa and vaguely slaps the air with the back of her hand. How did you find me, I find myself saying, just to say something, not really

interested. Aaahh, she plays mysterious, hands open. I
have informants, she says. I smile. For the few minutes
we spend in the car without settling on a destination,
we continue to exchange short, worn phrases that don't
reveal much: All good? This is mad, isn't it? Yes. And you?
You're the same. You cut your hair, I'm going to say and
Eloísa's going to show me the cross tattooed on her neck.
To help us, or so he doesn't have to listen, Axel turns on
the radio and skips nervously from one station to another
until he is grabbed by the anthem of the summer. That's
what he calls it, and turns up the volume.

After many false turns in search of somewhere in
the neighbourhood, Eloísa orders: Park here, I'm starv-
ing. We end up in a taxi drivers' bar a few blocks from
the building, next to a funeral parlour. Jaime again. We
sit at a table next to the window. The place is a pastiche
of styles. Eloísa takes me by the hand and for the third
or fourth time comes back to the same: What are you
up to, you daft cow? Her nails are bitten, painted black.
Well, I say, I'm here. She insists, she wants me to tell her,
I have no way out. I try to sum it all up in one phrase,
I chew it over but can't find the words. I got bored of
the countryside, I say and she laughs. And the old man?
I hesitate, three, four long seconds, as if saying it out
loud: He had an accident, He was run over by a truck, He
was killed on the road. The problem isn't the novelty of
death so much as the reflection it entails, the obligation
to recreate the grief, to put on a sorrowful face, because
not even Eloísa, who never held him in high regard, could
escape the platitudes. Did you chuck him? I'm succinct:
He died. And her: You're fucking with me. She's going

to say something else, but the waiter appears and saves her. The guy, a small bald man with a squirrel-like face, questions us with his chin, Axel asks for the menu and the man looks at him as if insulted.

Eloísa returns to the subject of Jaime, she squeezes my wrist and winds up the story with a short phrase: Man, what a head-fuck, I'm sorry. Really. She shakes her head as if saying never mind. How long has it been? she asks and answers herself: It's like three years, that's mad, she'll say it a hundred times. She herself has much to tell. Her parents separated, her mum went to live in Misiones and her old man stayed in the house with her and her brother. My eyes are gone, hypnotised by the silvery pearl. I'd like to see it properly, I'd have to ask her to keep her tongue still for a few seconds. She says that one day she got tired of all that horse shit and got the hell out of there. Now everything's really good, she speaks to her old man occasionally and everything, the bastard hooked up with a girl of twenty-three who works for the council in Luján and they live in a horrible but airy little apartment. After all the mess, they sold the house, did you hear? Yes, I say, although I didn't hear anything, but I witnessed the demolition which is more or less the same. She explains: They split the cash, fifty-fifty, and gave a little bit to me and my brother, do you remember my brother? I nod although when I try to visualise him a motorbike comes into my head.

There's no doubt, if the Eloísa of my memory was talkative, the current version is several times more power-ful: her age and the city. She barely takes a breath. As I listen to her, or at least pretend to, half of it is swallowed by sheer velocity, I take one of her cigarettes without asking, an old habit, part of the re-encounter. As in the Fénix, smoking is an effort. It's as though Axel isn't there; he spends the whole time entertaining himself on his phone. The waiter comes back, this time Axel keeps him there, issuing a series of commands about how he wants his burger, which gradually put the guy in a bad mood. With ham but no cheese, with tomato but no lettuce, a dribble of oil, French bread, good and crusty, mayonnaise on the side. Eloísa orders two Fernet and Cokes and a portion of chips, she decides for me and asks if I'm ok with it when the waiter has already gone. Axel returns to his mobile, Eloísa to the conversation.

From Open Door she moved to a place near La Plata, the name of which she can't remember; she was there for a few months staying with a boy she met in a bar. Half musician, total dope-head. Until she found out that the guy took part in Umbanda rites. He was a real nutjob. She kept wandering, a long summer in Misiones, a season in Uruguay, too quiet for her, and finally she ended up in Buenos Aires. Lots of nightlife, lots of weirdos. I hooked up with a thousand guys, she says. I smile. What didn't she do. She repeats twice: What didn't I do. She worked at just about anything I could imagine: bars, restaurants, telephonist, a motorbike place, a service station, even as a hostess in a high-class brothel. Only a hostess. Legs, you know it? Then she spent about six months working as a promoter for a mobile-phone company in Liniers, a bunch of sharks. And she began sleeping with a forty-something photographer, a cool guy who got her work at events. Parties, presentations, stupid little things. She met Axel at a wedding, she was waitressing, tray-carrying, as she calls it, and started telling him how pissed she was. Then, hearing his name, Axel raises his eyes from the screen for the first time and nods twice in confirmation. He has a strange face, a false square, his eyes not entirely in line, the nose reddish, scaly, covered in blackheads, the mouth large, dry lips. Seeing them together, their features, the clothes they wear, their way of talking or staying quiet, it's hard to think of two more different people. At first glance, it seems as though a kind of mutual pity must have brought them together.

The Fernet and chips force Eloísa to take a pause but she immediately picks up where she left off. She talks to me about the neighbourhood, my neighbourhood, which she knows well through a very good friend who has a second-hand-clothes shop. I'm distracted by an Uuuhhhh coming from a nearby table. Two old men sitting next to each other, drinking some kind of aperitif with soda, have started pulling at the remote control. The television is right above us on a high wall mount. It's showing a football match and one of them clearly wants to change channels, the other resists but ends up giving in. Now the screen shows a ship sinking at sea, a group of helicopters hovering over it like flies.

ECOLOGICAL DISASTER
300 TONNES OF CRUDE OIL IN
THE PERSIAN GULF

Eloísa goes to the toilet. I'm left alone with Axel who, without letting go of the phone, pressing keys blindly with his thumb, suddenly smiles at me, but says nothing. Since he doesn't sustain eye contact, I focus on a large, recently squeezed spot that's perfectly equidistant between his brows, a third eye. A fine scab is forming at the edges, the still fresh blood coagulating in the centre. The slight difference in skin tone between that area and the rest of his forehead makes me suspect he is wearing some kind of make-up. I'm not sure.

I take advantage of the interlude to look around me. The thing that grabs my attention most is the cabaret-style bar with gold studs, dark wood, the deep-red cushioned edging making you want to sink an elbow into it. The drinking-den effect is continued with a row of burgundy-coloured stools and the bottles multiplied by the mirrored walls behind the counter, liqueurs, wines, whiskies, grenadine. Further along, built into the wall, there's a grill, as large as a double bed. From a distance, I can make out a couple of chickens and a piece of steak, that's all. A grill of that size must have functioned to its full potential at some point, or perhaps not, it could be a project that failed in the attempt. Even more disconcerting is an arrangement of vines, garlands and pineapples, somewhere between Caribbean and Amazonian, swinging above the bar. Another jungle.

So, how's the city treating you? Axel is speaking, he surprises me. I turn to look at him at the same time as he discards his phone on the table, opening and closing his hands as if the muscles have cramped from so much tapping. Yeah, I say, it's fine. And the zoo? It must be something spending all day there, isn't it? Like a film. Yes, just like a film. He wants me to tell him an anecdote about animals, but everything that comes to mind involves humans, Iris in the jungle, Canetti deliberately turning to shit, Yessica and her fake tits. I invent something about a goose that tried to escape and was caught crossing the road. Axel laughs loudly, grunting like a pig, a piece of burger in his mouth.

Meanwhile, a man with no legs enters the bar, travelling on a kind of skateboard, but square, like a mobile platform. He's wearing glasses with green lenses, like jam-jar bottoms; rather than seeing better it's as though he doesn't want to see at all. He stretches out his hand. He passes us and Axel pulls a face of repulsion, he clenches his fists as if he were in pain too, it's unclear why, whether it's the legs, the misery or the stumps. Something is torturing him. In his hurry to get rid of the poor fellow, Axel puts his hand in his trouser pocket and instead of taking out what he was looking for, he spills a load of coins on the floor, some notes too. The cripple devotes himself to collecting it all, moving with amazing dexterity; Axel makes as if to bend down but aborts the movement halfway. Perturbed, he plugs his mouth with bread, chewing as best he can, jaws full, and refuses energetically when the man gestures to hand back everything that fell. He tells him with signs to take it all, that he wants nothing more than for him to get out of his sight quickly. The process leaves Axel exhausted and sweating, fists clenched on the table, not even craving his mobile. I'll be right back, I'm going to buy cigarettes, he says, and flees.

Eloísa takes advantage of Axel's absence to tell me about him. He's really quite alone, she says, confirming my intuition about how the couple got together. It's

highly likely that Axel would say the same about her. Pity
for pity's sake, that sounds about right, after everything.
You have no idea of the money they have, not a clue, she
continues. Axel's parents live in Miami, they left after
a kidnap attempt on his sister. Eloísa saw her once: An
aberration. Axel wanted to stay because of his girlfriend,
Débora, another moron. The boy handles the family's
money, but as for doing, he does nothing. Did I tell you
they own a jeweller's? They're shit-deep in money but
really stingy. Stingy, I repeat, surprised to hear Eloísa
use that word. Stingy, she repeats: Tight-fisted, penny-
pinching, miserly. And she continues: As you can see, he's
a real druggy. I've seen him out of it hundreds of times,
practically dead. But I love him – pah, I don't know if I
love him; I like him and we have fun. I live at the back of
the house, we see each other when we want to and when
we don't, we don't. Seeing him return, Eloísa pretends
not to notice and says in a whisper, as if it were another
confidence: Can you imagine what Miami must be like?

They drop me at the door of the building. Eloísa asks
me what my work schedule is like. She says she'll drop
by some day so we can go for a beer. She notes down her
mobile number for me again, on a piece of paper this
time. Before saying goodbye, she takes out a half-smoked
joint and hands it to me. A little present. Getting back
into the car she sticks her head out of the window again.
Axel says goodbye too, with two short, sharp beeps. They
disappear and I'm left like an idiot holding the door with
my ankle so it doesn't shut on me. I think about everything we said, everything we didn't, I think about the
past, everything that is no longer and never will be again,

I think about how each of us had to devise our truth in relation to the other, a comparison of before and after. And that's the reason for all the affectations, the smiles, the embarrassment, the surprise, the And you? This is mad, and I promise. All those words.

FIFTEEN

Saturday afternoon, the last day of the year. A few blocks before the zoo, in passing, I hear one taxi driver saying to another, as they sit in their cars, that a temperature of forty-three degrees has been forecast. That it will be a record, the highest for fifty years, and that the emergency services have declared an orange alert. Dog days, he shouts and accelerates. No matter what, if December's like this, the chances are that January will be worse. Record or not, the heat is certainly making itself felt and at times it seems unreal. It must be between two and three o'clock, I'm in the shade and yet this blouse, too heavy for the summer, is sticking to my back, chest and armpits. Few people dare to look round the cages in the sun: one bold woman drags five rebellious children behind her, a pale adolescent passes with a sketchbook and two tourist couples enter the reptile house sweaty and happy. Since the activity is almost nil, the fiery breeze sends me to sleep. I'm alone; Yessica was feeling unwell and they gave her the day off. My blood pressure's hit the floor, that's what she said. Esteban didn't appear either. The only person I saw, passing in the distance with a broom, was

Canetti, who in an attempt to escape the heat went to sweep behind the toilets, a zone he always avoids because of that intolerable sewer smell.

Suddenly, above the muffled hum emanating from this incendiary cloud of heat, I hear an exclamation followed by a metallic clatter. I'm gonna bust you, you utter bastard, is what I hear. Less quickly than other curious bystanders, but still attracted by the din, I leave my hideout and take three steps forwards without venturing beyond the edge of the shade. The scene is being acted out right in front of me, next to the drinks stall: on the ground, there's a blond guy surrounded by a table and some chairs that fell along with him; a few metres away, a skinhead in a vest, a hefty guy, hostile expression, keeps tossing out insults in that rough voice that dragged me from my lethargy. He's one of those skinheads who shave to disguise premature balding, to seem harder or more virile. In the second row, each man has his cheerleader. The blond guy has a little boy with curls, even blonder, of six or seven who snivels behind his back: Daddy, Daddy, he repeats, I can't work out whether reproaching or wanting to protect him. The other man is accompanied by a girl with back-combed hair, a fuchsia top and a leather miniskirt that comes down to where her arse meets her legs. Near the blond guy I can now see the remains of a hot dog, the sausage rolling slowly down the slope towards the lake, to the delight of the otters.

Think you're clever, dickhead? the skinhead persists. The blond guy doesn't seem particularly willing to fight, you can see the fear in his face, he'd rather the other man calmed down; for that reason he holds up his right hand.

However, because the skinhead isn't pacified, nor does he feel sorry for the man who fell down, quite the opposite, he threatens to continue hitting him and a security guard arrives to join the struggle without much success. But even though the skinhead gets angry, the intervention is of some use, because although he continues with the insults, he seems to give up on the idea of coming to blows.

The scandal attracted the attention of Iris, who left her post and approached me, raising her eyebrows. Behind her appeared a few people who had left the queue for the sea-lion show. But since I didn't know any more than what I could see, I could only offer the typical, vague conjectures that people tend to venture about the origins of any fight.

It was then, in that moment of distraction, as I was holding a silent dialogue with Iris, that the blond guy stood up and did something of which no one would have thought him capable, not those who were following the saga nor his son, nor even the man himself, much less the skinhead, who was now talking to the guard and gesticulating eloquently. The guy grabbed the base of a Coca-Cola sunshade that had toppled with him and in one movement that was as quick as it was furious swiped at his rival with a blow directly to the legs. Less from the force of the impact than from the surprise, the skinhead fell backwards and almost caught his neck on the edge of a raised flowerbed. Taking advantage of the fact that his aggressor was on the ground, instead of running away, the blond guy plucked up his courage and went to confront him, without releasing the sunshade, like a medieval knight brandishing his lance. What's wrong with you, what's wrong with you, he said. Iris let out a laugh, out of nerves, because of the ridiculousness of the situation, a noisy guffaw that she immediately repressed by putting her hand over her mouth. While the curly-haired boy continued crying, the girl in the miniskirt shouted Juan, to warn the skinhead of the attack. The young father's warrior-like attitude didn't last long. The skinhead's expression contorted like a latex mask. We saw it clearly, Iris and I; this time we hadn't been able to resist moving a bit closer. In two precise manoeuvres, with the speed of a ninja, no doubt born of some kind of training in martial arts or self defence, the skinhead disarmed the blond man of his sunshade, stood up and gave him a flying kick that clobbered him in the jaw. The guy collapsed, taking with him the only table that was still standing. Allowing him no time for anything, the skinhead leapt on the blond guy with all his ferocity: he kicked him in the stomach, the legs, the head, as if he were avenging some old family feud. The skinhead was so beside himself that not even the guards, of whom there were two by now, nor Iris's aquarium colleagues could contain him. Only when the other man stopped reacting, trembling, his mouth and one eye bloody, did the skinhead allow four men to take control of him. One of the guards called for help on his walkie-talkie. One man held the blond guy's head between his knees until the ambulance arrived. After a while, the police arrived in a patrol car, scaring the ducks with their siren.

The blond man was barely conscious, completely broken. They carried him into the ambulance on a stretcher along with his son. The skinhead was arrested.

As the remaining group of onlookers gradually dispersed, the girl in the miniskirt stayed where she was, unburdening herself into her phone. Since Iris and I, not meaning any harm, were looking in her direction, she wheeled round to snub us and, in an instant, without pausing in her rant, she got her footing wrong and broke a heel.

Incident over, and with all traces cleared so that no one would suspect anything had happened, Canetti hosed down the area. The boy from the bar told us his version of events. From the looks of things, while the skinhead had been in the toilet, the blond guy had made a move on the girl in the miniskirt at the food stand. Not even a move, he had paid her a compliment. It would seem that the girl told her boyfriend and the rest was history. We stayed there discussing it for a while, it was really Iris and the boy, I can never remember his name, Cristian or Marcelo, discussing who had been at fault. According to Iris, the blond guy was a stupid chancer. The boy, on the other hand, defended the father and laid the blame on the skinhead. He was out to kill him, he was saying. I saw his face, I knew he was out of it. They couldn't understand how he had been able to keep hitting him, on the ground and with the kid right there. He was really messed up. I say nothing, I keep scouring the ground in search of a bloodstain that might have been missed.

On the stairs of el Buti, a large hand falls on my shoulder and grips me. Benito hands me a bit of paper with a hurriedly handwritten note. I don't need to read it to recognise Eloísa's writing: Tonight party on a boat, it's going to be great. Call me. That's what she says and she leaves her phone number again. Thanks, I say to Benito who is waiting for a response like a messenger from another century.

In the flat, Herbert and Simón are playing at torturing a moribund beetle on the bathroom floor. When he sees me, Herbert blushes. He moves, as if wanting to hide what they're doing. I don't know what he thinks I'm going to reprimand him for. I ruffle their hair in greeting and with that they are forced to uncover the insect, pinned by three toothpicks. I don't censure them; I don't see anything bad in it – dirty, perhaps, but not bad.

I lie down to rest. The ceiling reflects the network of tree branches and the movement from the street at a speed I've never seen before. I make an effort to distinguish outlines, but abstraction always defeats me. Wanting to imitate that very quick, animated sequence, I try to blink in synchrony: completely impossible. I give in. The original landscape is disintegrated by this inverted projection and a new one created. A brief siesta and it's eight o'clock.

Herbert is still in the flat; they've abandoned the beetle, now they're entertaining themselves scratching each other's heads, in turn. Aren't you leaving, I ask. I'm in no hurry, I'm not training today. I wash my face and begin to hear the first bangs. Iris is arriving soon; I ask Benito to let her in, I can't be bothered going down, in fact I'd like to be able to sleep a little longer. It was a struggle to convince her but she eventually agreed. She tried to insist that we eat in the hotel, but I had already decided. The truth is that she doesn't like this building at all. She arrives loaded down with bags: fried chicken, olives, cheese, crisps, chocolate-coated peanuts and two bottles of cider. She's taken aback when she sees Herbert, not for any particular reason, she just doesn't like surprises. At half nine, Sonia appears, scolding her son from the door. What are you thinking, staying this late. I'm about to leap to his defence, say that I invited him, but I close my mouth. It's a matter for mothers.

Before eating, we smoke the half joint that Eloísa left me. Iris refuses twice and finally accepts. It has an immediate effect on her. Her eyes narrow and she enters a state of childishness close to stupidity. A long way from her usual extremes, exultant or ill-humoured, for a while she becomes almost autistic. The joint overshadows me too. We devour without pause, no chatting, everything we have.

At half eleven, we go out onto the street. At the entrance to the building there's a long table and by the kerb, a barbecue with steaks and a heap of flaming coals. Bottles of cider pass from hand to hand. A whole host of people I've never seen before and never will again come in and out of the door. A broad-shouldered woman with sequins stuck to her body moves off diagonally without showing her face. I could swear she's the famous Eva, but there's no one here I know who could confirm it. Firecrackers and gunshots, it's hard to tell which is which, mingle in the air. On the next block, the Ecuadorians, as they're known in the neighbourhood, are holding their own party. Tosca is the only one who doesn't show her face, she stays in her hovel. The rest, in varying degrees of joy and lethargy, parade unceasingly in front of us:

Benito, Sonia, Canetti, Mercedes, Herbert, Perico and the hard kids, in a gang. Simón trots after one of the little girls with Asian faces. The layers of reality, all I can see, lead me to a hallucinatory, acid-trip limbo. A firecracker, and I fall to the ground all at once.

Iris, a better drunk than at Christmas, less melancholic and more fun, insists that we go up close to see the Ecuadorians' dummy being burnt. We stay there a good while in the heat of the bonfire, which I see in duplicate, like a miniature, in Simón's pupils.

The snake nightmares return. This time just one, a python with a man's head and luminous eyes that pursues me, fattening the pipes of el Buti. I wake up on the verge of asphyxiation, almost with the dawn. I find the antidote in insomnia. The remedy in obsession. To combat snakes: more snakes. Sitting up in bed, I grope for the big book by Albertus Seba. Making myself comfortable, as I leaf through, I feel something pricking my groin. A pencil with zoo animals on it, I don't really know how it came to be in my pocket. Everything is linked. I go back through the pages and one of the illustrations is covered by a transparent sheet that triggers an immediate impulse. I start tracing a snake that occupies a whole page, the *Corallus hortulanus* or garden tree boa. That's how the year starts for me.

SIXTEEN

Third of January. Dawn breaks, sticky and oppressive; it couldn't be more humid. I go to the bank to pick up my first pay cheque. They gave me a card but the cash machine swallowed it. Iris, who's on a day off, will stay with Simón in the hotel. Before I leave, she gives me instructions: how to get there, where to get off, not to queue twice, and above all to avoid being served by the cashier with the moustache who always manages to find a problem. The ID, the signature, the system, there's something new every time. Best to arrive half an hour early and queue in the street. It's worse later, so she said.

I take the subway at Pacífico. Progressively, as I descend underground, first at the ticket window, then crossing the turnstiles, on the escalator leading to the platform, the viscous heat at ground level doubles, triples, until it reaches its peak inside the carriage. Without being quite full, there are a lot of people and as we approach the city centre we are increasingly crushed together. Someone comments: It must be about fifty degrees in here.

There are three people around me with whom I can't help maintaining physical contact. In front of me, behind me, arms, back, even the head of a boy with endless dreadlocks who will spend the entire journey rearranging his hair and scratching everyone else's faces with it. There are men in suits, ladies with bags, a down-and-out, a group of percussionists who don't really know where to put their drums. There's a girl who's unbelievably dressed, the seams of her trousers on the verge of bursting, a fat man sleeping, his cheek plastered against the window, and a very pregnant woman who provokes a ripple of sympathy as soon as she gets on. Strong garlic breath wafts through this atmosphere, impossible to identify which mouth it comes from. I breathe as best I can; I hope it's over soon.

Between Callao and Tribunales, more or less halfway, the train stops dead. Not violently, but still forcing us into a swaying motion that continues until we find our balance as a mass. Two minutes pass and the thing that causes irritation, ill humour, in some cases anxiety, is not knowing what's happening, or how long we'll be left stranded. Some accept it with resignation and, as well as sighing, they adopt bored expressions, checking the time on their mobiles with no hint of rebellion. Others, because that's the way they are, a matter of temperament, start talking loudly, sound off about the subway workers, speculate, swear at no one in particular.

One man, the most agitated, he must be about forty with lots of curly grey hair, overplays his annoyance and, clearly without thinking about it, bangs his fist against the emergency box and pulls the red lever which peals out a shrill alarm, extremely high-pitched, as if to scare off rats. The man is met with synchronised disapproval.

His intended heroism, the fact that he assumed his anger on behalf of the rest, makes him the target of all eyes. The hell is almost eternal. Fifteen minutes of enclosure, siren and sweat. Just about at the limit of what we can tolerate, just before someone carries out the threat of fainting, those standing next to the windows notify us of a movement of torches at the edge of the tunnel, they calm us down. Here, here, repeats one man and taps at the glass with his finger, fearing they'll pass us by, the way it happens in dreams.

When one of the doors is finally opened, the inevitable occurs, an avalanche of which no one seems to be the cause. Some raise their arms in a gesture of innocence. Two men with helmets and grey overalls try to contain the passengers' anxiety, they ask for order, they don't say women and children first, as they do during shipwrecks in films: Calm down, everyone will get off. They erect some steps and the carriage slowly drains of people. One at a time, they say, but people still push and shove. Because I'm in a corner opposite the exit, I'm one of the last to leave. As I get out, I look both ways. Our rescue scene is multiplied along the rest of the train, forming the typical image of an exodus of refugees.

The underground peregrination is a mini adventure. The guy who pulled the lever returns to his role from the shadows, he won't let up carping. Around me, others weave hypotheses about what happened. A blonde woman who is leading two girls, also blonde, by the hand, daughters or granddaughters, the darkness won't allow me to see, is talking on the phone, relating the events, and she mentions a power failure, I don't know where she got that from. A third person ventures the theory of a suicide. He says it loudly, with a touch of vindictiveness. I think: a suicide halfway between two stations doesn't make much sense. One of the percussionists starts humming. His friends encourage him with applause, the boy lets himself go and raises his voice:

> *I am the miner*
> *The miner am I*
> *I am the miner*
> *And I sing as I pass by*

At Tribunales we are informed over the loudspeaker that it wasn't a suicide or a strike, the blonde woman was right: there was a failure on the medium-tension lines. The man who protested on everyone's behalf, the guy with grey curls, now I can see him in his entirety, stomach too bulky for the length of his shirt, doesn't believe the explanations at all and continues with his lecture, now directing it at the loudspeaker as if it were a subway employee.

On the surface at last, the air could be described as fresh, even though it isn't really. An illusion that doesn't last long. I buy mint gum at a kiosk. I hardly ever do, but I don't think twice, I need it like water. As I chew, I feel as though the gum helps me dissolve all those smells that seeped into me during the journey, including the taste of garlic, which I can sense in my own mouth as if it had invaded me by osmosis.

Five blocks separate me from the bank where I have to collect my pay. I walk along the pavement under an extremely large sun in the opposite direction from the few cars that are cruising down the avenue. Before entering, I glimpse a swarm of bodies through the window. I go through the automatic door, which takes a second too long to open, as if it's too lazy to keep detecting people, and a dry, icy blast of air gives me a nasty shiver. There are queues criss-crossing in all directions. I have to ask three times before I'm told where I should stand. A security guard points out the longest line, which is snaking from the entrance to the cashiers. I join it.

It's the first working day of the year, which explains the hordes of people. I think about turning round and coming back tomorrow, but I reject the idea quickly; I'm already here. To entertain myself, I observe my surroundings methodically, from one side to the other. A green mural depicts a profile of South America on its side, sick or resting: the prominent forehead, the sunken eyes, the pinched mouth, the long, delicate chin. In front of me is a row of cubicles separated by partitions not even a metre and a half high, each containing a desk, a computer and an anglepoise lamp. In each one, a customer and a bank employee are facing each other. Apart from two cheerful women, probably friends, the faces on both sides tend towards discomfort. A bit further along, it opens out into empty space, with a round flower bed and a palm tree illuminated by a yellow spotlight. Artificial, real, I can't tell. I'm tempted to go and touch it to find out, but I'd have to abandon the queue and ask them to keep my place, a lot of fuss.

For the three quarters of an hour I'm going to spend in line behind a boy with headphones who doesn't stop nodding his head, my gaze wanders between the supine Latin America, the sleepy faces of the sales executives, Nelson, Víctor, Shirley, and the highest leaves of the palm tree that bend where they meet the ceiling. With about ten people between me and the finishing line, I start studying the cashiers. In the centre is the moustachioed bursar I'm to avoid. If I get him, I can let the person behind me pass in front, pretending not to notice, searching for something in my bag, pretending that I'm caught up in the cordons, having a coughing fit. To his right, there's a redhead with a small mouth and her hair in a bun; on the other side, a boy who if it weren't for the suit and tie you'd say was a teenager who's skipped school. I think about Canetti and his story of feigned madness, his ill-fated plan, his treacherous psychologist, his deserting wife, also about his limp, the trees he was employed to catalogue, the sweeping job he managed to get at the zoo. I try to imagine myself in the place of one of these people, but it doesn't fit.

Finally it's my turn. I sigh in relief: I've got the young lad. He's not at all friendly, you can tell he's been trained that way by his boss. I hand him the cheque, my ID. Do you have another form of identification? he asks. I smile at first, convinced he's joking, but from the stiff look in his eyes it would appear he's being serious. You can't read it at all, the photo's blurred, he says, picking up the document between his thumb and index finger. I look him in the eye, arch my brows, I apologise with a purse of my lips. While he does what he has to do on the computer in order to give me my money, he complains repeatedly in a low voice, muttering, as if he doesn't dare say what he wants to. He counts the money and opens his mouth but without raising his eyes, he's talking to the banknotes: I'll pay you this time, take it as an exception, next time you can forget it. That's what he says: Forget it.

The return trip is fast. No incidents, protests or bothersome noises. As if I had travelled into one city and returned by another.

On Friday morning, we go to look for Herbert in his flat because I have to be at the zoo to receive some new animals at one o'clock. In the corridor, before I knock on the door, our footsteps are marked by fast harp music. Herbert sticks his head out. He's flushed, his fringe stuck to his forehead, a black and yellow striped football shirt with a ring of sweat in the centre of his chest. I ask him whether he can come down a bit early. Yes, yes, but I have to change. He runs off and leaves the door ajar. The sunlight exaggerates the contrast between the half-finished flat and the resplendent domestic appliances. Mercedes appears in shorts and vest, his arms covered in tattoos and scars. It takes him half a minute to notice us. He ignores us, or doesn't see us. Until he suddenly says: Argh, what a fright. I justify myself: We're waiting for Herbert. Come in, he says with a smile of rotten teeth, and stretches out his arm offering me a *maté*. It's Paraguayan *tereré*, he says. Delicious, delicious.

Mercedes is a mysterious type, there are all kinds of versions of his past in circulation. Tosca calls him murderer, dirty and treacherous. According to her, he used to work in the port in Asunción, until he had to leave in a hurry. He was a docker, she reckons. She says he came here from Paraguay after killing two guys. The husband and brother of one of his lovers. Stabbed them to death. She says he has something like seven children back there but he doesn't even know most of their names. When he arrived in Buenos Aires, about fifteen years ago, he was poor, he showed up one day looking for work and she did him one favour after another. She offered him a roof over his head and introduced him to his wife. What else? Mercedes became something like a bodyguard to el Buti, the boy who was beaten to death, then he lost his way. He began dealing drugs, he went mad. Now he runs everything from here and occasionally goes out in a fake taxi, taking his son as a front. He makes him lie down on the back seat so that his legs don't go to sleep. Because of the football. It was much worse before, he had a troop of little sods coming and going at all hours with their packages. Their packages, Tosca repeats, shaking her head. They've all been arrested, I can't say anything. Just imagine. They want to see me dead.

Mercedes sits at the table and puts on some reading glasses that are too delicate for the size of his face. He opens a jotter and starts noting numbers in columns. From a box on the floor, out of my line of vision, he removes blister packs of medicines bunched up with elastic bands. He looks for something and goes back to making notes. I stand in the centre of the room drinking cold *maté*. Suddenly he says: And how's the little tearaway behaving himself? Fine, fine, I say quickly although I'm not entirely sure whether he's referring to Herbert or

Simón. And Sonia, I ask for the sake of it, to fill the void. Hospital, he replies without lifting his eyes.

Searching among the thousand things on the table, Mercedes lifts a teatowel and uncovers a revolver with a black grip and silver barrel. I'm struck not so much by the weapon itself as by its size. Really chunky. Mercedes carries on searching as if nothing had happened until he realises and raises his eyes, covering the revolver with his huge hand. Don't be scared, he says. It's in case someone really angry turns up. I show them the shine on this and they're suddenly tame. I smile, because of the shine part, but also because I feel that in some way he's here to protect us. On our side. Herbert appears and Mercedes changes the music to see us off, like a boy who wants to show all his toys at once. Instead of the harps, he now plays a mix of *cumbia* and reggae that accompanies us to the stairs, gradually diminishing until we reach home.

> *Iii'm not going to cryyyy*
> *No no no no*
> *Iii'm not going to cryyyy*
> *For the love of that woman*

SEVENTEEN

This place is hell, says Eloísa as soon as I close the flat door. She invites herself, as is her custom, turning up unannounced one afternoon. First we chat in the street for a while. She talks, I listen, Simón prowls about. She tells me about New Year, the party on the boat. Chaos. The idea was for us to stay moored there, but the owner, a friend of Axel's parents, got really pissed, raised the anchor and off we went sailing down the river. And in the middle of the night we ran aground. You have no idea, we didn't get back until five the next morning. A total blast. You're a bitch for not coming.

Eloísa wants to see my house, is so insistent that she finally convinces me. I drop in to Tosca's to let her know I'll be down later for her injection and, though I'm not sure I should, I introduce Eloísa to her. Tosca beckons me, wagging her index finger: As long as they don't stay, bring anyone you want. But don't make a racket. Then everyone will find out and they'll start bringing their whole clan.

How gross, says Eloísa climbing the stairs, quite loudly, so that she can be heard. No one shows their face.

And once she's inside: How can you live here? I shrug my shoulders and keep them raised, sustaining the I don't know. Why don't you stay with me? There's more than enough room, she says. And I realise that while she's talking to me she doesn't even notice Simón playing in a corner. As if he doesn't exist. I don't know whether she does it on purpose or whether she genuinely forgets I'm not alone. She keeps pressing: Doesn't it give you the creeps? I keep watching her without replying and she justifies herself: I mean, because of the filth. She wants to know how I ended up in the building. I tell her a bit: the Fénix, Canetti, Tosca, the injections, I don't say cancer, I say illness, Tosca would say the spud. Or the big bad spud, if she's in a very good mood. And that's it, I conclude, things turned out this way. She goes over to the window, tries my mattress, then back on her feet she opens the bathroom door: Anyway, it's not that bad, she says, her eyes wide, remembering something. I brought you some amazing little flowers, she says and pulls a small bundle wrapped in cellophane from her jeans pocket. She shows me the marijuana buds skewered on a little stick, she gives it to me to smell. Strong, yes. Amazing, she corrects me. I hand them back, she starts crushing the flowers with her fingers and, just like that, out of nowhere, she starts talking about her grandmother. Actually, about the wardrobe her grandmother had in her house, just like the one here, wide, enormous, with curves and cut off at the top. As I listen, I try to recall but I can't remember whether in our previous life, three or four years ago, she ever mentioned her. I could swear she didn't. The wardrobe was in the room where her grandparents had slept ever since they were married – in separate beds. Weird, huh? When her grandfather died, Eloísa occupied his bed whenever she stayed over. Identical, identical, it's mad. Yes, I say and think about Jaime's wardrobe, not exactly the same as this one but, now that I try to visualise it, quite similar. Very tall, with mothballs rolling loose along the shelves and all those clothes, ingrained with dirt, which I never dared to bag up, from the days when Jaime wore suits and had a wife. It's probable that Jaime and Eloísa's grandmother bought their wardrobes from the same furniture shop. The mystery is how this one came to be here. The only thing I know is that I'll never be able to fill it. Unless I set myself that goal, to keep a promise, on a whim. With borrowed clothes, old blankets, junk.

You never called back, Eloísa complains as she lights the joint and the aroma of marijuana, the ceremony, alerts Simón, who has been ignoring us from his play corner. He raises his eyes and gradually, intrigued or out of boredom, approaches us. Eloísa takes the first drags, one short and sharp, the next long and sustained, until she runs out of air. As if shushing in reverse. She releases the smoke, becoming rather cross-eyed, coughs and finally says: What a bugger. Simón sits down on the wooden bench, we stay standing. The situation is funny, the disproportion, the ratio of strength, Simón seems like a dwarf emperor. Eloísa passes me the joint and laughs, I don't know whether it's at that, at something else, at everything.

As we smoke she tells me about Axel. You have no idea what that house is like. A mansion, like three normal houses, she says. Total luxury. Four cars, motorbikes, a telly like a cinema screen, a maid who cooks for them and sprays air freshener everywhere, A baby smell that kills you, she says, another employee, younger, who cleans the bathrooms, the ornaments, the bedrooms, a gardener who works Saturdays, and Axel, who's wasted all day. Poor guy, she says. He's attempted suicide a thousand times. Pills, speed, coke, meds, he takes anything. Didn't you see his eyes? And his skin, like a lizard. He thinks he's a hard bastard because he goes to the slums to buy drugs. He's a show-off, she says.

And what are you doing there? I ask. She inhales the joint deeply and releases a cackle mixed with smoke. I don't know, she says, just laughing my arse off. I started as an assistant for the film Axel was going to shoot but then it came to nothing. I told you, didn't I? Actually, he keeps saying he's going to do it, he's always getting together with people. It's a story about pot-head extra-terrestrials. A load of nonsense. Now I'm half friend, half assistant. I keep him company so he doesn't feel so alone, I kind of help him with life, she says, suddenly subdued, her cheeks slack. I wonder exactly what it is she does. Whether she'll answer the phone, go shopping, pay his bills. Bathe him.

Axel's parents, Eloísa tells me, are Jews. Good people. He's Jewish too but his parents are much more Jewish. They have this massive house but they're never home. They travel once or twice a year, they live in Miami. When she says Miami, Eloísa raises her voice, she gets excited. They buy and sell apartments there. They left the jewellery business here, because they have a jeweller's, did you know? Yes, yes. Eloísa doesn't know them, she's only seen photos, she says they look like a couple of retards. Axel doesn't work, he occasionally wanders in to get money, there's another guy in charge, very old. And there's Débora, the girlfriend, a snob, they say they're getting married next year.

Eloísa moved into the house about six months ago. The first night he didn't even touch her, they watched telly until the morning, really high, then they spent the next day in bed because it was Sunday, eating and trying to fuck but he couldn't get it up at all. Monday came, then Tuesday, a week, and she ended up staying. Now they have the occasional screw, says Eloísa, but it's over almost before it's begun. He puts it in and can't last a second. I reckon he's gay, he doesn't want to admit it to himself, he's dying to be fucked, you can totally tell. But he's a good guy. He doesn't seem like the kind to treat you like shit, although I don't know, you never can tell. He's strange. He goes to a psychologist three times a week, he takes sedatives and he's always nervous, worried, it's hard to believe with all the dosh he has.

Eloísa lights a cigarette and starts imitating Orfe, the maid who has lived in Axel's house for forty years. She stands up, puts a cushion under her T-shirt, walks like an orang-utan, blowing saliva bubbles. Simón looks at her seriously and Eloísa tries to make him laugh. She pulls silly expressions without managing to raise a smile. Monkey face, madman face, deformed face, stretching her mouth with her fingers, zombie face, just showing the whites of her eyes, moving her ears, and finally she gets a grin out of him. Then Simón, as if annoyed at having given in, gets down from his throne and returns to shelter in his corner.

I'm hungry, says Eloísa. There isn't much; I offer her a packet of coconut biscuits. Despite my worst fears, they're quite good. Not crunchy, but edible. We want more. Checking the larder, which occupies a shelf in the wardrobe, Eloísa discovers a tin of peaches in syrup, which we open with a knife and a piece of tile. Three halves each, two for Simón.

Oh no, I've arsed up, I promised Axel I'd be back by ten to go for dinner with him at who knows whose house, says Eloísa as she taps a message into her mobile at top speed. She stands up, strokes Simón's head in passing and hurries me to see her out. Oh, I almost forgot, she says and removes a telephone from her pocket. Here, you can't live without a mobile. She hands me a red handset and a charger with the cable wrapped round it. The number is on the back, badly written but legible. Because I don't reach out immediately, she takes me by the wrist and places it in the palm of my hand. Relax, take it, the house is a cemetery for phones.

Before she leaves, on the pavement: Next week there's going to be a great party. Axel's turning thirty, you have to come. I say yes, I although I doubt I'll go, just so that she doesn't insist. The word party seems so distant to me, like a fantasy.

Next to the garden boa, which I trace again in the morning, there are two branches. Two types of the *Mimosaceae* family, the one on the left has medium-sized, unruly leaves, the other has small, abundant foliage, similar to that of a jacaranda. I think for a moment about including them in my drawing, but no, I leave them out. The tracing functions as a sedative which is closing my eyes very slowly. With the book open on my abdomen, like the body of a dwarf with fins that embrace me, an amphibious, affectionate dwarf, I have a perfect dream, without people or animals. A sweet dream that entertains me all night, making me laugh. A dream I can't remember at all.

EIGHTEEN

Going against his usual urge to dismantle, Benito fixes up a sound system he found discarded on the street. Almost in a good mood, with unfamiliar enthusiasm, Tosca makes me go through her papers in search of a little disc, that's what she calls it, of the best arias in history. Verdi, Puccini, Leoncavallo, Mozart and Bizet. I have one of the real ones, too, but I outlived it, she says and nods towards a record player covered in screws, nuts and all those strange pieces that Benito collects. As I prepare to inject her, Tosca asks me to get on with it, she wants to listen to her favourite aria. Put on number eight, she says. Do you know it? Yes, I lie, then check myself: I'm not sure. I like it, I don't know whether it's the music or seeing Tosca offer me her inner arm with unusual sweetness, more than sweetness, tragicomedy, in an overacted trance. I break the phial, fill the syringe, eyes on the needle sucking up the yellow liquid, and I'm transported when Tosca recites, out of time: *La vita è inferno all'infelice.*

Beni, play it again, says Tosca and carries on talking, this time about singers. She delays the moment of injection, she's babbling, the happiest I've seen her. Not Gigli, not Caruso, not Di Stefano, Tosca points out where she keeps her shellac and vinyl records. I get up and move towards the box under the television: That one, she says, that one there. Tito Schipa. He was a friend of my father, from school. The Yanks loved him. She hands the record back to me: I don't play those any more, they're beautiful but not very practical. She also tells me about someone in her village who sang at funerals. *La voce dei morti*, that's what they called him. A certain Vito Potenza. Potenza, Potenza, she says twice, her eyes on the ceiling, as if summoning him, as much as her swaddled neck will allow.

As well as a music lover, Tosca's father was, in all: inventor, fascist, herbalist, businessman, *Commendatore*, Mason and a violent man. He was also a frustrated artist, says Tosca, rolling her 'r's, dramatising the word. An arrrtist. For him, listening to one of his records was a ceremony. He did it in a room at the back of the house in Flores, which they bought when they arrived in the country. An enormous house, stretching from one street to the next, never-ending. He would shut himself away, naked, or covered in a sheet, Roman-style, and spend hours with the volume up. Occasionally with a friend or relative, but almost always alone.

Mussolini was a superman, Tosca tells me her father used to say to her. Almost a Garibaldi. Poom. Ahead of his time, a martyr, a genius who kept bad company. And she searches in the drawer for a portrait she always keeps there of her father, just graduated from military school on the day the Duce visited. She says: *Il Duce.* She can't find it. The drawer falls out, Tosca swears. Mixed in with the photos I'm picking up from the floor there are crumbs, rings, coins, sulphate batteries, a Cantonese restaurant menu, a lottery ticket and various knobs of used denture adhesive.

Instead of Mussolini, her father appears next to an Argentinian president to whom he was advisor. She can't remember his name, I don't recognise him either. Something to do with foreign trade, exporting grains. Two bald men, pale and heavy browed, in evening dress, white suit, black bow tie and with decorations pinned to their chests. Tosca becomes enthusiastic and shows me more photos, hurrying through some, lingering on others, and I'm curious to see what's coming next. Most are of her father: boarding the corvette *Esperanza*, at the foot of a warplane, at a community dinner, at the wheel of a racing car, eating an ice cream in Plaza Flores. She makes no comment about the women; I'm left to wonder whether one of them could be her mother, she doesn't even mention her. Next to a teenage Tosca, already fat, poses her sister Violeta, identical but slim, both dressed for a party in a park lit up at night. Did I tell you about Violeta, she asks and I nod, although she reminds me of the doctors and the metastasis anyway. Poor thing. The hair was the least of her troubles, she looked great in the wig, more beautiful than ever. She looked like an actress.

There are photos of Benito as a boy, the exaggerated head announcing his deformity. In an amusement park, hugging a ball, on the beach buried in the sand, sepia photos, colour prints, Polaroids. She never tells me anything about her life, whether she married or not, about Benito's father, and I don't dare ask. I sense something difficult, tragic, and if not tragic then sad at least. Among the photographs there's a little picture card of the Virgin of Syracuse, a miniature replica of the poster hanging above the headboard of the bed. She tells me again about the tears, the miracle, the woman who became blind before giving birth, I don't interrupt her or mention that she's already told me.

Switch it off, she shouts to Benito. Without music, the void makes itself felt. Too many memories, says Tosca and spits on the floor near my feet. It's not the first time I've seen her do it. At the start, I thought it was all in my mind. But no. Long, fast gobs, like a llama, like transparent vomit.

Once the drug is injected, instead of sinking into her usual lethargy, she speaks again after a minute, as if the will to keep telling stories is stronger than the depressant effect of the morphine. She stumbles over her words, confused, until, breaking off suddenly in the middle of a sentence, she drops. She asks me for another half dose, Don't make me beg, all these anecdotes have consumed her strength. Then yes, she closes her eyes without preamble or progression, in a few fractions of a second, like a light being switched on and off. I stay for a second watching her: her brow furrowed with deep wrinkles, the fleshy nose, the cheeks merging with the jowl, the lips withered, the chin reddened as if she's just shaved. She has a hairy mole next to the corner of the mouth, three black, erect hairs, one white and fine. The face of an old, spent woman, all her years weighing down on her. And I can't help travelling back to the girl who was, with that dark opera-aficionado of a father, a devotee of miracles. The same woman as now, her grimaces perfected by repetition, the same flesh, minus some teeth or dentures.

Distracted by a screech of brakes outside, I look behind me. On the television, always silent, there's a black-and-white cowboy film. A duel in the middle of the desert. They meet under a tree and take their paces with their backs to each other. A half turn and they are face to face, hands on hips, holding their belts, they weigh up the right moment to move their hands to their pistols. Bam, bam. The man who remains standing lowers his weapon and contemplates the horizon, expressionless. He returns to the tree, leans against the trunk and in two steps, without hesitating, puts the barrel of the gun in his mouth and shoots. Another bam. The screen becomes black: The end.

Tosca is sleeping deeply, breathing like a cat with a cold. It's late. Benito has been invisible for a while. He must have gone to bed. I stand up and check in passing that the walkie-talkie is still on and transmitting that hum full of interference that surrounds Simón's sleep. I stick my head out into the hall, no sign of Benito, the bed is empty. I enter the bathroom holding the beheaded phial firmly in my hand so that none is spilt. I sit down on the toilet and without hesitating inject myself with what remains of the morphine. Oof, my body turns into a lava flow. From my brain to my feet.

Where were you, Tosca will say and I'll smile, for the first time I'm the one to disconcert her. A smile that comes from inside me, roaring. I'm going, I don't know whether I say goodbye, my legs are weak as anything.

Rubbery. In the corridor someone passes in front of me, challenging gravity, in slow motion. Someone the half-light won't allow me to see. I smell a strong scent, sickly and intoxicating. The smell of soapy sex. Eva again, I suppose; she delights in the mystery and pauses before going outside to receive the full light of the streetlamp: her naked, grainy back, endless arse, the blonde wig covering her shoulders. I follow without seeing her face. She takes a step forward and closes the door with her heel. I linger where I am for a moment longer, hearing the strident clash of the chains against the corrugated iron. Afterwards, the silence of this place.

I turn round and face the staircase in a warm nebula. I place a foot on the first step and feel as though a pile of soft people is bearing down on me. I advance clumsily against this unfamiliar density. Agitation forces me to stop and take a breath. I raise a hand to my forehead and am surprised by the sweat. As I rest on the first step, I breathe deeply and tell myself that such a tiny amount can't have caused this much confusion. I forge on and immediately suffocate, my cheeks feel like balls of fire. I reach the flat on all fours.

Lying on my back, the ceiling runs away from me. Simón too, increasingly far from my feet. I close my eyes and my head starts spinning. Everything becomes a bottomless tank the colour of morphine, a yellow sea, dirty and bubbling. I touch the arm I injected but I can't feel it, not the arm, or the injection, or the vein, nothing. Just a prolonged sleepiness and a multitude of particles coursing through my blood at the speed of light.

NINETEEN

Grey day, with warm, fleeting showers, like rehearsals for a storm. Something of a relief amid such oppression. The zoo is almost empty, only a handful of people feel like trailing round with a raincoat or umbrella – defeated or desperate mothers, tourists whose remaining days are numbered. I stay at the back of the reptile house drinking *maté* with Esteban; if someone appears I intercept them on the path to ask for their ticket. Yessica had to go to cover someone in the children's play area. Esteban tells me about the flat he's renovating so that he can go and live with his girlfriend. He divorced a year ago, his daughters stayed with their mother. It was for the best, he says, so that things didn't end too badly. He talks to me about sprung floors, about low units with worktops and sliding doors, for which he's already paid a deposit, the electric grill he's thinking of installing on the balcony, airtight PVC vents. As I listen to his monotonous, forced voice describing the spaces of his new house like the Stations of the Cross, living room, kitchen, utility room, I move my head rhythmically at intervals of six, seven seconds, so that he feels he's being listened to, so that he doesn't

lose the thread, to justify my presence. He says that from
the balcony you can see the tower in Parque de la Ciudad.
Know where I mean? The train passes right in front, but
since it's on the thirteenth floor you barely notice. He tells
me a neighbour says it's just the occasional rumble and
he gestures with his hands as if strangling an imaginary
victim. I smile without understanding. I like the sound
of trains, it's like life . . . isn't it? He answers alone, convincing himself: And you can get used to anything. He's
quite right about that, although I don't know whether
it's more a case of everyone getting used to whatever
comes their way, which isn't quite the same thing. I keep
the comment to myself, it doesn't contribute much. The
good thing is that they can't build anything to spoil my
view, it's state land. It really gets the sun, he says in a
fit of optimism, his arms open as if about to hug me but
without following the gesture through. Now he's drinking
maté. He sucks the straw and, with a final smack of the
lips, he informs me: Come March, it will be exactly twenty
years until I pay off the mortgage, fixed payments with
fairly reasonable interest. The sprung floor, the futon,
the slat blinds, the girls' room, the train tracks and the
neighbour, the loan signed in the notary's office, the new
girlfriend and the ex-wife, in my mind all these things
accumulate in the three rooms, which I imagine to be sad
despite all the sunlight. Esteban smiles, he doesn't stop
smiling, he wants to be happy again. And from the way
he looks at me, stretching his eyelids wide, he's waiting
for my approval, a word of encouragement I don't manage
to utter. Luckily, three successive beeps come from my
mobile, arriving just in time to rescue me.

Message from Eloísa: By myslf, y dont u cum over? Excuse me, I say in order to move away from Esteban. Halfway between the tortoises and the exit, I stand for a while contemplating the boa constrictor, which seems to be dreaming with its eyes open. I'm at work, I finally write. Eloísa again: make something up dont be such a spoilsport. A diminutive Chinese couple trot up to me under a cape the shape of a bat. I check their tickets, they look at each other, they smile at me. Opposite, at the food stand, a typical family, father, mother, boy, girl, are waiting under the awning for the rain to stop, each with an ice cream in their hands. The distance and the curtain of water won't allow me to see whether all four ice creams are the same.

It's exactly a month today since I started work. I've never missed it, I've never arrived late, I've never objected to any task, even mopping the aisles of the reptile house one day when the cleaning staff was on strike. I think of a plausible excuse to escape: feeling unwell, tooth-ache, an urgent matter. I can say that Simón has a fever, that's believable, Esteban witnessed my phone beeping. Better to say I'm feeling dizzy, it's vague yet convincing, you never know what it might be a sign of. I leave it fifteen minutes, a reasonable time for the symptoms to appear. Eloísa doesn't persist with the messages. I suppose I have to speak to Esteban but I'm not sure, perhaps I need to see someone else, a supervisor, head of personnel. Yessica appears, back from the play area and in a state of pure ill humour. There are girls who shouldn't be allowed to breed, she says. They should have their uteruses forcibly removed. I tell her I'm not feeling well. She raises her brows distrustfully, hand on the walkie-talkie, she avoids looking me in the eye. She exposes her gums like an angry mare. She must sense my escape plan and is objecting in advance. It takes me a while to find Esteban, before I recognise his voice on the other side of the wall. I go round and see him chatting to the polar-bear keeper, still the same subject, his only subject. This time it's the transparent screen he's thinking of putting in the shower. Think it'll be expensive? he finishes saying as I interrupt the conversation, craning my neck forward with my hand raised. Is something wrong? Esteban asks. Unintentionally, I come out with a voice that is subdued, an invalid's voice. No, it's just that I don't feel very well. And he, with an unworried gesture, almost affectionate, touches my shoulder without it quite being a caress and tells me to go to the sickbay. Go and see if they'll give you something. There's nothing for it but to do as he says. I repeat Esteban's words in front of Yessica: I'm going to see if they'll give me something. I don't give her time to answer, I leave her chewing on her foul mood.

The sickbay is attached to the office where I had my first interview. The idea of bumping into the man from human resources isn't a pleasant one. I only saw him the once but every time I remember his oily face, spiky hair and dark-circled eyes like a goblin's, my repulsion grows. He seemed a poisonous type. As I approach, I slow down, I think several times about turning round, disappearing for a short wander and then going back to my post. I can say my dizziness passed on the way or that they gave me something and that's that.

I knock on the sickbay door, once, nothing, second time too, the third time it opens. I'm received by a tiny woman in a white apron who can't be more than five feet tall, wet hair, long-suffering eyes and round glasses. It's hard to tell whether she got caught in the rain or whether she's just had a shower and hasn't dried herself properly. From the way she picks up the pen, but mainly from the way she drums her fingertips on the desk, I can tell straight away that she's not going to be friendly. I'm listening, she says after asking my name and ID number. I'm feeling dizzy, a bad headache, I invent. Since when? A few hours, I say. Anything else? Fever? Cough? Muscle pain? I shake my head. Is your vision cloudy? A little, I venture. She wants to know whether I'm taking any medication, antibiotics, antihistamines, sedatives. Nothing. She asks for my arm to take my blood pressure. She inflates and deflates it in silence and without raising her eyes from her notebook says: It's fine, bottom number's a bit high.

Do you think you might be pregnant? Impossible, I reply and for the first time she meets my eye. A sarcastic look, I don't understand why. Then she starts writing and remains silent for a couple of minutes. She doesn't examine me, it's all just words, she doesn't use the stethoscope on the desk, nor does she take my temperature. She drops the pen, producing a metallic clatter, and speaks again: Whatever you want. I can give you something for the headache, or I'll write an order for you to go and have some tests. It's your body, that's what she says, and for the second and final time she shows me that pair of bloodshot grey eyes behind the lenses.

I leave the sickbay with an order for the laboratory. I try to decipher it under the drizzle: full haemogram, haematocrit, cholesterol and urine. And on a separate sheet, HIV: While we're at it, so you can forget about it, that's what she said. I raise my gaze and find myself looking at a bronze statue. I bend down to read the plaque: Eduardo Holmberg. Holmberg again. In a suit and hat, between an elephant and a dwarf giraffe, a monkey on his shoulder and a scorpion on his arm.

At the entrance to the reptile house, Esteban and Yessica are waiting for me. She sent me to get some tests, I say, holding up the papers. Now? interrupts Yessica, who has definitely discovered my ruse. Go, says Esteban. Take care and let me know if there's anything I can do. Yessica turns into fifty-something kilos of hatred.

When I'm out on the street, I text Eloísa. On my way, give me the address. The reply comes in five seconds, as if she's doing nothing but sending text messages. To find Axel's house, I get my bearings from one of the stallholders at the zoo door, the one with the stuffed toys. He doesn't send me on a direct route at all. If you don't want a lot of traipsing you have to take the subway and a bus or bus then subway. Since it's stopped raining, I decide to do the last stretch on foot.

Where Avenida de los Incas ends or begins, I cross under a bridge and walk uphill, skirting a small plaza stippled with young jacarandas. As I approach, I try to guess which will be Axel's house. Is it the chalet with the palm tree out front, the one with the bare brickwork, a white one with creeper-covered balconies, or the one concealed behind a very tall fence, as high as a man standing on another man's shoulders? Right enough, it's the one that's hidden from view, the grounds must occupy a quarter of the block. Before ringing the bell, I notice the two signs next to the entrance. The first says: Beware of the dogs. The other one is in English:

DON'T EVEN THINK OF PARKING HERE

Eloísa's voice rings out from the future, robotised. There's no Who is it? Come in, she says, through the garage. And the railing slides back on its own. First, a garden with curved beds, grass shorn to the ground and a path of paving slabs leading to the garage. To reach Eloísa, who is waiting for me on the threshold of a small, half-open door, I have to go round four cars: a pickup with tinted windows, a silver convertible, a jeep and a vintage car. Further along are three bicycles hanging from a rail and a red motorbike, one of those big ones. Eloísa embraces me and kisses me on both cheeks, as if we were meeting again after many years. We climb a spiral staircase that leads to a large kitchen, immense, like a train carriage, ending in a large window overlooking the park. A couple of pines, a magnolia tree and, at the back, a covered barbecue area with a straw roof. Finally, says Eloísa. It was an effort but you came, was it difficult? I shrug. I thought you'd got lost, she continues. No, I say and I'm about to relate the sequence in the sickbay but I check myself in time.

I was going to mix a Fernet, you want one? Each of us with a glass in our hands, we leave the kitchen and settle in the everyday dining room, too luxurious to be for every day. Each wall has its picture: a *mappa mundi* with cheeses instead of countries, a temple with a golden cupola and a field of sunflowers. In the middle of the table there's a dish of fruits made of rubber or wax, I can't tell which. I grab an apple, I squeeze it slightly and bring it to my nose as if I want to smell its aroma, Eloísa laughs. She laughs at me.

We spend a long time chatting about everything and nothing. Actually it's she who talks, I listen and enjoy myself: a television programme she watches every afternoon, where couples argue live on air, the trips she'd like to make, a spot on her neck that won't stop oozing pus, her constant horniness, that's how she puts it, from when she gets up until she goes to bed, and once again, Jaime's death. How did it happen. Was I sad, did I love him. Did he leave me any cash. I tell her about the accident next to the Camel sign. Yes, I totally remember. I don't say anything about the eviction, I make up a story about the house being sold and me receiving a part. She insists: Tell me the truth, were you in love? Yes, I say, and her response: I don't believe you.

Come on, she says to me presently, let's go and see Axel, he'll want to say hello. I stand up and follow her, thinking that she told me she was by herself. We pass the dining room, I brush the back of my hand along the edge of the table, glass, marble and gold edging, I fleetingly count a dozen chairs. Before we advance, Eloísa points out some towelling booties, like flat slippers, for me to slide across the parquet. Over the table hangs an enormous crystal spider. We cross the living room in a semi-darkness that suggests an uninhabited house. I can only see outlines, a horseshoe armchair fit for a small crowd, a coffee table with a ball of smoked glass in the centre, the rest, the ornaments, the pictures, the details, escape me. A few lines of light are just managing to defeat the lowered blinds.

Eloísa guides me by the hand to a door on a different level. She opens it without knocking, Axel jumps and almost drops the headset he's wearing, earphones and microphone in one, but he has quick reflexes and manages to rescue it in time. On the computer screen I can see the face of a girl or a guy, it's not clear, moving like a spastic doll. Axel blushes, as if we'd surprised him naked. I move closer to greet him and he tries to stand but half-way up he is tugged back by the cable of the earphones, which, out of apathy or because he's very engrossed in the conversation with the girl or guy, he doesn't think to remove. The kiss takes place in the air, without contact. Axel covers the microphone with his hand and murmurs: She's driving me crazy, I don't know how to get rid of her. Fuck her once and for all, then delete her from the chat room, Eloísa tells him and Axel responds by spitting out a laugh that spatters us both with saliva. A laugh of embarrassment, his own and someone else's. Axel is one of those people who never makes eye contact for more than a second or two. He gives the impression that if he did, he would immediately come apart. His strength lies in appearing nervous, upset, always somewhere else.

In Axel's room, everything is the opposite of the rest of the house, neither spacious nor luxurious. He has another room on the first floor, Eloísa will explain to me, the real one, but he never uses it, he moved downstairs because he feels alone up there. He spends all day on the computer, he's a freak, says Eloísa. As well as the computer – there are actually two of them, one black, the classic kind, another small and portable – there's a single bed, a television, shelves with books and CDs, some recently bought, never opened, still wrapped in cellophane, various bottles of perfume and a cork board with photos: Axel with friends, Axel and his family, Axel skiing, Axel looking wild against a black background, Axel and a blonde clinking glasses on the deck of a cruise liner. Next to the window hangs a painting: a man in a suit and tie walking a bulldog on a leash, each with a third eye. Like Axel's everlasting spot. It's one of Débora's paintings, I find out later from a magnetic postcard on the fridge door. Scenes of daily life, drivers, bank tellers, families leaving the cinema, street sweepers, all kinds of people, common and clairvoyant. Mystics, that's what the series is called.

Back in the living room, I bang my knee against the foot of a grand piano camouflaged in the half-light. I can only see it now that Eloísa has switched on a candelabra with seven artificial candles, flickering bulbs that give the illusion of flames. Oh. Shhh, she says, pointing out a mahogany-coloured urn. It's Axel's granddad, she says arching her eyebrows, her index finger forming a cross with her lips. We shouldn't wake him.

Another Fernet and Eloísa takes me to the basement: Come and I'll show you the bunker. Beneath the garden there's a tunnel that links the games room and gym with the barbecue area, where Eloísa's room is. It's a narrow passageway, all concrete, with fire extinguishers and exposed pipes. About halfway along, Eloísa moves ahead of me, types a code into a keyboard and the wall opens. A secret door. Remember, in case the world ends, she says and whispers: Four three two one, j k l m. A trap for idiots. For five seconds, the time it takes Eloísa to find the switch, all I can see inside is a solid black hole. The neon tubes flicker and light up one by one: an underground house. To one side, there are two rows of truckle beds with pillows and blankets. Between the beds, oxygen tubes with masks hanging by the mouth. In the centre, a folding table, a mini library, a small television and a sofa bed. The kitchen looks new: electric oven, extractor fan, a washing machine and a power generator. Look at everything his parents keep down here, says Eloísa as she opens the larder, they're totally bonkers. Tins of sardines, soups, pre-cooked meats, dehydrated chocolates. Eloísa grabs a vacuum pack of peanuts. Before we leave, she leads me to the bathroom, which is quite ordinary, except for the shower, a cylindrical cabin with a mixer tap.

We return to the surface and Eloísa explains the underground shelter in her own way: It seems that Axel's old man has a bee in his bonnet about the war. The grand-dad, the one in the urn, was in a concentration camp and they went for something like twenty years thinking he was dead. They found out he was alive pretty much by chance, through a bank account or something like that. And since they got it into their heads that the Nazis were coming back to bomb Buenos Aires, utter nonsense, they've been really unhinged, says Eloísa, tapping her temple with her index finger. We skirt the barbecue area along a path made of tree-trunk rounds, dodging the pool and the deckchairs. Grill, showers, hammocks, another kitchen and a small room with cane furniture, a reed curtain and a mattress on the floor. Eloísa's room, just like a beach house. My bed, she says, and flops on her back. More chat, more Fernet and a joint as we watch a programme about couples, the one she told me about a while earlier. Hang on while I have a shower, I'm disgusting, says Eloísa at one point and I think that sooner or later we're going to kiss again and see each other naked. There are times when it's all I wish for and then I don't even want to think about it.

It's getting on for eight, I think about Simón and Herbert. I don't know what I'm doing here. I take advantage of Eloísa still being in the bathroom, I gather my strength and decide to leave. I'm going to leave her a note but I can't find paper or anything to write with. Anyway, she'd never understand me, better to leave like this, without telling her. I jog across the garden, pass quickly through the kitchen to the garage door. Between the cars I realise that I'm trapped. With no keys or buttons in sight, I have no way out. I'd like to disappear, to teleport myself, to never have come. But there's no way out. I go back inside, perhaps Eloísa is still in the shower, that would simplify things quite a bit. I stick a foot in the kitchen and with a short, sharp Ohh of true fright, Axel raises his arms in shock like a trainee ghost. Sorry, I say, and he juggles so that crisps don't fall out of the packet onto the floor. No, no, *I'm* sorry, he says, I was somewhere else. And Elo? he asks. I point out back. I was leaving, will you open up for me? Yes, yes, he says distractedly and passes in front of me, his trousers hanging low with the crack of his arse on show. White and green skin, a vision that reminds me of the slogan of the Evangelical church: *Helmet of Salvation*, I murmur imperceptibly.

Guiding me between the cars, Axel complains at the lack of space. Yes, I say, incapable of making any comment, not about the convertible, or the pickup, or the jeep, or the collector's model, nor about the hanging bicycles. I could say: What lovely cars, they must be worth a fortune. But no. Axel opens a panel next to the door and presses buttons rapidly. Come back whenever you like. Yes, yes, thanks. Bye and bye. I escape quickly, without looking back. On the other side of the bridge, calmer now, standing in a queue of three at the bus stop, I receive a message from Eloísa: WHERE DID U GET TO GIRL???

TWENTY

Let's go for a walk, Iris suggests at the gate to the zoo, when we've already said goodbye and are about to head our separate ways. Tomorrow we have a day off, it's the first time we've both been free at the same time. We can go to the river, she says and I open my arms, embracing the idea without really knowing what Iris means by river.

Too early, she comes to el Buti to pick us up for our excursion. Because Simón is still asleep and I take a while to dress him and force breakfast down him, we make her wait some twenty minutes for us. That's probably why, for the blocks separating us from the main avenue and almost the entire bus journey, Iris remains silent, ignoring us, as if she wasn't with us. Just in case, to spare myself a reproach, I don't ask. Iris definitely has a strange sensitivity, unfathomable, capable of taking offence at the slightest thing. Yet at the same time she is always generous, or not so much generous, more like needy, with an urgent compulsion to share.

The bus limps forward. Along the back seat, Iris, Simón and I, in that order, receive a blast of air up our legs which, no matter how we twist our necks, we are condemned to inhale. Suddenly, we gain some speed for a few blocks only to be paralysed again in another traffic jam. Although she's still annoyed, at least now Iris is glancing over her shoulder at me, furtively, almost friendly. No one complains, no one rebels, no one gets off to walk. Nor do we, beginning to drift off to the hum of the engine and the movement of the bus which rocks as if we were sailing.

Very suddenly, without ceremony, because we have reached the end of the route, the driver shouts from the wheel: Post office. He doesn't exactly say post office the way anyone would say it, he aggravates and prolongs the o of office into a wild cry. We get off rather dazed, as if landing from another galaxy. Iris, who is quickest to come to her senses, leads the way to a supermarket opposite a dark plaza crammed with dwarf trees. I make out an *ombú* tree that must be a century old perched at the top of a slope; there are also eucalyptus, which are the tallest, a lime and a row of silk floss trees with very swollen trunks. Canetti's lessons are still fresh in my mind. Iris takes care of the purchases, we wait for her outside, Simón making a pile with some broken floor tiles, me, my gaze lost in the distance where the trees end and everything else begins.

Cheese, bread, apples and Coca-Cola, Iris reels off as she leaves the supermarket with a plastic bag in her hand. And a salami, she adds after a pause, rather aggrieved. We return to the point where the bus dropped us, we skirt the post-office building, cross a small, bare plaza without a single tree, the antithesis of the last one. We stop at the foot of an avenue with heavy traffic: lots of buses, lorries with trailers, containers. Waiting for the lights to change, Iris covers her ears with her hands, leaning slightly so Simón can see her. Her mood has finally changed. Iris isn't one for joking, in fact it's an effort for her not to be serious, except when she comes undone and explodes. That must be why Simón is observing her warily.

We pass two narrow train tracks disguised by tall weeds that no one has cut for a long time; we are confounded by a roundabout with no traffic lights which we dash across, until we reach the bridge straddling the canal. A white, modern bridge with steel cables of increasing lengths just like the strings of a fabulous harp. To the right, between the old renovated docks, a group of very high towers dispute their supremacy, some of them finished, the majority still under construction. A world of cranes, scaffolding and cement mixers. There are twin buildings separated by a clearing of sky and linked by high walkways. One of those flats must be Axel's, the one Débora is decorating for when they live together. Eloísa has been there, she described it to me drawing the shape in the air, like a semicircle with windows to the floor, the city on one side, the river on the other. She says she was returning from the casino once, with Axel and his friends, Berni, Andy and someone else, the time Axel lost something like three thousand dollars at roulette. She says that when they reached the flat they were all pretty drunk and they called Cohen, a guy who had been a tutor at Axel's school and who is now the group's dealer. He showed up with three girls who didn't even look like whores who stayed until seven in the morning for two hundred pesos each. Eloísa only did drugs, she took crack from a never-ending rock, but she didn't screw anyone, nor did Axel. How's he going to screw if he's a total poofter? He had two girls on top of him and still couldn't get it up. His friends, meanwhile, Cohen and the others, fucked them frontways, backways, left their hair full of milk. Eloísa watched, she took photos, filmed little videos, that's what she called them, little videos, and masturbated a bit. At most she touched someone's tits. But always staying outside the game: it wasn't worth it.

By the time we reach the ecological reserve, Simón is already hungry. Iris complains, she says we're going to have our picnic by the riverside. He can't wait ten minutes, she mutters between clenched teeth. It's not a question, nor is it directed at me, it's a statement loaded with irony. I appease Simón with a banana I've brought squashed in my pocket and we push on. On one side there's a dry lake sprouting with reeds and a few swamped ducks, on the other, an embankment with commercial premises installed under an arcade. Almost all of them are shut, only a few have their grilles raised and one man is lighting up a barbecue still empty of meat, his stomach on show. There is also a group in their sixties wearing shorts and bikinis, forming a semicircle, their skin shiny, oily, tanning themselves even though they don't look like they could get much browner.

After a brief exchange of glances, we decide to take the path to the right, a wide, muddy trail populated by cyclists, explorers, pensioners and a parade of strange characters ranging from loners to exhibitionists. Suddenly the city falls silent and the illusion of nature begins. Along the path, between the flame bushes, is a series

of platforms with coin-operated telescopes like standing machine guns. Simón climbs each one and tries to
manoeuvre the device. Come on, Iris will repeat, nothing
but impatience.

A very slim boy, his ribs clearly visible, emerges
from the reed bed scaring mosquitoes away with a white
T-shirt. His face is red, too inflamed to be just from the
heat. Feeling he's being watched, for fun, he sticks out
his tongue and jogs off exaggerating the movement of
his arse. I seek out Iris's eyes, she averts her gaze to the
pampas grass. After twenty minutes' walking, we turn left,
uphill. With no trees to protect us, we are the inevitable
target of a sun that is gradually becoming cruel.

The slope unveils the river in layers. There's no
breeze, or anything resembling one, the heat won't
back down. The water is an immobile sheet, like brown
cement, cocoa paste, with no waves, not even the merest
fold. Searching for a spot in the shade to settle down in,
stepping among the people who arrived before us, Iris
grabs me by the arm at the same time as she forces out
a sentence, staring at the ground: I can't believe it, she
says twice. The second time she also swears in her own
language.

It's Yuri and Olga, uncle and aunt of Draco, Iris's
boyfriend who went to the south and never returned.
Yuri overplays his surprise, Iris and Olga sink into their
chests, unashamedly externalising their unwillingness
for this meeting to occur. They glance at each other,
mutually accusatory, as if one of them had planned it. It
is impossible to avoid them, and we approach. Iris greets
them with three kisses, cheek to cheek. She introduces

me, I say hello with my hand and go after Simón who is running off towards the riverbank.

Squatting on this beach of rubble, debris and hardened litter, I catch a glimpse of a future that's bad but not terrible. I allow my gaze to roam, from the horizon to my now bare feet, from my feet to a regatta of sailing boats crowded near the middle of the river and back, right here, to a group of boys bathing amidst the twisted iron. I turn my head for an instant and the cut-out of the city, blurred behind the vapours exhaled by the earth, gives the impression of another future, more typical, without much mystery.

Simón goes to play by the water's edge. I half close my eyes: voices, shouts that sound like pleas for help, a ship's horn and the hum of the particles in the air which I imagine to be shaped like tiny embers. I turn round again to look for Iris. She's still standing, with a weary expression, staring straight ahead. Like a young girl being scolded by her parents. I think about Draco, the story of the separation, whether she'll be telling them how it all happened, or the opposite, whether they will be providing her with details. A crossroads of recriminations. Iris will reproach them for her boyfriend fleeing, they'll complain that she didn't accompany him southwards. She'll talk about the cold, that's why they are now measuring her up from under their brows as if saying that's no reason to leave someone and inside they'll be thinking: Abandonment for the sake of it; after everything, it's fair enough. Iris has already seen me, I feel as though she's about to call me over, she'll want to include me in the conversation, I swiftly flick my gaze back to the chocolaty river. I wonder how you say abandonment in Romanian.

Simón has taken advantage of those seconds of distraction to escape from my sight. He's hiding or being hidden by the landscape. One of the two is using the other. I'm not going to shout, I wouldn't know how. I wait, to see if he appears, surely he'll appear, but he doesn't appear. I stand up and walk without alarm, accommodating my flip-flops between the holes and the stones. I look both ways, nothing. I'm no longer looking for Simón but for the green of his T-shirt. Any green. I let myself be deceived by false clues, but they don't offer the right measurements, always the wrong width or height.

Left or right. I choose the bank, I take fifteen paces and I should be starting to worry, admit that he's lost and ask for help, and then it's almost as though someone places their hand on my shoulder, calling me. I turn my head and discover Simón next to a bush five metres from where I was sitting. I walk over to him. He doesn't say anything or look at me with reproachful eyes. His face merely suggests a: Where were you going? I'd explain but best not to, it's like Iris with Draco or Draco with Iris. You don't know who left whom, who is the mother of the blame.

Simón guides me behind the bush and between two pieces of concrete rubble and some remnants of bricks rounded by the water, the wind and everyone's footsteps, he shows me a small cemetery of beheaded dolls. Three, four centimetres long, made of ceramic, some with old-fashioned dresses, Egyptian, Asian, others naked, an army of little mutilated dolls awaiting burial or reanimation.

Legs, arms, loose limbs as well. I think that someone must have reunited them, the river couldn't put them together so painstakingly. Simón fills his arms with dolls and I don't know why I censure him, I tell him not to grab so many, Not so many, I order, but I offer no reason. And he answers me with a look that says: Poor things. Yes, poor things.

I check that Iris is still with Draco's aunt and uncle, but her attitude of ten minutes earlier, so fed up at having met his relations, is now one of happiness. In fact, she sees me and calls me over, arms open, almost euphoric. Yuri and Olga barely speak Spanish and when they do it takes quite some effort to understand them. Olga is ash blonde, with slim legs, freckled skin and severe eyes. Very similar to Iris, the antithesis of Yuri who never stops joking and laughs hard. I witness a litany of anecdotes and complicities which I try to guess from their expressions. Simón entertains himself with the little dolls, building them a cave in the sand. Hunger grabs us. Without consulting me, Iris decides that we'll share lunch with them. Two picnics in one. We contribute our cheese, bread, salami and Coca-Cola. From them, hard-boiled eggs, pâté, more bread and a bottle of pineapple cider which they have brought in a foil cooler. Yuri tells us that it's hullabaloo every night in the hotel where they live. He says hullabaloo with an incredible accent, as if he were beating his tongue against the skin of a drum. Always something, he says, and I think I understand him saying that a few weeks earlier a woman fell from a balcony on the building and embedded her head in the roof of a taxi. Olga, who as I will find out later is Yuri's second wife, he has at least twenty years on her, laughs with her hand over her mouth. Iris pulls a disgusted expression.

We scoff everything in minutes. We toast with the pineapple cider, which despite the thermal bag is warm when it reaches my mouth. The conversation continues but I throw myself down with my face to the sky, the voices reach me without translation, in a strange but transparent register, in which words are beyond meaning. At one point I could swear Iris is telling them the story about the fat woman who got jammed in the hanging walkway in the subtropical rainforest. The phrasing, the highs and lows, the exclamations, remind me of the way she told me.

The sun changes position and leaves us without protection. We react in unison, forced into movement by the glare. Simón? Right here, burying the little dolls. A moment of indecision: over there, further this way, in that little wood, I suggest. In the end, Yuri and Olga go their own way. The goodbye is short and cold, as if resentment has finally won over. We take a path cutting through the reed bed as far as a flowering *ceibo* tree. Canetti again, and his catalogue of trees. Simón doesn't take long to fall asleep. We lie on the grass, feet up on a bench, blood on a steep slope to the brain. In silence, we are bewitched by the network of leaves and flowers that separates us from the sky, until our eyes close. In my dream, brief, very brief, a small, flattened bird appears to me, its feet separated from its body. And yet it moves, dragging itself like a reptile.

The need to pee cuts short my siesta. I walk a few metres along a trail, I lower my trousers and knickers, squat and release an effervescent stream of piss that smells of pineapple cider. Through the pampas grass, I see the smudge of an animal passing, making the ground crunch, a chinchilla, a rat or a weasel. I can't make it out. Closer to me, a hole, the burrow. I don't lie down again, I sit next to Iris, who is still sleeping, her skin tattooed by a thousand nervous filigrees: all the shadows of the *ceibo*. I observe those features of hers, from other lands. I start caressing her head, I use my fingers as a comb to clear her face of hair. I smooth her eyebrows, I measure her lashes and notice those tiny hairs magnified on her lips, a little blonde moustache, microscopic. I stay like this for a while. Suddenly, frightening me, as if instead of waking her I had set fire to her, her eyes open, she looks straight at me. She smiles when I jump and I pass my hand over her forehead again. She lets me do it. That night at Christmas and some fantasies come to my mind, and very naturally the need rises in me to kiss her. She sees it coming and doesn't stop me. She reacts belatedly, when our lips are almost brushing. She moves my mouth away brutally, gripping my jaw. It disconcerts me, not the rejection, but the fact that it was expressed like that. So violently.

TWENTY-ONE

Herbert shows up with a bruised eye. A large, mature plum. Simón looks at him impressed, as do I. He allows himself to be examined, frowning with a mixture of pride and shame. I don't ask anything, I let him speak. He says he was elbowed during a match. And he clarifies: At training. I offer him a glass of milk, he drinks it in one go, almost closing the healthy eye; the other stays alert, halfway open. Simón points at his own cheekbone, as if his hurts too. I move away, they start playing. I'm going shopping, I say. And, with one foot outside, I ask: What do you want to eat? They both shrug at the same time and they remain like that, stony, transferring the doubt from one to the other.

At the supermarket on the corner there's a commotion of police cars and ambulances. I see it coming, first in scale, now life-size. I'm about to go and do my shopping elsewhere, but curiosity wins over and I stop behind the police cordon. Slightly further along is Mercedes, he doesn't see me, doesn't recognise me, or maybe that's just the way he is, rough, laconic, not one for niceties. Looking straight ahead, concentrating, he keeps

TWENTY-TWO

Party at Axel's house. I allow myself to be persuaded, partly by the many messages and partly by my slight boredom. I arrive early, for the preparations. At the entrance I'm welcomed by a Martian and I realise I should have come in fancy dress. Eloísa didn't mention it, but it's too late for me to change my mind. There aren't many people yet, Axel's best friends, the intimate circle, Andy and Berni, both dressed as transvestites, I'm going to get them mixed up all night; Débora, with studs and a red mohawk, a punk; Cyntia, her best friend, a galactic girl. Eloísa is an urban Indian, her head adorned with fluorescent feathers. Axel is dressed as a rabbi: long artificial beard, jacket and black trousers, Mexican-style hat and a white silk shirt, which as the hours pass will become stuck to his skin with sweat.

Because I'm in civvies, T-shirt, jeans and sandals, Eloísa gesticulates when she sees me, laughing hard. Her laughter is the wrong way round, at seeing me without a costume, the opposite of the rest. Come on, she says, we fix ourselves a Fernet and she leads me outside. I didn't know, I say as we cross the garden, illuminated by torches and candles floating in the pool. Eloísa, who is already quite drunk, laughs again enthusiastically. I do too, infected. In her room there's a load of clothes, shoes and accessories piled on the mattress. Discarded costumes that have been left there for situations like this. After rummaging for a while, she makes a decision. I let her dress me in a skirt with Islamic swirls, a sequinned bodice and a belt with medallions hanging from it. And a piece of tulle to cover half my face. That's you, she says. Now we need make-up. Otherwise you'll look sod-all like an odalisque.

As she paints my eyes and lips and applies blusher, I crumble a lump of marijuana, separating the stems and seeds. The swift movement of my fingers over my cupped hand produces an annoying, delicious tingling. We smoke as she does my hair. Eloísa takes two steps back to look at me properly, she exhales and releases a guffaw mingled with a cough. You're a right whore, she says proudly.

We lie down on the floor with our legs bent. Iris comes to my mind; we lay like this in the grass under the shade of the *ceibo* tree before the kiss that never was. Some of them are pretty much freaks, Eloísa is telling me. But I get on well with them. I look around and realise she's made some changes to the room, even though it takes me a few minutes to pinpoint what they are. She's put up a poster, a monkey dressed as a train driver mounted on a multicoloured elephant: *The Magical Circus*.

We go back to the party. My head feels hot. In the short time we were shut away, a lot of people have clearly arrived all at once. We lost track of time, says Eloísa. Now there are groups of boys and girls in the garden, most of them in costume. Two devils, more transvestites, a rocker, a mermaid, the usual nuns, priests, police officers, a skeleton and some less common disguises: a cardboard woman, a dice man and a dog girl with a leash around her neck who asks to be taken for a walk. Others, rebels, or unaware like me, have come as themselves. The joint hits me hard. All this lucidity is driving me crazy.

We enter the house and Eloísa lets go of my hand. Be right back, she says, ushering me towards the living room and she exits through a door. Illuminated with intermittent spotlights, a mirror ball and the distorted lights that mask the floor, the space seems like somewhere else, very different to the room I saw a few weeks ago. The dining table is perpendicular to the wall and serving as a bar. Instead of the photo frames and menorahs there is a long row of cups and glasses, a dish with cherries and another with prawns. I try a prawn, it's tasteless. And the first thing I notice: the urn with Axel's granddad's ashes is no longer there. They must have put it somewhere safe from a potential breakage. Seeing me dressed like this, Axel throws me a Wooowww that invites a few glances and he offers me a red drink. Daiqui, he says with a twisted smile. I accept so that he won't insist.

More and more guests are arriving without costumes. I don't think anyone would notice if I changed back into my own clothes. Eloísa appears holding a guy by the arm, half prisoner half thief, stripy suit, a cap on his head, beard painted on with burnt cork. She introduces him like this: Marito, a genius. Later I find out that he's in charge of the warehouse for the jeweller's, that he was the family's driver for a while and that he's like a brother to Axel. Just like in the country: Jaime used to have Boca whenever he had a barbecue, that half friend half employee, half compadre half foreman, who worked for him but who also shared the table. Marito has very dark, frizzy hair and dun-coloured eyes. He seems, just like Boca, to be a good man, trustworthy.

Back in the garden, Eloísa rolls a fresh joint, we sit on the grass and the aroma is a magnet. We are joined by a girl dressed as a castaway: long face, bowl cut, tits like watermelons. Leyla is a designer like Débora, they met at university. She makes clothes, prints, what she's wearing for example, blue leggings with dragons and flames. She laughs hard, just like Eloísa, mocking some of the people who pass near us, especially the cardboard girl. Honestly quite ridiculous. The chat takes us anywhere, chignons, pancakes, potted orchids and horoscopes. Leyla is a horoscope aficionado, she's done several courses, she knows how to read tarot, runes, the I Ching. She asks my sign. Virgo, I think, I say not joking, and the two of them laugh in chorus. And ascendant? I shake my head, no idea. What time were you born? At dawn, I throw out to satisfy her. So you must have an ascendant in Gemini, she ventures. You're a bit stubborn, are you?

Clapping and whistling reaches us from the house. We draw closer. In the centre of the dance floor, Axel is brandishing a microphone. He thanks everyone for coming, he says he loves us and forgives us. You know I love you all. And he adds a few words in Hebrew, or fake Hebrew, that sound like a sermon. I'm going to sing you one of my favourite songs, he says and signals to the DJ, a guy with greying hair and a baby face. A classic, he explains and forces his already hoarse voice. The song is in English, almost everyone knows it apart from me. He makes an impressive sight, veins just under his skin, eyes out of orbit, deranged. About to cry, crying, Axel trembles as if he's about to break into pieces. The ovation will be interminable, a competition to see who can shout loudest, who can come up with the most ingenious comment. Gay-boy rabbi, Berni or Andy shouts at him.

Then the party really comes undone. Loud, catchy music. Installed behind two computers, the grey-haired guy circles his arm in the air, encouraging people to dance. Initially, there's a certain degree of timidity, until some of the more forward guests, Eloísa naturally, begin to move, overacting an enthusiasm that ends up infecting everyone else. I watch for a while, but faced with the very likely occurrence of Eloísa dragging me in to dance, I retreat and go outside again. I sit in an intermediate area between the house and the garden, a kind of terrace with deckchairs and large pots full of canes. Near me there's a boy dressed all in black, a priest or executioner, his back to me, next to a girl dressed as a clown who's facing my way. They are holding hands, staring at each other, serious despite the costumes and the deafening music, as if making a real confession. The girl can't get over her bewilderment, she shoots out a hundred questions a minute: Are you serious? I can't believe it. But how did it happen? Did anyone know? They're talking about someone else, sick, dead, I can't tell. I think about the mother, the father, also about a girlfriend or pal. Why

didn't you call and tell me? The boy shakes his head in a
continuous movement. And, with a snap of the fingers
to materialise the idea of the unexpected, he concludes:
It was just like that.

Cohen, the dealer and former tutor, arrives. Dark
glasses are the only element of disguise. I need no intro-
duction. An average-looking guy, hooked nose, four-day
beard, who flees from the crowd. He makes no greetings,
he prowls around for a moment before taking refuge in
Axel's room. A minor celebrity.

I spend a while wandering, from the kitchen to the
living room, living room to garden, to the barbecue area
and back no fewer than five times, I go to the bathroom
to pee, I entertain myself there for a while with the jet
from the bidet, I take advantage of the opportunity to lose
the tulle veil, hiding it in the laundry basket, I go and get
another strawberry daiquiri which I leave somewhere,
very sweet, undrinkable, I have a fleeting conversation
with Leyla who asks me whether I brought anything
to smoke, an exchange of words with the barman who
suggests I have a gin with mint, a brief simulation of
dancing which I abort as soon as a hand grabs my arm
to draw me onto the dance floor, putting up an effective
resistance.

It's ten to three, I notice on the kitchen clock, I
decide to leave. Near the exit I'm intercepted by Eloísa.
She grabs my wrist and drags me to the basement. The
light downstairs is terrible, like an interrogation cell.
My eyes won't adapt properly. Andy and other friends
of Axel are playing ping-pong with obstacles. On each
side of the table there are chaotically placed objects: a

bottle of vodka, a pack of cigarettes, condoms, a couple of mobile phones. They laugh as if in a cartoon, bending double. Eloísa disappears along a corridor and leaves me watching the game. Now the ping-pong group is joined by a girl dressed as a peasant, very drunk, who sways from one player's shoulder to another so as not to fall.

I'm almost falling asleep when Eloísa reappears, rapidly descending the stairs and nodding for me to follow her. She disconcerts me, leaving from one side, returning from the other; she comes from upstairs when I could have sworn she was down here. We go into the dressing room on the way to the sauna. We try to enter but someone is holding the door shut. It's me, says Eloísa; it still doesn't open. She insists and finally they give in. Axel sticks his head out, frenetic, nose running as usual, those red marks around his nostrils more pronounced than ever: Come in and shut the door, he says. He's with Débora, Cyntia, Leyla and another girl. On a yellow plate, on the steps of the sauna, Axel tips out the contents of a little plastic tube full of a glinting powder. Cyntia smiles hello with a mouthful of braces, Leyla gets excited. Axel divides the drug into a series of lines which he invites us to take with that rasping snore of his, like a contented seal. A guru. In turn, we bend down to inhale. When it's my turn, Axel warns me: It's fierce. I take it since I'm there. A bitter taste descends my throat. I'll leave you to it, he says and disappears. From the other side of the door a chorus begins: Aaaxel, Aaaxel, Aaaxel.

What if we light the stove, says Eloísa, but there's no consensus. Go on, go on, and eventually she gives in. The crystals in my nose and the cigarette smoke cause a sneezing fit. For five seconds, one after the other. The girls laugh, I feel two flames behind my eyes. Eloísa leaves and returns like lightning with a bottle of vodka and a ping-pong ball. She suggests a game. You have to pass the ball with your feet, anyone who drops it has to take something off. To begin with, apart from Leyla, the girls can't be bothered, they sigh and exchange glances. Eloísa: It's just a bit of fun for a while, that's all. Ok, they agree, but without the clothes part, without taking anything off. The game is more fun than expected. I get the feeling this isn't the first time Eloísa has played, she's by far the most skilful. We don't even complete two rounds before we're all falling about with laughter. Now it's the vodka bottle being passed from hand to hand. We drink from the neck, even Débora, who takes a slug and shudders from the burning sensation. Eloísa tilts the bottle and takes a long gulp which culminates in an Aaahhh, poured out as if she were spitting fire. The feet game fizzles out. Leyla challenges us with a more daring variation. Now it's passing the little ball from mouth to mouth, hands on the back of the neck. This time Débora and Cyntia require no convincing. We do that for a while, like fish out of water, mouths gaping, lips brushing, until Eloísa goes off the rails and gives a love bite to Débora, who pushes her quite hard. You're really crazy, bitch, she says, her mohawk crushed. They exit in a line, Leyla too, in solidarity with her friend.

More vodka and my eyes go from so much dizziness. I lose my senses, the grain of the wood undulates as if braiding itself, I hear deformed words: *catalep, tolomintes, monlocita*. I look again: Eloísa has her legs open, knickers down, passing the ping-pong ball over her groin. It's all rather blurry to me but I can still see how Eloísa puts the little ball into her cunt, which swallows it whole without chewing. A trick. Now she squats and expels it, trying to get it to land in the wooden pot at the foot of the stove. She tries once, twice, three times, she laughs alone, she runs out of air. I think that yes, like the girls said, she's mad. Totally mad. I leave the sauna, Eloísa doesn't follow me. The basement is empty, there's just a couple kissing at the mouth of the tunnel leading to the bunker. I climb the stairs quickly and cross the slippery floor, a pool of sugar, lemon and mud. It's as if my head has been cut from my body.

In the living room they're dancing in circles, unruly, costumes dishevelled. A potpourri of Jewish music. Axel is in the middle shaking his fake locks, minus his jacket and hat, face swollen, about to explode, glued to a bottle of whisky which he keeps pouring into his eyes. He shakes his head like a loony, he jumps, he stamps, he gives a war cry and when he can see again, despite everything, there is still some kind of emotion in his gaze. Around him there are two circles, one within the other, spinning in opposite directions, arms interlinked, screeching like magpies. Speed disintegrates the rings and the dance becomes a violent pogo with Eloísa in the vanguard, magnificent Eloísa once again, hurling bodies against each other, with punches, elbows and flying kicks. Débora ends up on the floor with a burst lip and a bloody mouth.

The accident paralyses everything. First, someone dressed as a labourer tries to administer first aid but since he can't stop the bleeding they decide to take her to A&E. Axel is white, shaken, looking for keys and money like a madman. They leave for a clinic in two cars, Axel, Cyntia and Débora in one and another three nameless guests in the other.

For a while the party is left without music. Eloísa replaces the boy at the bar but no one wants anything any more. I sink between cushions, drunk like never before, wanting to disappear. I close my eyes and fall into a spiral that spins with exasperating slowness. Yet I'm very much here, alert. I catch distant phrases with incredible clarity. Speculation about who it was that kicked Débora; lots of people name Andy, who was really out of it. Slowly, timidly at first, gradually more decisively, the DJ starts playing music again in order to move past the incident. Background music that carries on until the end at a medium volume that discourages dancing. Eloísa wakes me up with a slap on the leg and takes me by the hand to the garden with a bottle of beer. I want to leave but confusion keeps me. Near the pool there's a group of bodies doing I can't tell what. We move away from the party for good and settle in the deckchairs at the barbecue area without saying anything else, faces to a sky full of weak stars.

I wake up I don't know how much later with a stitch that twists my stomach. A device, a robot, something that sneaks into my dream and as the minutes pass becomes too real, unbearable. Something lodged in my gut, a giant parasite. Tic tac tic tac. In passing from sleep to this partial vigilance, I fantasise that I'm going to live with this thing beating inside me forever. Perhaps vomiting will relieve me. I have to try. Eloísa is still in the deckchair next to me. She's sleeping with one hand on her forehead and her mouth half open. Fighting the migraine that suddenly erupts, I measure the steps separating me from the basin next to the grill. I stand up in three slow movements, extremely slow, and walk along the brick path but I don't reach my destination, I stop at the foot of an outdoor shower. I barely lean over, the retches come out by themselves until I've released everything, like a saturated sanitary towel. Just like the night before Jaime's wake. Unstoppable vomit. I try to aim for the grating but that's worse, I soil my skirt. I grab tightly on to the shower pipe, trembling with cold despite the heat. I breathe deeply, consciously, and gradually start to revive. I turn on the tap and the cold water on my face, in my eyes, running down my throat, completes the resurrection. I have no strength to change, I carry my clothes rolled into a ball, like a stolen baby.

My journey home is eternal. Three quarters of an hour at the bus stop without being able to make the decision to walk. I arrive at daybreak, the sun filtering through the holes of the city. Torture. At the entrance to the building, my medallion belt gets caught on a bolt and I'm stuck for a while unable to unhook myself. I climb the stairs in slow motion. From the landing on the second floor I can make out Mercedes with a cigarette in his mouth next to the door of our flat. I pause in search of an explanation, but since I can't find one, I keep climbing. He sees me, and when I'm close he throws me a nod, raising his chin. Like a priest, a mafioso. Sonia also welcomes me with a hard gesture, of concern or reprimand. I raise my eyebrows to find out what's going on and she steps aside. The first thing I see is Herbert standing squeezing his chin with a frightened expression and then Simón, lying naked, his forehead covered with a damp cloth, body like a leaf. Sonia speaks quietly behind me, warming my ears: His temperature's soaring.

TWENTY-THREE

It takes a moment for the penny to drop. The scene is disconcerting: Simón is on his back, shivering; Mercedes is smoking by the door; another woman is spying from the shadows; Sonia is scaring me; Herbert is pale, back against the wall. Everything is spinning, inside and outside too, the wardrobe, the faces, the bucket, the light bulb hanging from the ceiling which blinds me for an instant whenever I look at it. Blind, stupid, lost. Finally I react and kneel down. I take Simón's hands, cold and clammy, I say: Simón, Simón. I remove the damp cloth, I kiss his eyes, his forehead, he's boiling. I pick up the sheet, wrinkled at his feet and I'm about to cover him but Sonia steps forward and shakes her head from above. Best not, she says.

I look at her with annoyance, as if she were guilty of something. I can't stand the fact that she's giving me instructions. I can't stand myself, dirty, worn out, mouth like a swamp. Impossible to disguise the stink of alcohol on me. I'd like to go back in time. Sonia tries to make Simón drink some water. I'm grateful for her good intentions, her care, I regret having given her a dirty look. I gradually find out what happened. Herbert says Simón woke in the middle of the night crying like a baby. Having nightmares. And because he felt so hot, he was concerned and went up to call Sonia. When the two of them returned, Simón was shivering and had vomited on the pillow. Sonia immediately realised he had a high fever and undressed him, changed the drenched sheets and opened the windows to allow the air to flow. Simón vomited again twice, the last time just a thick, white paste. That's what Sonia tells me, she's kept a bit on a cloth to show me. She also says she thought about making him a herbal tea to calm the pain, sure that he had an upset stomach, but she preferred not to do anything. Herbert brought a thermometer from their place and they took his temperature. He was as high as forty, they wrapped him in wet towels and brought him down to thirty-eight. They also gave him half a teaspoon of Novalgin. I'm about to ask why they didn't call me to let me know, but I stop myself in time, I didn't leave them the number of the mobile I didn't even have with me. I'd prefer not to know whether they tried to find me. I venture a hypothesis: It could be the heat, sunstroke. Sonia insists: I think it's a stomach upset, we can make a herbal tea from *burro* or common rue, it won't do him any harm, at worst he'll just throw it up. I look at her in silence, unconvinced. For the time that follows, a long time full of doubts and suppositions, I stay by Simón's side, without touching him so as not to make him hotter. Dozing, at times he half opens his eyes and looks at me from his feverish sleep, silent, interrogating me: What is happening to me, what is this thing that's coursing through my body, this new thing I've never felt? It's the first time I've seen him really sick; until now he's only ever had coughs, colds and scrapes, never anything serious.

We need to bring his fever down, says Sonia, then we'll see, and she passes the damp cloth for me to cover his forehead again. In contact with the cold fabric, Simón shudders, tenses his muscles and my head fills with dark thoughts. The minutes pass, the thermometer shows 39.3, the vomiting starts again. More cloths, more towels, more water, and when there finally seems to be an improvement, Simón starts to shake uncontrollably on the bed, showing the whites of his eyes, demonic. Sonia shouts at me: Put him on his side. And when I don't react, she pushes me away and does it herself.

The convulsions pass, we calm down a bit, I decide to take him to a hospital. Agitated, upset, Sonia starts pacing the room until I see her bend down in a corner and hear her say as if enlightened: That's it. She comes over to me and shows me the little ochre ball she's holding between her index finger and thumb. He must have swallowed a poison bead, she says with the excitement of someone revealing an enigma. Ask him, she orders, as if it has to be translated into another language. I don't really understand what she's talking about, I try all the same but Simón is gone, in another reality. I insist a couple of times and finally he nods his head. Yes, he ate one of those little balls which I now see are scattered around the bedroom floor like old, unexploded ammunition. Sonia says we need to find out how many he put in his mouth. She asks Herbert. It certainly wasn't with me, perhaps it was before I arrived, he says and looks at me. I can't remember having seen anything either. Sonia suggests I consult a healer, she doesn't call her a healer, but a woman who knows how to cure this kind of thing. I'd prefer to go to hospital.

First, it occurs to me to drop into Tosca's, she must be awake by now. We leave Simón in Herbert's care, giving him instructions not to let the cloth fall off his forehead. As we descend, Sonia tells me about poison beads. They are the fruit of the paradise tree, they come in through the window, she says and concludes: In large quantities they can make you retarded or paralytic. I enter without knocking. Tosca is watching television, Benito is sleeping at her feet, curled up on the floor like a fairy-tale pet. I explain the situation. Die, he won't die, says Tosca and repeats what Sonia said: We need to find out how many he swallowed, the best thing is to take him to hospital to have his stomach pumped. And looking me in the eye: Inject me, girl, hurry, then go, you never know what might happen.

Upstairs again, we wrap him up well and I carry him to the street. Mercedes is waiting for us at the entrance to the building at the wheel of his fake taxi. Sonia comes with us too, Herbert stays on the pavement, he says good-bye with his arm raised and his lips drooping, annoyed at not being allowed to come along. The car journey is torture, Simón keeps vomiting that phlegmy cream and I'm not always successful in getting his head out of the window. He dirties his clothes, my legs, the upholstery too. Mercedes complains in a low voice. He curses in his own language, that sharp Guaraní he uses at times, and accelerates, ignoring the traffic lights.

Sonia decides for me, we're going to the hospital where she works. The doctors are good, she says, and she silences me when I say I think it would be better to go to the children's hospital. It's not very far, ten, fifteen minutes, it feels like a century. We go through a tunnel underneath the railway lines and come out on a very wide road between a piece of wasteland with weed-covered ruins and a supermarket as big as an airport. Further away, there's a group of high-rises with balconies overlooking the void. I look so that I don't have to think.

I get out of the car carrying Simón in my arms as if he's war-wounded. The hospital signs calm me: *A&E*, *X-rays*, *Haemotherapy*. There's no way we can be seen quickly, in spite of Sonia's influence. None of her acquaintances are around. They're all new doctors, she complains. At the paediatric emergency window they ask me for Simón's symptoms. What's he got, that's what they say. High fever, we can't bring it down with anything. They register us, no one shows their face but they did warn me: You'll have to wait a while. We have an emergency, a boy who's really serious.

Three quarters of an hour until we are called by a tiny female doctor. I tell her: vomiting, fever, convulsions. Any history? I don't know whether to tell her about the poison beads. She strips him, takes his temperature, listens to his heart, checks his eyes, his ears, listens to his breathing and finally, as I'm dressing him again, she puts a syringe full of a pink liquid in his mouth. Seven point five, remember in case they ask you. I pluck up courage: My neighbour says it could be these, I say and show her a couple of the little balls I brought in my pocket. They call them poison beads, I murmur, I think he's eaten some. The doctor observes them without touching. Ok, she says, disregarding my contribution. First we'll do some tests and then we'll see. In any case, we'll check with toxicology later.

We stay in the small consulting room, Simón lying on the stretcher, me, standing, unable to move much because of the passing nurses, doctors, more patients. A girl with a cut on her forehead, another with a sharp pain in her groin that won't allow her to stand up straight and a blond boy with lots of teeth and a dislocated elbow. Since there's no orthopaedic specialist in paediatrics they're going to be waiting a good while until the adult consultant, with a twisting and flexing manoeuvre, slips the bone, after two refusals, back into place. Magic.

When I'm beginning to suspect the doctor has forgotten about us, she comes up from behind with an order for a blood test for Simón. We take a number in the clinic, it's at forty-five and we are seventy-three. I entertain myself with the mobile, the calendar, the games, the alarms. A girl with Yessica's hair passes and I remember the vipers, I clearly won't be able to go to work. I send a message to Iris so she can let them know, Simón sick, I write, and her reply: Serious? I don't answer. We get a friendly male nurse with a thin moustache and swollen bags under his eyes. He uses a rubber dinosaur to try to distract Simón, who is still half zombie, incapable of anything. It isn't easy to find a good vein, the man sweats, switches arms, from left to right, he scratches around with the needle, Simón cries and kicks his legs as much as his strength will allow him. Then he surrenders. I wonder whether it's really necessary to poke about quite so much, if there isn't something brutal about this way of doing it. Looking around, the tubes, the drips, I find it hard to believe that there isn't a more modern method. The man puffs, he grabs his head, it seems like he's about to give up and just then, that red, dark, thick liquid Simón has inside him which I've never seen before begins to run along the tube. The nurse covers the puncture with lint and warns me: Don't be scared if he gets a bruise, it's normal. With a filled test tube and a note saying Urgent, he sends us to the central laboratory.

Three flights of stairs, I knock several times at a flaking door until a side window is opened. A horrible man with the worst breath ever sticks his head out. Do I look deaf? I apologise and hand him the blood. The machine isn't working, I can't promise you anything, he says and shuts the window in my face. We wait on a bench with our feet dangling. I don't know how long. Simón curls up using me as a backrest, I read and reread a poster about the prevention of sudden death syndrome.

With the results of the analysis in my hand, we return to A&E. On the way I see the doctor who attended us, minus her apron, in sandals and miniskirt. She is in a hurry, tapping at her mobile, I intercept her as she's getting into her car. She can't place me immediately, I help her: The boy with the poison beads, I say. Ah, yes, sorry, I didn't tell you, the guys from toxicology, so she calls them, are at a conference, they'll be back tomorrow, so you'll have to wait. I have the test results, I say and show her. The white cell count is a bit high, we'll need to keep an eye on that, she says. Take it to the head of

A&E. Meanwhile we'll keep him under observation. Don't worry, it'll be fine, it might just be a bad virus. Or a bit of stress, but best to be sure. I can't work out whether the stress thing is serious or a joke.

Simón gets hot again. Another syringe of paracetamol and he falls asleep by himself, without pats or caresses. He takes a nap on a stretcher and I wait in an adjoining room with very high ceilings. I could also willingly fall asleep. A woman speaks to me from behind, I hear her voice before I see her face: What did they find? Nothing, he's got food poisoning, I say with determination and the woman looks at me doubtfully. If they're keeping him in it must be for something, they don't have beds to spare here. I'm about to say that he hasn't been admitted yet, that he's just under observation, but I stay quiet. Mirta introduces herself and indicates a door with a bronze plaque that says Mothers' Room. In there you've got a kitchen, TV, fridge, there aren't many of us today, there will certainly be room for you to stay. There are some armchairs, failing that, the air beds. She takes me by the arm, she wants me to see. I don't go in, I glance in from the door: a strong smell of fried food. The vapour leaves a trail like a jet plane. I locate the origin: a spitting pan on a hob just below the wall-mounted television. Around an oval table two women are drinking *maté*, engrossed in the news, one of them very old, the grandmother of some child, I think, the other almost still adolescent, a sister or premature mother. Mirta insists on showing me the facilities: There are hot showers from seven to ten, the laundry is at the back. There, she says, pointing out two trunks, is where the blankets are kept. In a low voice:

Keep an eye on your things, there's always a thief lurking about. The clothes horse was swiped yesterday. Back in the corridor, without my asking, Mirta tells me she came in for a consultation about some spots that appeared on her son's face and he's been here three months. His cheeks went red, his lips swelled and his temperature rose every night. First they told me it was a virus, then that it was an allergy, they did some X-rays and an electrocardiogram and they discovered a heart murmur. In the end they came up with Kawasaki syndrome. Do you know what that is, she asks. I shake my head but she doesn't tell me, she moves her hand like a windscreen wiper giving me to understand that it makes no sense for her to explain. They've already given him two bypasses, chronic cardiac insufficiency. It looks like we're heading for a transplant, she says in a strange tone, almost proud, as if the gravity of the situation gives her a certain status. It's not easy to find a donor of his age.

Afternoon in the hospital is nothing but desolation. After two, there's hardly a soul there. The few people who cross a corridor or enter and exit a door, porters mostly, just accentuate the feeling of emptiness. Simón has been moved to an intermediate care room, a stage between A&E and formal admittance, as will be explained to me later on. There are around twenty beds facing each other in two rows. In the middle is the desk for doctors and nurses, a cluster of apparatus and monitors. You almost always have to wait a couple of days for a bed to become free, you were lucky, I'm told. Before entering, we have to rub our hands with alcohol and put on surgical masks. There can be no more than five mothers at a time so we have to take turns. As Simón's fever lessens, he starts to become aware of where he is and doesn't like it. They connect him to a saline drip. Annoyed by the needle stuck in his wrist, he tries to rip out the cannula in one go. I hold his hand so that he doesn't wound himself. We stay like that for a while, until he gets used to it and falls asleep again.

I go out to the courtyard and witness a cat fight. Someone calls me from the end of the passageway. I can't see properly; the stained glass of the chapel projects a diffused light that has a clouding effect. Here, says the voice. I stay where I am, unable to make anything out. Sonia advances down the corridor and becomes visible. I smile and walk up to her. I was looking for you, she says and makes as if to give me a kiss on the cheek but stops halfway. How is he? Better, they've brought his fever down and he's been sleeping for about two hours. I also tell her about the blood tests. Come on, she says and I follow her. We go through a swing door between the pharmacy and the chapel that leads to a wide staircase to the first basement level: operating theatre, resuscitation room and, at the back, the morgue. We walk towards it, but branch off again, going down another flight to the boiler room. Smoke and rust. Sonia guides me to a room which she opens with a key and locks from the inside. No one comes here, she says in a conspiratorial tone. A couple of chairs, a standing lamp, a small table. High up, a ventilation grille. Would you like some *maté*, she asks. I accept and Sonia opens a metal cabinet with lots of shelves from which she removes the *yerba*, an electric kettle and some sachets of sugar. With this movement, she exposes an arsenal of medication: boxes, blisters, pills, pills and more pills. Of all colours, shapes and sizes. Also a collection of phials held by the neck with rubber bands: morphine, oxytocin, diclofenac. The kind Tosca uses leaps out at me from the pile.

Sonia unplugs the kettle, brews the *maté*, spits the first mouthful into a bucket, sucks the straw for a second time and passes it to me. They've been wanting to throw me out for a while now, she says, justifying herself. Did you see the orange girls? They've been here a year, contracts, they pay them peanuts, there are new faces every day, they bring them in to gradually wear us down. There's just me and one other left; there used to be about fifteen of us, almost all of them ended up resigning. Well, I'm staying and I take care of my own business, she says. I'm not harming anyone, am I? I shrug, it doesn't look like it.

I spoke to the woman, she says, and clarifies: The healer. Ah. She told me you have to make an infusion with the bark of the paradise. The antidote alongside the poison, that sounds reasonable. Like with the snakes, my dreams and the drawing. It occurs to me that I'm bound to find a paradise tree in the hospital garden. There must be one here, I say, but she disagrees energetically. It has to be the same one – if not, it won't work. I'm beginning to doubt the healer's remedy, it's a touch fanciful. Sonia says that if she'd known she would have brought some with her but she was only able to speak to her when she got to the hospital. Before we leave, I ask her for something for my headache. She offers me a grey pill especially for migraines.

I go back to the ward, Simón is awake, sitting up in bed with a glum face. The nurse: I think he was looking for you. She also says that a doctor came by wanting to see me. Another says: Bring him some comfy clothes. I buy him a vanilla yoghurt which he doesn't even try and I flee back to Sonia's hideout to see if she can stay with him while I go to the flat and return. No problem.

I take a taxi. The man spends the whole journey talking to someone on his mobile through a device stuck round his ear like a caterpillar, headphone and microphone in one. He gesticulates, letting go of the steering wheel, as if the other person could see him. I pay no attention to what he says. I just retain the phrase nasty piece of work.

I enter el Buti at a run. I make quick work: clothes, money, biscuits. Before I leave, standing at the door, I take a look at what remains of the emergency: a mountain of towels, an upturned glass, the bed is beyond dishevelment. I drop into Tosca's to inject her with morphine, but she tells me she sorted it out herself and lifts her blouse to show me her pricked stomach. But it's not the same, dear, chalk and cheese. She asks after Simón: And the boy? Still there, I say. She distrusts doctors, they like the sound of their own voices. On the pavement, walking to the corner, I remember Sonia, the paradise tree and the healer. I retrace my steps a few metres, rip a piece of bark from the trunk and put it in my trouser pocket.

Back to the hospital in a bus that drops me ten blocks away. I enter the ward and Simón is surrounded by nurses. Sonia tells me she was about to call. It's gone right back up. I give a questioning look; they answer with a mix of confusion and contempt. I stay at the margins as they perform a series of procedures on him, they clean him with cotton cloths, they insert and remove the thermometer, they make him take more of the pink syrup. I go out into the corridor and approach the first doctor I come across and as chance would have it, it's the head of A&E. I tell him about the fever, Yes, yes, he already knows. Let's see how he does overnight. And he informs me that he's already sent him for some X-rays to see how his lungs are. He also says he spoke to the folk from toxicology and that it can't be those little balls. We can rule out an infection. And I should stay calm, they're monitoring him, he says and leaves. Eight o'clock comes round and things get worse. Simón peaks at forty again. They give him an analgesic in a drip that leaves him half stupid. He doesn't want to eat, he refuses everything I offer him. I stroke his forehead, I console him in his ear, I tell him it will be over soon, I start to feel afraid. A nurse tells me off for all to hear, showing me with her finger: Not like that. I make myself comfortable in the chair and feel the piece of bark digging into my leg. A cleaner finds me a glass of hot water which he borrows from the doctors' kitchen. I cross the very dark garden. I stop under a light, split the paradise bark in two and submerge it. I sit on a bench and wait. Ridiculous. The water is barely tinged, very light brown. I return to the ward enveloping the glass between my hands as I blow near the surface. Simón is asleep, I have to wake him up for a bit to make him drink the tea, concealed from the nurses' eyes. I try to put myself in his place, imagining what he must be feeling and thinking, but it doesn't get me anywhere. I stay by his side until I'm thrown out. I don't understand how anyone can sleep in all this light.

With the night, the void of the afternoon becomes sinister. Or charming, it's difficult to say. Few lights illuminate the courtyard, the tall trees, a fig, a rubber plant, lots of bushes. Along the drains, bordering the corridors, rises a white smoke, sporadic, like the breath of a subterranean beast. It must be the boilers that surround Sonia's hideaway. An ambulance approaches, the siren intensifying. I have a sugary coffee sold to me by a man at the taxi rank. It's a heavy night, with no moon or stars, just clouds. A cave. I take two steps along the pavement. From the darkness I hear whistles that could be directed at me, I can't be sure; I turn back just in case.

A security guard blocks my way at the entrance to the hospital, where am I going, My son, I say and he moves aside unwillingly, shaking his head, as if I were mocking the law. A small troop of gloved women is moving along the corridors in orange uniforms, Sonia's competition. They clean the floors, sweep the ramps and stairs, carry enormous bags. The smell of disinfectant makes me dizzy. I carry on, not quite sure where I'm going, and when I'm opposite the chapel, this time I push the door with the stained glass. A large lady is praying or sleeping, her arms resting on the plateau of the start of her stomach, her hands covering her face. It's a modest but pleasant chapel which, you can tell, was built without many resources. The finishes are irregular, the benches are different styles, as are the lamps, a mishmash. The altar is a plank with trestles and the cross couldn't be more restrained. Two crossed pieces of wood, no varnish or Christ figure.

A young couple enters holding hands, they sit down in the first row. They talk loudly, they converse as though they were in any other place, not noisily, just normally, a long way from prayer.

A mobile phone rings and I take a while to accept that it's mine. The lady I thought was asleep turns her head, indignant. I squeeze the device firmly, reprimanding it, to muffle the sound, like someone gripping the hand of a child who won't shut up. I stand up and reach the exit quickly. In that couple of seconds a chilling shiver runs through me, I think about this morning when we were admitted to hospital, the moment when the woman behind the barred window noted my details, my name, my telephone number. I think about Simón, I think the worst. Once I'm outside, I look at the screen, a message from Eloísa: IM FUCKED YOU?

Tiredness drives me into the mothers' room. I'm scared to fall asleep, I feel as though if I close my eyes I won't open them again. The place is crammed, there are bodies all over the place, many have already gone to bed, others are playing cards, the rest are watching television, a quiz show. The woman who spoke to me in the afternoon, the transplant one, gestures to me with her hands, her eyebrows, her lips, as if saying: I'm sorry. I find out that some children were diverted here from a provincial hospital after a bus overturned. Grab one and lie down there, she says pointing out the pile of air mattresses. She also insists I take a blanket, and I do, even though it seems absurd in this heat. In the corridor, following the example of others who have been left outside, I recognise the couple I saw in the church.

I settle down next to an old lift under a large window looking over the top of a tree I can't identify. Large leaves, dark green, drooping branches, Canetti would be able to tell me. I lie down on the bare mattress and take a while to get used to the rancid smell of the rubber. And yes, the woman was right, I feel cold, the humidity, the fear, those very high ceilings. I take off my sandals and undo my trousers, allowing the red stripe marking my waist to breathe. The silence is terrible. The clacks, the hurried steps, the screeching wheels, the crash of chains when the lift starts moving. I'm so worn out and yet my body and my mind seem to have got used to resisting, incapable of ceding even a minute of vigilance. I curl up against the wall but sleep doesn't come. I haven't slept since the morning of the previous day. I shiver, boiling inside. Could Simón have infected me with whatever he has? I scratch my skin, dig my nails in deeper, I'm angry with myself.

I close my eyes and see Eloísa spitting ping-pong balls out of her cunt. One after another, like a warped factory. At the edge of breathlessness, she tells me there's still one in there. Jammed. I insert my hand, the whole arm, and she twists, killing herself with laughter. Her body becomes a glove, oily, soft, very light, for my giant's hand, a doctor's glove, a magician's.

In the middle of the night I wake up perplexed, trembling. Dying of thirst.

TWENTY-FOUR

Simón is better by morning, with no fever or symptoms of anything, without much explanation either. Before seeing him, I wake up in the corridor with a woman standing shaking me by the shoulder. I come out of a deep, painful sleep, as if I'd been beaten to a pulp all night. Coming, I say as a reflex, without knowing where or why. My body responds clumsily, torturing me with every movement. I only half hear the woman's voice, she's watching me from above. She says I'm wanted. I try to stand up, the sun is in my eyes, I button my trousers, I can't find my sandals anywhere. I pick up the mattress, fold the blanket, I peer through the bars of the lift with the impossible notion that they might have fallen, nothing. Who's going to take a pair of worn-out shoes? It's a mystery. In the mothers' room, quietly, to keep everyone from hearing, I explain what happened to me and the *maté* woman, the one who must be a grandmother and not a mother, points out a basket where lost items are kept. Stuff we find round and about, she says. See if anything will do. There's a trainer that fits, but loosely, some espadrilles that are too small and a pair of clogs that aren't too bad on me. They must be two sizes too big, but I can walk perfectly and when I feel them escaping I keep them on by standing on the tips of my toes. All morning I have the feeling someone is treading on my heels, when it's actually me click-clacking after myself.

A young, tanned, clean-shaven doctor is waiting for me with Simón, he introduces himself, he's that day's boss. He greets me with a smile. I tell him everything again, the fever, the vomiting, I tell him about the poison beads and he looks at me strangely but with interest. Yes, poison beads, he repeats with a rasping voice. I show him, I still have some in my pocket. How do you feel, he asks Simón, who from the seriousness of his gaze looks as if he's been addressed in another language. The man checks a chart, take notes, consults a new, small nurse about something. He's ready to go home, he says. But first we're going to do some tests just to dispel any doubts. Yesterday's white cell count wasn't normal, he reminds me. Yes, I know, and I think about how we'll need to go through the martyrdom of the needles again but apparently there's no other way.

Because it's morning, because Simón is much better and the danger has seemingly passed, in the light of day everything unfolds without complication. The blood flows. In the laboratory, instead of the fat man with rancid breath, there's a woman with oval glasses, too refined for her position, who serves us quickly and hands me the results in an instant. On the way out, as I start reading, comparing the figures with the reference indices, the woman anticipates my query: Perfect, she says. The white cells are all in order.

by the snakes who, after an hour, seem to look at me with different eyes. Conspiratorial, yet lying in wait. Before I leave, I take a turn round the nursery. The twenty-odd clumsy beings moving uncoordinatedly seem to lay bare the failures of creation. Like the death rattle of someone in agony. Minimal, spasmodic shakes. Like an organ that ticks out of time, or the opposite, that switches off under orders from the brain. Forceful to begin with, lazy near the end. I stay for a while watching them from the other side of the glass and suddenly a thought occurs to me that doesn't remain idle for long. The door, which I assume is locked, gives way. I plunge a hand into the incubator and grab a tiny lizard. A baby iguana which I enclose in my fist and sink into my trouser pocket until I reach the zoo exit.

I cross the street and enter the botanic gardens. On a bench at the edge of the path, I take out the iguana, which jumps from my hand and starts to crawl up my arm. I wrap it in a hanky and put it in my rucksack, safe from prying eyes and cats. On the way, I feel slight pangs of regret, but it's too late, there's no going back now. I justify myself as best I can. I think of something relating to freedom and captivity, although I end up in a muddle. I simplify things: a present for Simón to help him recover from the fright. I revise what I can remember about iguanas' diets: leaves, flowers, fruits and some small animals, slugs, spiders, worms, insects in general. They are very good swimmers and almost always walk alone. The adults reach two metres in length. I imagine it in the flat biting its tail, but that's a long way off. I go for the first option and buy a celery plant, the greengrocer won't agree to sell me any less than that, as well as a couple of green apples which it will surely like.

On the corner of el Buti, two guys are arguing and shouting, calling each other Coward, Son of a bitch, followed by Wimp and Retard. They are positioned in such a way that they are blocking the entrance and I don't dare say excuse me. The fight is taking place in an imaginary ring and they come to a truce by the kerb. Only now do I see a badly parked car and a motorbike thrown down on the pavement. I guess the source of the argument without knowing which belongs to whom.

I push open the flat door. Simón is on the bed, covered up to the nose, breathing noisily. By his side, Herbert is staring at him. It was obvious. A relapse, I feel stupid, I shouldn't have left him alone. Herbert speaks quietly and informs me of what I can already see: He fell asleep, he says. I crouch down and realise it's just tiredness, the trip to the hospital, the injections, the interminable night. I stroke his forehead, fresh, not a touch of fever.

I pay Herbert for the week and before saying goodbye I wonder whether to share the novelty I've brought home. I stay quiet. I don't know whether the need to hide the iguana stems from a fear that the robbery will be discovered and it will reach the ears of someone at the zoo or because pets aren't allowed in the building. I close the door properly and unpack the animal, which I hold in my hand for a while, unable to decide where to make a place for it. In the base of the wardrobe I find a flattened shoebox which I reshape by folding up the edges. I make up a mattress with pieces of toilet paper, I place the box between the toilet and the pipe for the bidet that was never installed. I leave the bathroom door ajar and join Simón's siesta. Sleep sucks me up like a black hole.

We wake at around nine, hungry. So much so that I forget the iguana and the desperation of having nothing to eat sends us out to the street. Friday night, there are already families queuing at the pizzeria on the main road. We sit on the last free bench at the counter. The television is showing a football match which Simón follows as if he's really interested. Herbert's influence. Then, as I chew, my brain reproaches me over the iguana. All at once: Esteban's enthusiasm, the other beasts, its blood brothers, the celery and the apples that are still in my bag. I hurry and encourage Simón not to eat in such a leisurely fashion, at least not today.

My fears are confirmed, the iguana has abandoned the home I proposed for it. I search in the corners, between the sheets, in another box, the one with Simón's toy cars, under the wardrobe, behind the gas cylinder, through the cracks in the skirting board, I even uselessly check the corridor. It doesn't occur to me to track it right there, thirty centimetres from its basket, next to the grille at the foot of the toilet. It was semi-abandonment. I pick it up gently and call Simón, who drags his feet, head drooping. I cover the animal with my hand and when I uncover it Simón freezes. He baptises it Uana. I tell him it's a secret between us two, I show him the little house I made. I chop a piece of apple and a stalk of celery which Simón puts in a bottle lid. We spy on it eating, fascinated, as though in the presence of a being from another planet.

TWENTY-FIVE

AM OUTSIDE, COMING? Eloísa writes like that, in capital letters, as if shouting to me from the street, at half six on the dot, when I'm already in the changing room getting ready to leave. I catch sight of her from a distance, very small, she doesn't see me, she's acting as though she doesn't see me. She's standing at the entrance with a giant bag of popcorn, sunglasses, flowery blouse and denim shorts, in between the pony and a purple dragon, or is it a dinosaur, handing out balloons with its snout. As I approach, now that she's waving at me with her free hand, I remember the last time I saw her. At the end of the party, lying in the deckchair, awake but gone, exhausted from always having to be the same. So theatrical. And yet again, as in the past, as with her adventures in the country, my attention is grabbed by that capacity of hers to re-emerge as though nothing has happened, burying everything, without blame or remorse, like an animal. The difference is that now, while the attitude is the same, behind her eyes, in her teeth, underneath her skin, you can tell that eternity is gradually wearing her down.

She embraces me and grabs a hand which she pulls to her pocket for me to feel it. I brought you a surprise, she says as we walk in front of the creature, I still can't work out what it's meant to be, and Eloísa sticks her tongue out at it as we pass, just for the sake of it, she can't help herself. I'm a bit embarrassed. Whoever's sweating inside the costume must be cursing her and overheating even more. We cross the road diagonally, heading for the plaza in front of a building made of mirrored glass with a large American flag flying high.

We sit at the top of a slope, at the foot of the pergola. Very tall banana trees, a weeping willow and a string of paradise trees border the avenue. Canetti's right, I'm beginning to hate them. Ta dah, says Eloísa and brings out a joint, thick as a fat finger. Flowers from the best garden. It takes a while to light it because a wind gets up, not strong but whirling, which plays with the flame of the lighter. A moment of calm and then another gust. In the sky there are white and translucent surface clouds, speeding northwards; others, higher up, are towers of grey foam that move slowly from the river towards us. Rain or refreshment, you get the feeling that something's going to happen. It's been like this all day, heavy and indefinite.

We smoke in silence, two draws each, it feels like it's never going to end. The rain doesn't come, instead we feel an unexpected relief on our skin. Eloísa speaks again, she can't bear the void. Did you have a good time the other night? she asks but she doesn't allow me to answer, she continues alone: Did you see what ugly bastards Axel's friends are, every single one. And work, how's it going? It's fine, I say, I don't mind it. She pauses to take a drag and I'm about to tell her about the iguana but I change my mind. I tell her about Simón, about the poison beads, the night in the hospital, What a bummer, she says but deep down she doesn't hear me at all, out of jealousy, because her mind's on something else or she's scared of children.

I wonder what it would be like if she kissed me now or if later on she felt like stroking a breast and started sucking it. I'd certainly let her do it. When she's in front of me, she reveals everything, unbridled, like at the party, telling me about her orgies and fantasies, it's as though I'm seeing her through glass, on a screen. Something similar must happen to how she sees me. She doesn't come on to me nor does she provoke me, and I don't look for it either. It's true that I haven't really been turned on for a while now, not even by Iris, who became more of a curiosity than anything else. I masturbate once in a while, so as not to lose the habit, in the same way I scratch my neck or cross and uncross my fingers when I don't know where to put my hands.

The high clouds pass by, the ones that looked like they were bringing rain, and the sky clears, tinged orange where the sun is setting. Far from the city. Sliding down the grass, we reach the flat ground and lie down on our backs, the joint goes out thanks to the humidity floating in the air. We stay like that for a while until one of us, her, me, I'm not sure, points out a group of women doing gymnastics. They form a circle around a boy in sports gear and dark glasses with a lifeguard's body who's giving them instructions about the exercises, providing an example of every movement. They imitate him as best they can, some skilfully, others struggling. Leapfrogs, flexes, abdominals and a quick jog to the pergola and back. From where we are lying, we see them come and go, heads where the feet should be, feet in place of heads. A silent film, hilarious. Sequences that are more than just clumsy, they're spastic, trainers, legs, arms, armpits and hips coordinating like endless marionette parts. But the thing that kills us is the arses. Sad, baggy, arses like faces, tight, chubby, with drooping jaws, chatty or circumspect, arses in action. Our laughter ends up choking us.

I could eat a couple of horses, says Eloísa, recovering her breath. We hoist ourselves up hand in hand. We skirt the group of gymnasts and Eloísa can't help mocking, releasing a forced, unnatural cackle, which I accompany with a discreet smile and increase my pace. To cross the road, Eloísa grabs my arm tightly as if she were wobbling and about to fall. A game, another game. Climbing onto the pavement again, feeling me cold and unenthusiastic, she gives a wink of disappointment.

The plaza is a mess, the traffic lights don't work, which everyone is using as an excuse for exasperation. Further over, Garibaldi rides on high. Undertaking a certain amount of risk, we dodge cars, motorbikes and buses and enter a luminous pizzeria without consulting each other. I go first, Eloísa follows behind, and as soon as she sets foot in the place she spits out another cackle. I turn round, she covers her mouth with a hand, with the other she points to my back. My T-shirt is sprouting grass, my hair too, as are hers. Before we sit down, as we shake our clothes in spite of the censorious looks, Eloísa, her voice choked, says: It looks like we've been rolling about like lezzers.

I go to the toilet, I pee a lot and carry on removing grass from my hair in front of the mirror. There's always a bit more. My face is red, my cheeks hot, as if I'd been running. I return to the table, Eloísa is flicking through the menu. I've got cash, she says, order what you want, Axel gave it to me to buy him some medicine I couldn't get, I'll tell him I spent it on the taxi and that's that. We are served by a very well-spruced waiter, as Eloísa would say: fake tan, fully waxed arms and highlighted hair. A boy who punctuates every phrase he utters with a movement of the shoulder, the left, the right, it depends, on the defensive, as if saying: What do I care. A local faggot, that's how Eloísa defines him as we watch him move away with our order: a pitcher of beer, here they call it a double jug, and a mozzarella pizza with anchovies. A real one, explains Eloísa so that there's no doubt and I understand the allusion to Axel, who is the fake faggot.

Let's go for a couple of quick puffs before the pizza comes, says Eloísa, nodding towards the bathroom. She wears me out. Imagine if one of them comes in. I'm referring to the old lady in a pearl necklace, chewing with loose dentures, the young woman with inflated tits and a television face or the girl at the next table who's giving us a dirty look, God knows why. Imagine, I insist, and now the two of us, as we did a while ago, lying on the slope watching the upside-down aerobics class, explode into laughter, which makes us the centre of attention once more, Eloísa beating her palm on the table, which sounds just like a drum roll, me, drinking beer to try to hide it. In fact, one of the waiters, not ours, who is reprimanding us with signals from his raised shoulder, allows himself to be infected and gives a hint of a smile which he aborts as soon as the man at the till points out an unattended table.

We gradually calm down, eyes red, tired from so much laughing, just in time for the arrival of our order. For a while, as we eat and drink beer without pause – the anchovies are more than salty, they're poisonous – we don't say much. We just smile every time the camp waiter approaches us, somewhere between solicitous and mocking, and gives us one of his contemptuous gestures as he asks if we'd like anything else. We munch away rather animalistically, not worrying about manners, mouths dirty, hands greasy, dripping tomato sauce. We paint the tablecloth with stains of all shapes.

Finally sated, we take a deep breath and Eloísa starts talking again. She says that Axel now wants to make her an actress in the film. What film, I ask. The film they're going to make with Andy, the one with the Martians. I told you. Oh, yes. I'm fed up of him, I'd move tomorrow but I don't have the money. I want to get the hell out of there, that's what she says. Yes, the house is really good, but having him wandering round all day is unbearable. He's a worm, she says, and the word resonates in me somewhere. She is interrupted by a black man, really black, from Africa or Central America, passing among the tables with a briefcase full of jewellery. Bracelets, earrings, gold chokers, as well as watches, fake and luxurious, blue backgrounds, silver-plated, with moons and suns. Eloísa tries everything. The black guy, who doesn't utter a single word, partly out of timidity, but mainly because he has earphones in and appears to have no intention of entering into contact with the outside world, is patient. Nor does he protest when Eloísa ends up saying, Thanks, maybe next time. He half closes the briefcase with two fingers and moves on. We take swigs of beer in unison and once more fall into silence. And what if we go and live together? says Eloísa suddenly with a foam moustache on her lip. I raise my eyebrows without stopping drinking but I don't say anything, nor am I going to. She doesn't insist either, she must have remembered Simón and rejected the idea quickly. She stands up: Be right back, I'm going to pee. I space out, head resting on my hand, my palate still burning from the anchovies, I look out of the window: a man missing a leg is crossing the street dressed in combat gear. People look at him with a mixture of repulsion and commisera-tion. He steps onto the pavement, I lose sight of him, I let my eyes zigzag along the pedestrian route disfigured by the heat, the tyres and the million soles treading it. An X-ray of a pair of sick lungs comes into my mind. I think about Tosca and melanomas. The gay waiter rescues me by very deliberately clinking the cutlery to wake me up.

Eloísa returns from the bathroom, both fists clenched near her temples and a wide smile, as if celebrating a goal. She says she's had a great idea and taps her forehead three times with her knuckles. Guess. I think about Axel's film. No, no. You want to do a runner. Warm, warm, but bigger, much bigger, she says, eyes clear, suddenly a child. I take a gulp of beer, I give in and she squeezes my wrist, lowering my arm. I put up a weak resistance, for seconds. She leans in to me and finally says very quietly: The jewels, you daft cow, we'll nick the jewels.

She asks me for a pen. Since I don't have one, she stands up and gets one at the till. She unfolds a paper napkin and starts drawing the plan of the house. The ground floor, which you already know, she says, living room, kitchen, Axel's little room and the staircase. What staircase? I ask with a silent gesture, lengthening my neck. The staircase. No, never saw it. She insists: Behind the piano. Well, it doesn't matter, she continues, you saw it but you don't remember. That's how you get to the bedrooms. On another napkin she traces the lines that separate the rooms, Axel's, his sister's, which is now a guest room, his parents'. Here's the bed, the bathroom on one side, it's enormous, it has a jacuzzi and everything, there's the dressing room. You have no idea. At the end of the wardrobe she marks an asterisk so hard that it perforates the paper: That's where the jewels are, in a safe behind a mirror. She waits for my reaction. I can't tell whether this is a sophisticated joke, so I stay quiet. She continues: I haven't told you the best part, I know where they keep the key. I must be looking at her with incredulous eyes, more than incredulous, stunned, spellbound. We'll get rich, understand? She makes the sign of the cross with her index finger over her lips and concludes: I swear in God's name.

The mix of marijuana, pizza and beer clump together in my guts to form one single, rancid, reverberant mass of taste that rises in my throat in the form of a retch. A false retch that still prevents me from closing my mouth. Walking the few blocks back to the building, I feel like I have a flowerpot on my head. More than that, my whole head has turned into a cube of dry earth. Hard. It's already night-time when I arrive. Simón and Herbert are sleeping together, back to back. I wonder whether they'll have eaten anything. Impossible to tell: there are no traces of anything, no smells, rubbish, dirty plates. I feel like a ghost.

TWENTY-SIX

The dream is so real that I wake up with vertigo and bad heartburn. Mercedes is pursuing us through the building. Herbert, Sonia and Simón manage to slip down the stairs, celebrating their freedom with playful laughs. He catches me with a swipe and drags me to the lift shaft. There, he lets go of me and skewers me with his hard cock, like a bull's, colossal. He fucks me in the air, right next to the abyss.

Morning in the plaza. Swings, slides, taxi drivers drinking coffee, too much sky for the city. Sitting in the sand, I take off my shoes and entertain myself burying and exposing my feet. My toes are covered in grains of sand that pile up on the skin like minuscule living beings. Thousands of little blond men with the singular mission of sinking and allowing themselves to sink. And at that moment, passing from one state to another, when the toes stop being toes, the instant at which the knuckles have no beginning or end, the deformity is revealed. My deformity. A different kind of decomposition, through concealment, that leads to the same nothing, the same mystery as ever. A horn beeps and it's goodbye abstraction. Simón is carefully swinging his motorcycling cat back and forth until suddenly he ducks his head and gives it a hard push, launching it like a rocket.

I shake my feet, leave the sandpit and sit on the cement border around the plaza, my back supported by the railings. I start emptying my pockets, between notes and coins I count eighteen pesos. Rolled into a ball, the napkin on which Eloísa drew her plan of Axel's house, the first floor, the bedrooms, the route to the jewels. She didn't stop talking for half an hour and I, somewhere else even before she started telling me about her plan, only caught words at random: *diamonds, dresses, shoes, Miami, idiot* and *happiness*. At times I woke up and paid her fleeting attention again. That house is a waste of time, no one ever notices a thing, who's coming in or out, Orfe, the maid, workers who turn up occasionally, the gardener, the pool boy, Axel and his mates, it's mental. It would be impossible for them to catch us, she was saying, increasingly serious, and it didn't sound like an idea that had occurred to her in a flash of inspiration, more like something she had been concocting for a while. I went back to daydreaming with my eyes open, the spicy taste of the anchovies still inflaming my palate; her lips moved at top speed while her hands, just as fast, moulded together the crumbs scattered across the table, forming a ball of dirty dough. Now Simón is moving from the swing to the slide, following the cat's lead. I fold the napkin in four and slip it back in my pocket. A souvenir.

We have lunch at a newly opened hamburger joint. The place is painted fluorescent green and attended by a family of women. Mother and three daughters, staggered in age, all very different, tall and thin, short and big-bummed, the youngest almost masculine. All four have the same arch above the chin. We sit at a table on the pavement and all the time we're there we have to fend off a dog that insists on pawing at Simón's legs.

At twelve, Herbert arrives with Sonia. I hurry to shut the iguana in the bathroom. Herbert already knows, I asked him to swear absolute silence. Sonia says, she finds it hard to tell me, you can tell by the preamble, that Herbert was sent home from school yesterday because his head is full of lice. He's infected, she says and lowers her eyes as if afraid of wounding me. I look at her with a forced expression assuming there's more to come. Finally she suggests that perhaps he's contaminated Simón. You should check him, she says. Of course. She takes a step forward, she doesn't trust me: Do you want me to take a look. I shrug. She approaches Simón, who is playing in a corner with a patrol car without wheels, she leans in, examines his head, her fingers moving very quickly among the hairs like a piano virtuoso. Then she raises her eyebrows, bites her lips, pulls an exaggerated face of fright: Come here, look, she says, I've never seen anything like it.

The rest of the day passes without incident until Iris calls me from her post in the aquarium. She comes out of her booth and, covering her mouth with her hand, says in my ear: I'm leaving. The whiff of sardines and my incomprehension make me take a step back. I question silently, with a nod. I'm leaving, I'm going back to my country. I ask for an explanation with both palms to the sky. My dad's sick, pneumonia, he's in a bad way, she says. Apparently what started as flu got more complicated when he was admitted with a hospital-acquired infection. He's alone, someone has to look after him. Yes, I say, and at the same time I think I remember that her mother died the day she was born. She never mentioned the subject again, and I didn't ask. Iris lights one of her white-filtered cigarettes and exhales, wrinkling her mouth. I'm going to use the money I've saved to pay for the ticket, she says with a melancholy that's different from usual – it's deeper, more theatrical. I have the feeling she's keeping quiet about something, I try to enquire but I don't get far. I ask her how she feels, whether she's sad, if there's something else. She frowns, shakes her head vehemently as if I'd insulted her. Sad? she repeats, hissing the 's' as if to spit. She leaves, once again she doesn't say goodbye.

Yessica tells me that Esteban is looking for me. She says it sarcastically, or jealously, I can't tell. It takes me a while to find him, I come and go along the aisles of the reptile house until I notice the sign for the nursery and everything becomes clear. The theft of the iguana becomes my only thought. Why didn't it occur to me sooner, it's so obvious, sooner or later this was bound to happen. I feel stupid, I don't even have an alibi. I knock at the door, there's no answer, I stick my head in, Esteban is on the other side of the glass among the incubators wearing a surgical mask. I can make out Uana's brothers and sisters in the distance, by now he must be crawling about the flat in search of a new hiding place to escape

Herbert and Simón's fanaticism. Esteban comes round to my side, removes the mask, greets me with a kiss on the cheek. We have a problem, he says. I stay silent. We've detected a virus, three turtles have died, we're going to have to transfer them urgently for a general disinfection. I'm going to need you, he says and breathes in. But he isn't finished. Oh, and another thing, he says, walking out. There's an iguana missing, did you notice? How strange, I say and he nods twice with an old-womanish expression.

At the exit, Iris is waiting for me. She raises her hand, she beckons me, she wants us to walk back together. The same subject as the afternoon, she adds details about the illness and her father's deterioration, they sent her a terrible photo. That's what she says, Terrible. I come out with a stupid phrase of consolation, Well, I'm sure it will do him good to see you. A few blocks in silence, we say goodbye at a corner. We must have a leaving do, I say. I don't like goodbyes, she hurries to answer.

I spend half the night hunting lice with a fine comb. Simón's hair is soaked in cider vinegar. It fattens them up and they burst more easily, Sonia's words. Well-developed adult lice, young lice that are difficult to trap, nits by the dozen, alive and dead, which I'm lining up on a sheet of newspaper soaked in alcohol. I wonder whether they organise themselves in some way, whether there will be parts of the head that are more attractive than others, whether there's any kind of hierarchy or government. Whether they'd be trainable, even sacred to some past or future civilisation. To begin with, I kill them without hesitation, squishing them between my fingertips, making them explode nail against nail, tst, tst. But with repetition, a certain interest is awoken in me and I start studying their behaviour. I try to mutilate them, keeping them alive, so that they can't escape from my sight. It's not easy. I follow their final steps attentively, guiding them to meet other cripples. They find themselves forced to pass through a labyrinth built of the corpses of their fellows. What must it be like to experience all this, their own agony and the death of the rest, with no awareness of pain, tragedy or killing. Lice, fleas, bedbugs. Life forms that, in planetary terms, are perfectly equatable to ours. When I finally finish, at least I think I've finished, I have in front of me a real cemetery of tiny bugs. A scaled-down extermination camp. The hunt leaves me as exhausted as I am excited. Sleepless, I clean the bathroom, I run a cloth over the floor, I soak all the socks I can find in the washbowl, most of them missing a partner, also my three pairs of knickers, including the ones I'm wearing. I go to bed at half three, naked, annoyed at I don't know what. Eyes closed, a row of morphine phials appears to me, floating against a black background like dancers in the darkness.

TWENTY-SEVEN

Excursion to Open Door. It's Eloísa's idea, she wants to go and see what it's like these days, she hasn't been back since her house and the shop were demolished. She suggests the two of us go alone, but I add Iris and Simón to the group, which she eventually accepts with a reluctant: If there's no other way. In fact, inviting Iris is a way to give her the send-off she doesn't want. It takes a couple of chats to convince her: A day in the country, I tell her, to clear your head. She answers sarcastically but finally agrees.

We arrange to meet at Once station at half ten in the morning. Eloísa arrives forty-five minutes late. Simón and I kill time with a hot dog each for breakfast, Iris watches us in disgust. As we wait, I realise I'm making the assumption that they've seen each other before, the time Eloísa came to get me at the zoo. I was never able to tell whether that was the case or not, but anyway, the thought of an encounter between the two intrigues and excites me. But when Eloísa arrives, our hurry not to miss the train allows no time for introductions, everything happens at a run.

We sit on a group of seats facing each other and after Eloísa's excuses, saying that she sent me about six messages even though I didn't receive one, and Iris's monosyllabic complaints, we enter a long tunnel that silences us for a while. We each retreat into our own little world. Eloísa, who has only slept for two hours, covers her hangover with a pair of Carey sunglasses, disproportionately wide for her face; Iris looks out of the darkened window, full of distrust; Simón is too lively, kicking my knees to mark his boredom. I distract myself comparing noses and ears. Pointed, twisted, flattened, piggy, like magpies, like plug sockets, porous and smooth, mousy, funny, ridiculous, endless. Ears with noses.

At Liniers, a white-haired man gets on, blue shirt, polka-dot tie and braces. He's dragging a little trolley holding a black leather case. He sits in the middle of the carriage, two metres from where we're sitting. The man unfolds a stool and takes out a shiny, red accordion, which he places on his legs on top of a flannel. Before playing, he regales us with a short brotherly speech. He talks about our mission in the world, our duty to love our neighbours and God equally: He who loves one and not the other is at fault, he says, and searches for the eyes of the other passengers, who in most cases avert their gazes. When he falls silent, the music comes: a *chamamé*, a tango and a *milonga*. Eloísa becomes enthusiastic, as does Simón; Iris watches with eyes like an extraterrestrial's. Before leaving, the man recommends drinking a cup of chamomile tea every night and a glass of lemon juice in the morning so as not to die trying. He says: So's not to die trying. Then he passes the hat. I have a few coins for which he thanks me too effusively, so that the others can't fail to hear. Safe journey, bless you.

Change at Moreno. We get on the new train as it's starting to move. Another hour, which we use to doze. A parade of beggars and hawkers. We arrive in Luján at around two, too hungry to walk round, we make do with a little bar opposite the station. We have escalopes and chips for lunch, today's special, the only option. Eloísa starts interrogating Iris. About her country, the people, how they dress, what they're like, who's the most famous Romanian, what's her favourite dish. *Frigarui*, says Iris and Eloísa takes three attempts to say it properly. Iris explains that they're like long hamburgers that sometimes have vegetables in them and which are eaten with bread and yoghurt. Eloísa puts two fingers in her mouth, as if to vomit. It's delicious, Iris retorts, almost offended. I eat quickly, and as I listen to them talk I begin to realise that the situation makes me slightly uncomfortable. I cross the small plaza with Simón so that he can climb on a strange wooden structure, I can't tell whether it's intended for exercise or for children to play on. This is the very spot where I stood waiting for Jaime one of the first times I came. Almost unchanged, except that on the corner, instead of the ice-cream shop, there's a veterinary surgery that looks as friendly as a dog baring its teeth.

We take a bus that goes around the plaza. In order to see the whole basilica, Iris has to bend down and twist her neck. Big, she says. Eloísa, who's in the seat in front, turns round at one stage, pointing out a place I can't see properly, a chemist, a launderette, and says to me: Remember? We get out at the entrance to the loony bin. Eloísa offers a bit of explanation to Iris, who becomes laconic again. You have no idea what it's like, she says. Unbelievable. Without discussion, naturally, we take the dirt track bordering the hospital, as if going home. The sun is strong but not quite as hot as before, a truck passes and envelops us in a dust cloud. At the crossroads, more or less equidistant from Jaime's farm and the site that used to be occupied by Eloísa's parents' shop, I trace a parabola in the air with my raised arm. I look at Iris, as if telling her about it. Pretty, she says.

Eloísa insists we go to what used to be her house first. She wants to see what was left after the bulldozers did their thing. Almost nothing, a few traces with which to mentally reconstruct the place: four posts that according to Eloísa mark the limits of the store, the tracks of the driveway and a bunch of corrugated-iron sheets in a pile, which we assume are the remains of the shed. This is mad, Eloísa cries, and just when I'm wondering if it will affect her, what kind of emotions it might rouse in her, a few steps further over, eyes on a copse of eucalyptus, kicking the ground just like Simón, a girl again, she raises her head, looking straight ahead: This was always a shithole, she says, at least it's worse now. I smile, Iris looks at her askance, uncomprehendingly.

We retrace our steps towards the farm. I avert my eyes to delay the first impression. In the distance I can make out an army of strimmers diagonally sweeping the field, closer to us are two coils of steel cable and in between, the fig tree, parched but still standing. Two seconds later, reading my mind, Eloísa comes back with another Remember? Simón leads the way, running, he recognises his territory. About thirty metres from the gate, the same as ever but painted white, a security booth has been installed, minimal and plastic. A strangely uniformed man comes out: black shirt buttoned to the neck, like a priest, baggy gaucho trousers and military boots. Quite an ensemble. He doesn't smile, he reveals what teeth he has left, only the couple at the front of the upper gum, rotted by nicotine. He eyes us suspiciously, more timid than mean. He must have come from the loony bin. Eloísa looks at me, trying to contain herself, she's thinking the same as me. Some things never change. The loonies, the barriers.

There's no need for the man to open his mouth, we can't go through. I could tell him that I lived there until a short while ago, that I spent the last four years in that house and that this boy I'm carrying in my arms was raised there. But why? What do I want to see? What is it that I need to prove? There's no sense to it. Iris's eyes, which suddenly look a lot like Simón's, end up dissuading me. Rising high, blotting out the landscape of my recent past, an immense billboard promises duplexes, chalets, plots, golf, spa and country club. The house, the stable, even the furrows left by Jaime's pickup are still there, intact despite being closed off. I wonder how long it will take for the billboard to become reality. A year? Two? Perhaps less. I don't think I'll come back to see it. Eloísa suggests going to the stream, to the mulberry tree. It's a long way, I say that we'd be better heading back. She pretends not to hear me. Downhill, between the wire fence and the shadow of the stands on the polo field, my head is inevitably filled with images from before, happy, tremendous.

All that remains of the stream is a scrawny thread of water, everything around it has been filled with light, sandy earth; the tree is there but without leaves or mulberries. Dead or dying. We set up camp on the bank, to rest. Iris sits cross-legged, Eloísa and I lie on our backs, Simón wanders about. Eyes fixed on the blue void interspersed with an infinite network of branches, I lose myself in a journey through time. I think without meaning to about all the lives that came before which were necessary for me to be born. I come up with three or four names, nothing more. I try to think ahead, this thing I am, this link, how and where it will reverberate. Simón, and then what? Think about the jewels, Eloísa says to me quietly, rather witch-like, breathing close to my ear, which brings me down like a lead balloon. The jewels, she murmurs again. I bite a smile. Iris, watching us upside down, adopts a paranoid expression, she must think we're making fun of her.

Climbing the slope, I make out between the weeds half a dead dog covered in a cloud of flies. I act as if I've seen nothing, to prevent Simón or Iris or Eloísa noticing. I can guess the three different reactions and I prefer to avoid them all. Iris's shriek, Eloísa's excitement, Simón, naturally curious, wanting to touch it. We pass the entrance to the farm again, the man in the booth doesn't come out this time, I say goodbye with a fleeting glance, the sun is beating down, Eloísa pushes ahead. She says: Come on. She doesn't consult us, she just marks out our route, she bends down and slips under the wire fence. And? she hurries us on, palms up, balancing invisible balls. A cutting gesture from Iris, her shoulder raised, is enough for me to understand that she's not planning to follow, that I should do as I please. I don't feel like convincing her and allow myself to be guided by her prudence. Eloísa acts offended, walks under the stand and crosses the polo field diagonally, gradually growing smaller. Iris reprimands her silently, showing her gums. Simón won't walk any further, I'm going to have to carry him for what's left of the day. A cluster of dragonflies attacks us head-on. When we reach the crossroads, Eloísa is already a tiny speck, we still have a twenty-minute walk ahead of us and I regret not having followed her.

At a service station, recently opened on what always used to be wasteland, Eloísa is waiting for us with a can of Coca-Cola, chatting to a guy in a vest and mirrored glasses. Iris looks at her angrily, the same anger I feel towards her for being so stubborn. It's getting on for five in the afternoon, Simón wants an ice cream, Iris to go back, Eloísa for us to accompany her to a pool bar to see if anyone she knows is there. Going for none of these options, we walk the few blocks to the shopping centre and stop at a kiosk. We sit down with a giant bag of crisps on some brick steps in front of a hairdresser's: *Styles.* For Eloísa, we cease to exist for a while. She devotes herself to sending messages, one after another. She is electrified by the responses, which the mobile announces with the gasping of a hysterical girl. Finally she addresses us: There's something on around eight, you coming? She says she's going to meet her school friends and some other guys she hasn't seen for ages. And she adds: What will it be like to see everyone again?

I wake at dawn with a start: the iguana is walking across my cheek.

TWENTY-EIGHT

Time with tortoises. Giant ones, from Aldabra. Relatives of those from the Galapagos. The female isn't as restless as the male. Esteban taught me to distinguish between them, explaining something about concave and convex. A characteristic that allows copulation. I've spent two months coming and going without paying any attention to this naturally lit tank at the centre of all my movements, with its tree trunk, pool and mattress of rotten vegetables. Tomato, carrot, celery and a thousand mysterious little green pieces. The rain and Yessica's absence force me to find a pastime and my feet lead me to contemplate these two fantastic beasts. I stand in the corner, my forehead supported where the walls join, occasionally glancing up to see whether anyone's approaching and intercepting them in the aisle to check their ticket. Two minutes of observation are enough to humanise them, to project myself into the enclosure, into the slowness, to load all that weight on my shoulders. The female won't acknowledge me at all, always motionless by the side of the pool. The male, almost twice her size, he certainly moves, initially erratically, circling her, chasing something with black skin, it could be aubergine. I try to count the rings on the carapace to work out his age, impossible, I immediately get lost. A loud voice brings me back to my post. It's a tall, slim woman, her wrists covered by metallic bracelets, chink chink chink, and five children flitting round her like gnomes. I wait for them to disappear and return to the tortoises. The male, now, to my surprise, is up against the glass, right where I had been standing. Courteous or standing guard. When I'm face to face with him, not before or after, he stretches that aged alien neck of his and strikes the glass with his rapacious beak. He calls me, challenging, he wants something. And not just one blow, there are several, phlegmatic, but rhythmic, like a code. Here I am, he seems to be saying. A statement, a threat, a greeting. Since I can't interpret it, he stares at me and the pecking accelerates. I could swear he's saying something about captivity, his ancestors and all the humans he's seen pass by. As many living as dead, for me. Can't you see? They're all here, engraved on my retinas. Before he starts speaking, I lean towards his fellow beings, the land tortoises. Much more numerous, mobile and superficial, incapable of making eye contact. Terrestrial.

Eloísa asks me to meet her a few blocks from Axel's house. She writes: HV 2 C U URGENT. There are eleven text messages in the day and since I'm not going to reply to any of them, she calls: Why do you never answer, dickhead? She says we'll meet at eleven at the pizzeria before the bridge. I'm about to refuse but I stop myself. Since

Herbert is still at home I ask whether he can stay with Simón tonight. No problem, there's never any problem.

The bus drops me at the door, a minimalist kind of place, television high on the wall, facing mirrors from floor to ceiling, illuminated photos of pizzas and three guys eating standing up at the endlessly multiplied counter. Eloísa hasn't arrived. I prefer to wait outside, up on the bank at the edge of the train tracks. I look towards the avenue to see whether she's coming. Ten minutes, fifteen, nothing. A couple, a guy alone, another couple, two boys on skateboards. From the darkness of the bridge, a strange figure is becoming clear, it could be Eloísa but it isn't, much taller and with shining hair. The night spins out the intrigue and I take advantage of being on this slope to conceal my surprise. It's her: white fur coat, miniskirt, transparent silk blouse, high heels and a wig.

I walk down to the pavement, I question her with my hands and discover that she is also plastered in make-up. A rookie transvestite, slight, inexperienced, taking her first steps on the street. But Eloísa's bitter expression contrasts with her crazy appearance. I'm so fucked off with it all, is the first thing she says and she ushers me into the pizzeria. We sit on stools at the end of the bar. Eloísa takes off the coat, rolls it up and rests it on the foot rail. A thin, hairy, tame dog. However far away we move, all eyes are infectiously drawn to us. Eloísa is the target, of course, I'm just part of the package.

The fat cow caught me in the dressing room looking for the key to the safe, that's how she begins. She didn't see me, I'm sure, she came in two seconds later, but I really shat myself. You have no idea. I told her there was a fancy dress party and that Axel said I could use his old lady's clothes. Almost the truth. She says that Orfe kept watching her as she started trying on dresses, wigs and shoes. She wouldn't go away and Eloísa had the key in her hand and couldn't leave without returning it to its place. She was there for half an hour not knowing what to do. Total bummer. Finally I put on this coat and d'you know what the old bitch says? I shake my head. What are you supposed to be going as? she imitates Orfe's voice, like a stupid bird. A right whore I almost told her, Eloísa laughs loudly and as she talks and drinks beer she gets worked up like a man.

Now that we are no longer a novelty, we entertain ourselves watching television like the rest of the customers in the pizzeria. A hot-air balloon has lost control and is flying aimlessly, guarded by two aeroplanes that are trying to guide it to the sea. Underneath, on the screen, it reads: *Prisoners fleeing by balloon caught mid-air.* We fantasise that the ropes get tangled with the wings of the planes and they all go under together. The images are being transmitted live from Arizona. But our attention doesn't last long, the guy behind the bar, in charge of packing up pizzas, stretches out an arm, changes channel, sighing as if he doesn't believe any of what they're saying, and puts on a boxing match.

We get two slices of napolitana each and Eloísa returns to the matter of the robbery between mouthfuls. I'm going to have to kill her, she says and throws out a wild, foamy cackle. I laugh with her and, seeing her properly, I don't understand why she's still wearing the wig. And the key, I ask. All fine, the old bitch got tired and eventually left me alone. You won't regret it, she fires at me and I can't remember saying I would join in her plan. It has to be this Friday. Axel's going to the psychiatrist at one on the other side of the city and Orfe's going to cook with the nuns. There's no danger of anything. With just one of those rings we're made. For them it's a just a bonus. What difference can it make to them? Since I don't answer, she becomes bold and tries out a phrase that surprises even her: You'll see, we're going to start a new life. Eloísa is animated by what she has just said and repeats the last few words, over-articulating, as if she's found the slogan she was looking for: A new life, do you realise?

I offer no opinion, nor do I contradict her. I prefer to let things follow their natural course, then I'll see. I bet Eloísa gives up anyway, when faced with the delirium. A pause to chew and she returns to the subject: I have an idea, she says. Let's make a bed for the fat bitch, she deserves it. She means incriminating Orfe by putting a necklace under her mattress, or in her wardrobe, Yes, better in the wardrobe, between the clothes, badly hidden, so they can find it easily. She looks at me expectantly, she wants me to give my approval, but I stay silent. I don't feel like opposing her and I consent without meaning to.

On the way out of the pizzeria, Eloísa removes the wig, puts it inside the coat and hides the bundle behind a group of dense bushes at the foot of the bank. Another dog, this time stray and crouching. I'll grab it on the way back, she says. Who's going to take it? With no fixed direction, we snake through the dark streets lined with tall banana trees until we come out at a corner overpopulated with teenagers, in groups, alone, in couples, an obligatory meeting point for their nocturnal outings. It's Saturday night, I take a while to remember. In Eloísa's words: This is where the wannabes hang out because they don't know what the hell to do. In that couple of blocks, the traffic, both in the street and on the pavement, has become a kicked anthill.

We move away, some boys shout I don't know what at us from one pavement to the other. Eloísa answers them with a rough screech: Suck my tits. When it seems the night is taking us nowhere, Eloísa grabs me by the arm and leads me into a shopping arcade with the blinds down. Come on, she says, you won't believe this. A broad aisle with shuttered premises on either side, we climb a stationary escalator, more shops, all of them shut, fishing gear, tattoos, lottery kiosks, model aeroplanes. We pause at the window of a place selling masks and disguises: witches, monsters, presidents. Bugger, says Eloísa, I should have brought mine. And for a moment I try to imagine her walking all those blocks in the fur coat and wig. No, I just can't picture it.

Another escalator and, at the end of the corridor, a dark glass door with a neon sign: *Shantytown*. I slow my pace, wanting to go back. And Eloísa, who let go of me a while ago, sensing my resistance, takes me by the hand again and drags me to the entrance like a mother with a rebellious child. The guy on the door, in suit and trainers, draws back a plastic chain. Hi girls, that's what he says and shows us his golden front teeth. I have to get rid of my keys first, then all the coins in my pockets so that I don't set off the metal detector.

At first glance: a small stage with two towers of speakers, bodies and heads milling about, a circular dance floor with tiles that illuminate rhythmically, tables and chairs in corners against the wall, streamers, more bodies, a beach bar. It will take a couple of minutes for my eyes to get used to this new light, like a restless fog. Apart from a spotlight spinning on its axis, the rest, skirting boards, corners and outlines, are delineated by blue tubes that conceal everything that isn't white. Eloísa moves ahead of me and asks for a bottle of beer, which is handed to her capped with two red cups, from a child's party. There's a three-for-two promotion. We make a toast: To us.

The DJ takes it upon himself to keep the night lively too. He directs the dancing, arranges choreography, signals to someone, a couple, a man, a single woman, the guy in the palm-tree shirt, you in the fuchsia miniskirt, he makes it clear with a laser pointer and issues instructions. A god of the night. Let's see, let's see the brunette shake her booty. Where are those sharks? Work it, hotties, work it, he says, his voice serious, quivering, mouth stuck to the microphone producing a series of aquatic sounds, like seal kisses. And now for this sweet *cumbia*. It's going out with a subliminal message, so no one's gonna be left with the horn.

More beer, I hurry down three glasses in one go. I lose Eloísa somewhere, I wander round several times in vain until I locate her on the dance floor. I avoid her, but she's seen me, she stretches and catches my arm. I'd rape this guy, she says in my ear, pointing out a guy who won't stop smiling. His friend takes advantage of the opportunity to approach me, he takes me by the waist. I have no means of escape. I move, I pretend I'm dancing. The guy sticks his mouth to my ear to speak. You're so beautiful, he says, I don't understand the rest. A gap between songs, I excuse myself with a flick of the hand and aim for the toilets with the bottle under my arm. On the way, I hear: Get me a . . .

I pee with my eyes closed. A cliff appears to me and an old-fashioned girl in petticoats with her legs up who shows me everything. In the background, a mass of flares lights up the sea. Where did that come from? On my way back, I see Eloísa jumping in the centre of a ring of three guys who are blowing her kisses and moving very close to speak to her. I look for the darkest corner and start drinking beer, without wanting to but without stopping.

Where are you going? Eloísa shouts at me, leaning over the rail a second before I disappear. I gesture to say I'm leaving. And I exaggerate the modulation so that she can read my lips: I'm zonked. Come on, she insists but this time I stand firm, I'm not going to give in. She lets me go and warns me with her index finger: Friday, don't forget. Yes, yes, Friday.

TWENTY-NINE

The iguana is dead by morning. Stomach up, limbs rigid and splayed. It lived with us for nearly three weeks. I find it near the door, as if it had run out of breath during an escape attempt. It didn't adapt, lack of humidity, too much heat, who knows. It's also possible that it would have died if it had stayed with its siblings in the incubator, perhaps it was written in its genes. Luckily, I make the discovery before Simón wakes. I have time to wrap it in newspaper and put it in a box which I hide on top of the wardrobe. I'll work out what to do later, how to tell him. I'll invent something.

I put on some water for coffee. Now, after years of *maté*, I've started liking coffee. I'm hooked on the stuff during work breaks. I stay quiet, eyes on the soot-blackened kettle. Only that little snake of thick steam that leaves the spout with a strident whistle rouses me. Simón too, gradually moving into a sitting position, legs crossed, arms too, across that white, bulging abdomen, like a tiny Buddha. He surveys his surroundings with the typical disorientation of awakening, not so much lost as annoyed, contemplating the world indifferently, with no desire to understand it, as if reproaching its existence. But his disconcertedness quickly passes to whining and with his snivels everything swings back to the everyday: breakfast milk, a walk around the block if it isn't raining, improvised lunch, the long hours of the afternoon with Herbert, television sometimes, treats to eat, night-time and the battle with sleep.

It's a cloudy day, asphyxiating and gelatinous. A day that infects everyone equally with its dull oppression. Even Herbert, always so lively, turns up with a long face. As if he's slept badly. I've never seen him like this, I'm about to ask him if something's wrong, but I hold my words in time. I try to put myself in his place, best not to pester him. If he wants to talk, it has to come from him. I restrict myself to telling him that there are sausages and rice in the pan, that we've already eaten, he can help himself. Despite his bad mood, he issues a quiet thank you, through his teeth. I bump into Benito in the corridor, carrying buckets. He looks down at me from his great height, with a mixture of contempt and desolation. Hi, I say, and he responds with a grunt.

My arrival at the zoo only confirms this expansive wave of irritation. Yessica won't tire of bad-mouthing God knows who all afternoon, presumably some superior who ordered her to clean the toilets. The staff from the company in charge of hygiene is on strike again and this time they didn't even send an emergency replacement. At one point I approach her with intentions of solidarity, to offer a hand, but it turns out I only lend her my ear, scarcely a pleasure. I've never seen so much shit in one place, she says. It's incredible, as if they all agreed to come and crap here. I wonder, she says challengingly, gloved hands on her hips, raising her voice as if she wants those who have been here before us to know we're talking about them and apologise: Don't these wretches have bathrooms in their own homes? I'm an idiot, she mutters, her eyes red, about to burst into tears. It's my fault, I should have refused.

I walk past the nursery, I think about the iguana and the fact that I'm now faced with two deceptions for the same reason. Even Esteban hasn't escaped the tone of the day. He comes and goes along the corridors of the reptile house, cupped hand protecting his left cheek, without paying any attention to his little creatures, as he calls them when he's in a good mood. The despondency is justified in his case. I find out he's just come from the dentist, the guy took out the wrong molar and now he's in twice as much pain. Because of the infection that's still there and because of the needlessly exposed gum. At break time, seeing Canetti limp towards me clutching a coffee, I pretend not to notice, scratching my neck, and set off towards the bears. I'd definitely rather avoid him today.

Without stopping, I gesture to Iris to come and find me, although I'm not sure whether she notices. A few minutes pass and when I'm starting to convince myself that she didn't see me at all, I feel someone touch my shoulder by the elephants' palace, scaring me slightly. Iris smiles, her lips retracted, rather dismal. We walk round the lion pit, Hércules and Corazón, the decrepit male and the blind female. So sad, says Iris, and I'm not sure what she's referring to.

The time we spend together seems like a preamble to something serious she has to say but it doesn't come out. She doesn't look at me, her eyes dart in all directions, a broom bush, two posing flamingos, nowhere at all. I think about her father, I think the worst. I can't bear to ask her. Finally she speaks: I'm bringing forward my return home. I'm leaving next week. I'm sorry and I was right: His bones are gone, he can't even get out of bed any more. I'd like to console her, I'd hug her, I just stroke a hand. I search for her eyes, she seeks out the ground. Someone else would ask how it passed from the lungs to the bones. I can't get the words out. It seems worse than worse. I feel bad, for her, for her father, for not knowing how to act. We say goodbye at the entrance to the reptile house. Still silent, until she turns round and says quickly, without looking at me: It's a lie, a complete lie.

Another three hours of work and I have to pull at the same ball of wool a thousand times to try to unravel Iris. Which part is the lie? I wait for her at the exit and we start walking together towards the Fénix. At a kiosk we buy an ice cream each, strawberry for me, pineapple for her, and there's no need to ask anything, she spills it all out herself. Draco wrote to her from the south, he says he's working in a wine cellar and he met someone. A Belgian girl. Belgian? Yes, Belgian. They're saving up for an expedition to Antarctica. Iris talks and with each phrase she shakes her head, out of incredulity, but also with irony. She repeats in a sarcastic tone: Antarctica. I try to imagine Draco and this girl navigating between ice floes, on a sledge, wrapped in sheepskin, sheltering in an igloo, and all around them, white, white, white. At the hotel door, Iris explains as if it were necessary: My father is much better. I embrace her and finally she cries.

Back in el Buti, the issue is how to get rid of the iguana. I take advantage of the fact that Herbert, his mood much improved, is playing with Simón, throwing pieces of Styrofoam, and I climb onto the chair to grab the box with the packaged animal. Be right back, I say to the air, determined to put an end to the matter without hesitation and throw the creature out with the rubbish. As I descend the stairs, I'm struck by a vivid thought, a command that forces me to turn back. I discard the box down the lift shaft and with the animal enclosed in my fist I go up to find Herbert and Simón. Perhaps it's because of what Iris told me this afternoon, the fruits of her lie, it must be something like that. I call them over. I try to proffer explanations I don't have, I immediately feel I've said too much. I open my hand, exposing the body. Simón looks down at it, without conviction, Herbert draws his face close with a morbid fascination. I conclude: Animals are like plants and people, they live for the time they have to live, then they disappear. I don't say die. And Simón, who finally peels his eyes away from the green iguana that is now far from green, increasingly grey, stares at me and takes all the time in the world to fabricate a smile, at first timid, hesitant, barely a stretch of the lips, which as the seconds pass broadens into an infectious little laugh.

We discuss what to do with the body. Herbert wants to light a small bonfire, Simón insists on keeping it, I impose my decision to bury it. We descend in a slow procession, they act as escorts, I'm in the middle with the deceased. On the pavement, we consider our options: trees, flower beds, the fig tree in a neighbouring lot. We take a vote and the paradise wins. Without being asked, Herbert assumes the role of gravedigger. He uses his hands to scrape a well the size of a grapefruit, more than enough. I take charge of depositing the iguana in the pit and all of us, after a brief pause, a minimal, silent homage, with no speech or farewell, cover it with earth. Simón takes care of flattening the grave with his feet but there is still a slight mound, barely perceptible, blending in with the protuberances of the tree roots, which leave nothing smooth.

The dream of Eloísa and her greedy cunt returns. Playing cards this time, aces and kings, clubs, diamonds and hearts. She rolls them up and slips them in and I have to guess which card will come out. It's just a question of luck.

THIRTY

Friday arrives. Eloísa tells me to meet her at one in the afternoon. On the dot, she writes in the last of seven messages she sends me the night before. She also says: All ready, I got gloves. I don't reply, I concentrate on the drawing of the snake, the huge tome lying between my legs. The idea of the robbery is spinning round my head and even though it only ever sounds unreal to me, just another story, sometimes I become more practical and try to visualise it. I think of the consequences, the laws and the social aspects, about the benefits too, the money I could use for I don't really know what. The most sensible thing would be to give up before it's too late. When my eyes start to close and I no longer have a firm enough hand to carry on tracing the boa with its million scales, I grope for the mobile and two seconds before I regret it I text: Fine.

I'm punctual, as Eloísa asked me to be; at five minutes past I ring the bell and it's clear she's been waiting for me. The iron gate slides back with a sigh to let me through.

Her head appears at the back of the garage above the car roofs. She waves without speaking, nor does she say anything when we are face to face, she gives me a quick kiss and a manly pat on the shoulder. I can see her properly now we are entering the kitchen. Her hair is wet, combed slickly back, just out of the shower. She's dressed in a red vest top that clings to her body and dark blue jeans, also tight. She isn't wearing a bra. If I didn't know her I'd say she looked reliable and determined. It's as if the role of thief in which she's about to make her debut should be underpinned by a change of appearance, to give her courage and throw people off the scent. She asks if I want coffee, she doesn't offer me alcohol as she usually does, I suppose staying sober is part of the plan. I accept half a cup and as I drink I think that, in this mini gang we have formed, she would be the boss and I the henchman.

First, before the action, a brief conference in the everyday dining room. We go through some rules: avoid making noise and dropping things, nothing to attract attention, speak quietly just in case, leave everything in its place, even the slightest little thing, keep the gloves on until the end. Surgical gloves that Eloísa hands to me seriously as if they were a secret weapon. We just need to allocate roles, to decide how to carry out the coup. The question is whether I accompany her or keep lookout. The second option sounds more prudent but if I stay alone on the ground floor and someone enters it will look suspicious. We'd best go together, Eloísa concludes, we can always invent something. Say I wanted to show you the jacuzzi, some bollocks like that.

At the foot of the stairs, giving me to understand that from now on the real adventure has begun, that setting foot on the first step is already part of the crime, Eloísa shows me a clenched fist. A code of the underworld I haven't yet grasped. I respond as best I can, imitating her with much less enthusiasm. The curved, solid banister serves as a guide for my ascent, my latex skin gliding over the wood frictionlessly, as if it had just been waxed.

Upstairs, the walls are populated with family portraits, all the same size and identically framed. Axel's parents by the sea, him, heavily bearded, her, pregnant, hair long and uncombed. Cheek to cheek, they are both biting a slice of pizza, two perfect sets of teeth marks. Next to it, Axel and his sister, in little sailor suits. Teenagers, with braces, and more up-to-date snaps, the four of them together with slightly forced smiles. There are also black-and-white portraits, grandparents, great-great-grandparents, children from the past, Axel's ancestors. What are you doing? Eloísa calls me, sticking half her body out, two doors along.

The room is as immense as a room can be. Eloísa drops out of character and for an instant is the same as ever. She jumps and belly flops onto that limitless bed where four or five could easily sleep without bothering each other. What bastards, she says, looking at the ceiling. On the other side there's a chest of drawers with a collection of perfumes and silver figurines: an army of naked dwarves with very pronounced penises. Have you seen the state of the bathroom? I lean in: the famous jacuzzi next to the window, a massage table, the toilet with bronze seat and lid, luxurious but cold. In a corner, an exercise bike, handlebars folded. Ready, says Eloísa, rubbing her hands together. Once more she becomes serious and stands up determinedly.

There it is, she says, gesturing to a sliding door that opens in the middle of the wall. We move into a dressing room with a mirror at the back. To the right, women's clothes, dresses, skirts and coats, to the left, an endless row of men's suits, more or less identical, many grey, some black or blue. Eloísa moves ahead and unhooks the mirror. Ta-dah, she says as she uncovers the safe. Guess where the key is. She points out two rows with fifty-odd shoes on either side. Party shoes, heels, boots, sandals, clogs, slippers. No, I don't know. Another clue: It's red and for women. I don't answer. Eloísa takes a step forward, bends down, she's about to unveil the mystery.

And suddenly: a door slamming, a creak and another slam. Hide the gloves, Eloísa tells me, tapping me with her finger so that I keep silent. She's been knocked off course, she doesn't understand, she interlaces her fingers and twitches them, asking me for an explanation that naturally I won't be able to give. We allow thirty seconds to pass, immobile and expectant. Eloísa re-hangs the mirror on the wall and leaves the shoe in its place. Act as if nothing's happened, she says, leaving the room. From the corner of the staircase we see that the door to Axel's room is opening, he stays as quiet as us, disconcerted. Eloísa is quick: You scared us, dickhead, she says and raises a hand to her chest. Axel shrugs apologetically. What are you doing? he asks. She wanted to see, says Eloísa, nodding towards me. Oh.

Axel tells us without anyone asking that his psychiatrist, he calls her the girl, stood him up. She isn't answering her mobile, or her landline, she doesn't seem to be anywhere, she's been kidnapped as far as I can make out. Eloísa forgets about the jewels, she hides it well, and goes out to the garden: Be right back. Have you eaten, Axel asks me. I make a gesture he understands as a no and he brings a bag of crisps, a tin of palm hearts, cheese slices and Coca-Cola from the kitchen. They leave me alone in the middle of the house and I would flee like before but I'm scared of getting trapped again. Eloísa returns with her hands busy rolling a joint. She winks at me behind Axel's back, inviting me to stay calm, as she moves her lips to say: All fine. We smoke, we eat, we make ludicrous conjectures about the whereabouts of the psychiatrist. We laugh like good friends. Axel becomes animated and unfolds the giant screen to watch television. A flick through the channels and we get caught on a video clip: a guy in a motorbike helmet next to a cardboard tree. Magically, another guy appears at his side, a kind of hippy with a Creole guitar and his hair in his face. Between them, a desperate-looking girl. They sing: *There's someone living inside of me as if I were his house.* The chorus is catchy, Eloísa joins the choir, Axel la-la-las, I'm shuddering. I think about Tosca, about her tumour, the spud, which lives inside her as if she were its house. At the end of the song, the boy in the helmet is alone once more, steaming up the visor with his breath.

I'm off, I say at one point, assuming that it's getting late. Axel makes a joke I don't hear, at which he laughs alone. Eloísa walks me to the bus stop. Crossing the avenue, she pulls my arm: It's all good, he didn't realise anything was up. He totally bought the thing about me showing you the house. I don't reply, in fact I don't give her the pleasure of making eye contact as she wants to. Eloísa gets annoyed, my silence bothers her. We'll do it next Friday, she says and becomes bold: It can't happen twice in a row. We're immune. That's what she says: immune.

Under the bridge, without stopping, I tell her no. Best not. Why not? She squeezes my wrist hard. She repeats indignantly: Why not? Eloísa forces me to stop and I'm standing between her and a bed of curved bricks separating the pavement from the embankment. I try to think and I end up saying something that only makes it worse: Why don't you do it yourself? Eloísa becomes furious, she speaks with a fresh hatred. You're a shit, she'll spit out at least four times before she finally leaves. I cross the street. Before disappearing into the tunnel she shouts again with all her anger, her hands cupped around her mouth to produce a megaphone: Baaack-staaaaabber.

The heat pushes us out to the street during the night. Everything sticks to us, mattress, clothes, hair. Simón tosses and turns in bed emitting thin little whimpers, mouth closed, like a subjugated animal. I observe him from the corridor with the door open to see if the air is moving out there, until he sits up and looks straight at me with the face of a bad-tempered adult announcing that he won't stand it any longer. He gives up trying to sleep. At the entrance to the building there's a group who, like us, can't tolerate enclosure and have come out in search of unlikely relief. There's Perico, el Buti's brother, crouching under a tree; nearer us, more visible, a couple of teenagers drinking beer and a fat family with their radio blasting. Benito and Tosca aren't there; I wonder how they'll manage to bear the heat in that chaotic apartment with such low ceilings. I can see Canetti with his limping gait, coming and going, his head bowed as if he has lost something. Luckily, he doesn't notice me. We move away, streets, passageways, the train tracks. We reach a paved plaza where an indigenous camp is set up under the motorway and we turn back. I can't get it out of my head: There's someone living inside of me as if I were his house.

THIRTY-ONE

Leaning against the trunk of the paradise near us, where we buried the iguana, there's a broken mirror. In pieces. The part that's still intact is shaped like a shark fin. Or a wave, wide at the base, pointed at the crest. I observe it for a moment, I measure it up without touching, I crouch down and my reflection turns into another me, berserk and fragmented, asking for shelter. I make a decision. I climb the stairs with the mirror under my arm. Transporting it is uncomfortable and somewhat dangerous. I don't always remember to stretch my neck to avoid pricking myself. I think that if I trip, my natural impulse would be to block the fall with my hands and so the sharp edge would embed itself in my jugular or if I was lucky slice off an ear. A stupid death, a bit like Jaime's, but even more so, because of the manner of it and the spectacular nature of the bleeding. I think about Simón telling the story twenty years from now. Tragicomic.

It must be two, three in the morning. I have no way of finding out. My mobile says 17.33, I've never known how to set the time. I pace round the room with a new, unfamiliar restlessness I can't identify. I walk in circles, figures of eight. My gaze drops and the sight of my hairy legs reminds of the pink razor I bought at the kiosk a week ago. I spend a while looking for it until I discover it under the wardrobe, intact, unused, still in its clear plastic wrapping. On the label there's a fantasy aeroplane flying over a beach with flowers and palm trees. Travel to the Bahamas with your best friend, it says. To take part in the competition you have to cut out as many of the brand's logos as you can, amass points, send them in the post and wait for the draw at the end of the summer. I wonder what the deal is with the best friend, whether it's a manner of speaking, or whether whoever wins has to demonstrate in some way that this is her best friend and not just anyone. In my case, I'd have to choose between Iris and Eloísa, the problem is who would keep an eye on Simón. Tosca, Sonia, yes, more likely, we'd have to see what Mercedes said. I could also check whether in special cases they would allow a son instead of a best friend.

Sitting on the toilet, I soap my legs with cold water ready to shave them for the first time in quite a while. At least since Jaime's death. Partly because the hair has been growing with less vigour recently and doesn't annoy me. I do it carefully, taking my time. When I finish, I debate whether or not to shave my pubic hair. I move on to my armpits. I examine them in the mirror and I have to contort myself to see properly, accommodating my body to fit this capricious, quiet wave shape. Done. Clean, I feel strange, lighter, unprotected. On my knees, I now notice above my ears two clusters of white hairs sticking out in curls. Nowhere else on my head, just there. The novelty is not so much the white hairs but the quantity.

I've found the odd white one before, here and there, lost, premature, without company, as if in a panic about the passage of time. But this is different, it's not one or two or five, more like a dozen on each side. I spend a while combing them with my fingers and suddenly, because some part of me must be resisting, but above all because I have the urge to do some pruning, I decide to cut my hair. The scissors Herbert left here a couple of days earlier are to hand. He brought them to cut dinosaurs out of a magazine he found on the street. I begin rather timidly, with the mirror behind my neck, a rear-view mirror, layering the ends at the back. I continue with the sides, where the white hairs are, and the fringe. I cut prudently, I try to chop the same amount each time. Until without meaning to, lack of concentration or rage, the scissors slip from my hand and pull out a clump almost from the root. The incident paralyses me, I contemplate the bare patch, unable to decide whether it could go unnoticed. Something inside me starts to ponder a decision that initially seems like madness and gradually becomes the solution. An idea that my hand takes it upon itself to make irreversible with three violent snips. In less than five minutes my head is covered by a fine pelt of hair that must be no longer than three centimetres. The problem is that I'm limited by my joints, as well as the curves of the mirror, which prevent me from having a full view, condemning the cut to irregularity. I'm about to wield the razor and bring the matter to a close by shaving myself entirely, but a certain vision of the future stops me. Shaved, it strikes me that I would stop being me to a certain extent, would become a caricature of myself. And that must be the frightening part, being more me than I already am. In any case, I restrain the impulse in time and a few hours later, mid morning, Herbert will take care of evening out my new hairdo. In front of the mirror, I realise that he handles the scissors like a pro, much better than me. Simón says nothing, I think he likes it.

When she sees me, Yessica exaggerates her surprise, covering her mouth with her hands. Oh, she says, you look like a guy. Esteban notices too and tries to encourage me. It's great, a bit unusual, but it's great, he says, pointing at his own head. Iris releases one of her cackles, spying on me from the sardine stall. I put on the zoo cap to avoid more comments.

A quiet afternoon until the matter of the iguana re-emerges. The truth is that I was beginning to forget it, I'm slightly surprised without quite being worried. Yessica says that Esteban wants to see me, I should look for him out back. I discover that they're going to begin an internal investigation. It's not up to me, he says, rules. Because I was there the day the animal disappeared they're definitely going to want to speak to me. But I shouldn't worry, it's a formality. I nod in silence as I wonder who will be interrogating me. There's no way I can be found out, I left no clues of any kind, the creature is well buried twenty blocks from here. The only people who could incriminate me, and it would be a betrayal, are Herbert and Simón.

From then on, the iguana in all its forms occupies my head relentlessly. The situation as I see it, that is to say, depending on my mood, seems serious at times and at others, more often, a minor anecdote. And what if I tell the truth, confess? I try to imagine Esteban's reaction, I doubt he would be able to understand, to become my accomplice. I elaborate a speech to explain what happened, the word impulse comes to my mind. I had a sudden impulse, Esteban, I don't know what got into me, I would begin by saying. I'd tell him about Simón, about the poison beads, the fright of seeing him in hospital, under analysis, I'd say, in an attempt to move him, and that the need surged in me to provide him with a companion while I wasn't there. I could mention Jaime, the father who died a few months ago, the trauma of the move, so many changes at once, and more arguments to soften the blow. I know it was madness, almost as if someone else had done it in my place. The problem is that if I managed to touch Esteban and get him on my side, he would certainly suggest I return the iguana without reporting me. The death is inadmissible. I'd carry on lying about that. It escaped and that's it. It's even more believable than the burial, animals escape when they change environment. But I would only be able to cover up for so long; I feel like I'm in a labyrinth. I think about all this while, on the other side of the rail, with the yellow python curled up in the background, protected by the shadow so that none of the bosses can see her, so she says, Yessica paints her nails an angry red, those nails that are so long I imagine them giving painful caresses. Running down a neck, an arm, a prick, the very idea produces a shudder in me that I repress by gritting my teeth.

During the break, I bump into Canetti, more taciturn than ever. I'm thinking about quitting, I tell him. His reaction is delayed, his eyes glued to the embers of the cigarette dying between his fingers. I'm knackered, says Canetti and starts moving his shoulders as if saying what do I care. He talks about his pains, about all his misfortunes. What a shitty life, he sighs. I stop him short. I repeat: I want to quit. And he steps back as if I were about to slap him. It arouses his full interest: resignations, dismissals and working relationships are a very sensitive topic for him. He doesn't try to dissuade me nor does he encourage me to do it, he limits himself to advising me. He knows a lot about the subject: agreements, rights, regulations. He lists advantages and disadvantages: The important thing is to have a strategy. If you send a letter of resignation you lose, like in war, that's how he puts it. He takes a drag, releases smoke from his nose and mouth and continues: It's always better for them to fire you. And he adds, lowering his voice: You have to forge your own escape route, understand. Pull stunts, cause a racket without anyone noticing. Canetti's nature is too strong for him and despite so many losses, all those miserable years, as he calls them, the rebel seed has been kept alive in him ever since it occurred to him to hatch an illness to which in some way he ended up falling victim. A kind of silent, solo revolution, neither utopian nor idealistic, but practical and mocking, that of a fainthearted martyr.

At the end of the day, I see Esteban passing between the tables and sunshades. He walks rapidly towards the lake next to a zoo employee dressed, like me, as an explorer, speaking into his walkie-talkie and gesticulating with his free hand, giving to understand that whoever is at the other end is an imbecile. This is my opportunity to clarify matters, we'll see what happens afterwards. I take a step forward but I pause in the attempt, one foot in the shade and the other in the sun. Esteban notices my aborted impulse, and my indecision; for that reason he raises an arm and waves above his head at me, showing no hint of stopping, as if he already knows and prefers not to hear me say it.

After a week of silence, Eloísa rears her head again. She sends me two identical messages one after the other. I'm sorry, she writes, I'm really mental. And a third, at dawn: You kno I love u.

THIRTY-TWO

Herbert comes in kicking the door. He's in his pants, hair on end, confused expression and a pillow mark splitting his cheek in two. What time is it, I ask, my voice hoarse, sitting up in three beats. I have the book with the naturalist illustrations on top of me, making it hard for me to move. Mum says for you to go upstairs. I hear him fine, but I don't react, I hug my legs, I stretch to grab the sheet, screwed up at the foot of the mattress, and cover myself, I feel a bit embarrassed. It's as if he's speaking to me in a dream, there's no sense replying. He insists: It's urgent. What happened, I ask silently, raising my chin. Herbert says nothing more. Message delivered, mission accomplished, he turns round and is swallowed by the darkness of the corridor. I put on the first thing I can grab, the usual jeans and a black T-shirt with studs that Eloísa left one day and never reclaimed. I leave on tiptoe so as not to wake Simón, who is biting his lips in his sleep. A warrior's dream.

I realise that I'm barefoot as I'm climbing the stairs but I don't go back, I'm guided by the word urgent. In fact, if it weren't for the confusion caused by the abrupt awakening, I would almost certainly be speculating on what might be waiting for me up there. But no, I climb on blindly. On the fifth floor, I lean in, half opening the door. I risk a few steps and from the kitchen I can see Mercedes snoring, sprawled over the bed; closer to me Herbert is lying on his, his eyes tightly closed, as if what just happened was my own invention. I can't see Sonia anywhere.

I retreat. Motionless on the threshold, I hear a hoarse shout: Here, here. The voice is coming from the other end of the corridor, some four doors further down. I feel my way forward, unable to see much ahead of me until I make out Sonia beckoning with her hand. There's no time for greetings or explanations. I need your help, she says quietly, guiding me into the flat by the shoulder. Identical to Mercedes and Sonia's: dining kitchen, two rooms at the sides. The one on the right is empty, in the other there are three or four children sleeping on the same mattress, criss-crossed, superimposed. Between the bedrooms is the bathroom, instead of a door there's an iron panel which Sonia slides across to pass through, carefully so that it doesn't come apart. She makes me enter first, she's anxious for me to see: a naked woman sitting on the toilet, her head straining towards her legs, about to give birth. The last thing she wants is to go to hospital, Sonia breathes at my neck. The woman, only just noticing us, throws herself back, her fright slightly out of time. She has a tangle of black hair, very black, covering half her face. I give an Oriental-style bow of greeting, she ignores me. It really hurts, it's squeezing, says the woman, addressing Sonia, as if she doesn't entirely accept my presence. I move back, the conversation is between them. Don't you think we'd better go? The other woman shakes her head from side to side as if possessed.

We leave the room to deliberate. Sonia tells me that last time she was in hospital for three weeks because the stitches from her caesarean got infected. They cut her right up, she says. She doesn't want to go through that again, she explains and shrugs, I don't know whether in reprimand or sympathy. A silence and she confirms the latter: I'd do the same as her. Another pause and she nods. Suddenly she asks me: Are you up for this? I don't know, I say. I think about horses, cows and calves. Also about snake eggs. Yes, I don't know. It'll come out either way, says Sonia as if in jest, but not. We enter again, feigning impossible courage. Relax, I find myself saying, and for the first time she looks straight at me, child's eyes, sharp and shining. Sonia positions herself behind, I take her by the wrists, helping her to stand up. Now I can see her properly: the dirty stomach about to burst, that dark, flat belly button, arms and legs so limp. The woman is a girl of uncertain age, too young to have so many children, assuming that all those in the bedroom are hers. She has double circles round her eyes, a border of very dark skin and another of ash colour, reaching the top of her cheeks. A hardened young woman. Take deep breaths, release the air slowly, Sonia recommends, showing her what she should do, a sequence of brief rhythmic puffs to direct the pushes. The girl imitates as best she can but as soon as a new contraction comes she forgets about the breathing, her posture, the two of us, and doubles up again. I want to lie down, she says, surrendering. I can't take any more. I offer her my arm so that she can stand up while Sonia covers her with a towel. In moving, the girl translates her discomfort with a series of Ows followed by a strident click, swirling the saliva between the tongue and the palate.

We accompany her to the bed, she curls up in the middle, I wonder where the father can be. The two of us take refuge in the bathroom. Sonia sits down, taking the place of the woman in labour, she also seems defeated, she speaks to the tiles: I'm worn out, she says. For a while we are wordless. Sorry, I didn't know what to do. No, no, I say and venture: Perhaps it would be best to call a doctor, just in case. Sonia answers me by kneading the air with her hands, a call for calm: We're already here, we just need to stick it out.

Hold me, the girl asks from the bedroom. Another shuffle and each of us is in our position. It's coming, she says in a moan and her faces fattens like rubber. She becomes red, sweats incredibly, she contains a shout that takes a while to explode, silent first, then released with full force, violent, the way someone being shot must sound. Sonia's expression adds to the effort, the pushes. At the height of the trauma, the panel that serves as a door slides open and a hand at the end of a skinny, tattooed arm shakes a plastic bag which I grab without words. Before disappearing the invisible man utters a phrase of annoyance, his voice slippery with alcohol: Everything was shut, I had to go to the back of beyond. Sonia makes a nervous gesture for me to unpack the things quickly: a roll of lint, cotton, a bottle of alcohol, another of Pervinox.

A fresh round of contractions and now it really does seem to be coming. Pass me a towel, Sonia asks me and places it like a cushion under the girl's legs. We swap positions. Sonia bends down, rests her ear on the stomach, asking for silence as she searches for the heartbeat. She detects it, she smiles, reassuring the girl with her thumb up. Now she inserts two fingers into the vagina, index and middle, eyes on the ceiling. It's very close, she says mid exploration. Rest a bit, get your strength together, we're almost there. We rotate. Sonia behind, me in front. I crouch down. A moment of serenity and here we go. The girl's stifled cries, Sonia's fervent instructions for her to push and breathe, the hot flushes, all encourage me to clutch firmly to those trembling legs to keep them wide open.

What follows is so frenzied that I'm not entirely sure it really happened like this. Twice I saw the baby's black jelly head crowning, twice I thought it was coming. The third time, when I started to fear that nothing was going to come out at all, that we would need to call an ambulance, shoot off to A&E, something gave way. The head opened a path, dislodging itself, followed by the rest of the body with the momentum of its own weight. The shock was so great that Sonia had to shout at me before I acted: Put your hands out. And I did; if I hadn't, the baby would have ended up, newly born, on the floor.

The crying, the relief, the exaltation of the mother beyond fatigue, the cord across its neck, It could have been a tragedy, Sonia says in my ear, the atavistic face of the father who only now dares enter and blasts us with that unmistakeable cheap wine breath, Sonia's

300

watery eyes, my hands sticky with amniotic fluid, that new, silky body with its clusters of tiny fingers, Jonatán, that's what they'll call him, who attaches himself without delay to that tit with fat veins, the placenta which finally disengages like a warm, red, palpitating alien, it's all too much. Inevitably, it takes me back to Simón and his dizzying birth: my waters breaking on the steps of the cemetery, the trip to hospital in Jaime's pickup with the smell of decomposing petrol and the raucous voice of a nurse congratulating me: You just spat it out, girl, if only they were all like that. Saying goodbye, Sonia confesses at the threshold of her flat: That's why I got my tubes tied.

I return to bed with the dawn and that dark head emerging from the entrails overwhelms my mind like a sky parting in the middle.

THIRTY-THREE

Quarter past twelve in the human resources office. No one explained the reason for the appointment, I assume it's about the missing iguana. They keep me waiting in the same place I sat anticipating the job interview that first time. I don't know what I'm going to say, I don't have it very well rehearsed, I'll improvise and we'll see what happens. On either side of the armchair there is a novelty: a synthetic pine with felt squirrels attached to the branches and an aluminium magazine rack with copies of *National Geographic*, an animal atlas and a booklet published for the zoo's centenary. I open it at random, my eyes fall on a paragraph in an article called 'The Founding' and within three lines I've come across Eduardo Ladislao Holmberg. The man with the library that had the snake book, the man on the statue, the same man who wrote the novel about Martians. Mr Nic-Nac. Two pages are devoted to praising him without restraint. Energetic, philanthropic, erudite, patriotic and a humanist. At the bottom, a photo of Sarmiento: patron of the park, Domingo Faustino Sarmiento donated three black-necked swans for its inauguration. I continue leafing through the booklet and stop at 'The Monkey Mystery'. Apparently, at one time, the zoo's monkeys moved about the island without restriction, an arrangement that some time later was curtailed, leaving them stuck with the cages in which they have been kept to this day. The legend goes that in the summer of 1933, every morning, two chimpanzees would appear without explanation on the other side of the lake. The keepers were on edge for several weeks, because of the outrages the monkeys committed at night but above all because they were unable to fathom how they crossed from shore to shore when they couldn't swim. The authorities resolved to mount a night guard to solve the puzzle. The answer lay with the buffaloes, which . . .

A door opens and the greasy guy appears, forcing me to suspend my reading. Shall we? he says, and stretches out his arm to usher me into his office ahead of him. Water, coffee? Thanks, no. And how are they treating you? I smile. You've got a good boss. Yes, we get along very well. You caught the tough season, now summer's coming to an end you'll see how everything changes, sometimes it gets too quiet. Well, he says, let's get down to it. He broaches the topic without beating around the bush: Quite some business with the iguana, isn't it? I nod. A mystery, he says. I think about the monkeys. There's honestly no explanation, I say and immediately regret it, promising myself that from now on I won't volunteer anything, to avoid false steps that might give the game away. Let's see, we'll just run through it, he says, and moves the mouse, eyes on the monitor screen. Here it says that it was the thirtieth of January. Do you remember anything? I tell him about my routine, the trip round the reptile house, the gathering of lost objects, the doors that close and those that don't. And the nursery? Couldn't you have left it open without meaning to? I shake my head determinedly and during the silence that follows I'm convinced the guy's going to say something like You're not telling me the truth or Someone saw you. But no. Ok, he says, bringing the topic to a close, to my surprise. We'll have to keep investigating.

I called you in for something else, he reveals without looking at me, rifling through some papers piled on the desk. Silence. Here it is, he says, and starts reading to himself, running his index finger down the sheet to the rhythm of an electrocardiogram. You arrived in December, it'll be three months next Monday, won't it? The thing is that your contract's going to expire, he wants to know whether I'm aware of that. I lie: Yes, of course. What's your plan? I shrug, stretch my hands forward to suggest that I intend to keep working. Very well. He twists in his seat and tells me that they'll offer to renew my contract for another three months. Unfortunately at the moment we can't talk about you becoming permanent. But you never know, with things the way they are, he says, waggling his thumb. What I can tell you is that, as of next week, you'll be working in another sector. It's still to be decided, but they always rotate it fairly. Although he doesn't say as much, I assume it's because of the iguana, until the episode is cleared up. I accept without hesitation.

●

Eloísa tires of being friendly, my silence irritates her: Hey girl, what's up? I don't respond to that either. It's not that I'm annoyed or anything, I just don't know what to say, how to approach her again. I prefer to stay quiet. She wouldn't understand me, she gets angry quickly. She sends me half a dozen messages in one afternoon, she goes from When will we see each other? to What's wrong, bitch? And from there to an unceasing series of insults: Whore, Spoilsport, Fuck-up. UR SICK IN THE HEAD, is the last thing she writes. Then, she disappears.

In spite of herself, Iris has her send-off. Very intimate, Simón and me, no one else. The plane that will take her back to her country leaves at half three in the morning. Cheap flight, she says. The taxi comes to get her at twenty to one. It's a cool night, the first in a long time. The sky is amazingly clear for the city. I manage to count some twenty stars. We settle in the courtyard of the Fénix under the yellow lamp. Simón cavorts about until he runs out of energy. He goes to sleep by himself, without me having to say anything, suddenly adult. In an unusually good mood, the Spaniard lends us an airbed which we put at the end of the table. The characters passing through the hotel come and go, from the bathroom to the bedrooms, from the kitchen to the hall where the television is. Iris has bought ham, bread, Roquefort and two bottles of black beer.

She says that she went to work today as if it were any other day. She did her double shift, spent the morning in the subtropical jungle and the afternoon at the ticket booth for the sea-lion show. At six she presented herself at human resources to let them know she was leaving. When? she says the unpleasant guy asked her and she couldn't contain her laughter. We drink several toasts, we recall anecdotes, we laugh as we remember the encounter with Yuri and Olga. In Iris's room, lined up on the mattress, already sheetless, are the ticket, the passport and a plastic envelope with very colourful banknotes, presumably Romanian. Flowers, national heroes and planets. She gives instructions for me to send her telegram of resignation. I also have to pick up her final wage.

I'm leaving along with the heat, I don't know whether she's protesting or saying it with joy. The last goodbye is short, clumsy, almost non-existent. There are no embraces or effusions, just a superficial peck on the cheek. The night takes care of erasing any emotion. Iris opens and closes her hand from inside the taxi, a timid wave, like a diva in decline. See you soon, she says and I repeat as if at a mass: See you soon. The car drives a block and turns the first corner to the right, a brisk swerve that makes the tyres screech. I stay standing at the door of the hotel with Simón in my arms gripping my body with his arms and legs, absorbed in some undefined thought that flees behind Iris until the roar of a motorbike rouses me. The return journey is hell, Simón's weight tortures my back to an implausible degree.

THIRTY-FOUR

I'm going to die today, says Tosca early in the morning. She asks me to move closer, she speaks in my ear so that Benito can't hear. She crosses her index finger over her lips, making it clear that it's a secret between me and her. I'm about to respond, to say something that doesn't come out; I limit myself to arching my eyebrows and squeezing out a smile to reproach her for the thought. I hurry to prepare the syringe, I look for the vein and inject the morphine right to the last drop.

From the world of snakes, I was transferred to the farm. In the open air, unobserved, much more pleasurable. When Yessica found out, she caused a minor row, arguing that she'd asked to change sector a while ago and her seniority should put her before me. I tried to explain that they assigned me without asking, if it were up to me I'd have no problem staying, but it was pointless, she was indignant. Since I moved to my new post, she's stopped greeting me. There's been no further mention of the iguana. The subject comes to me every now and then like a ghost and I get it into my head that sooner or later some evidence is going to appear to incriminate me. I wonder whether my judgement day will come.

Working in the farm is very different. There are days when no one comes. Many people avoid the place, probably because it only has ordinary animals they've seen before. It's also true that a short diversion is required to find it, leaving the main path and climbing a ramp. I spend most of my time alone, sitting on a plastic stool under the shade of a straw roof. My companion is a short, heavyset boy, very introverted and fanatical about the job. He definitely prefers dealing with the goats, the donkey and the cow to dealing with humans. To begin with, I struggle to get used to the smell, that mix of dung and fodder that contaminates the air. Now that I've grown accustomed to it, sometimes I close my eyes, breathe deeply and smell something potent that fills me with vigour.

Behind the pens there's an L-shaped construction with barred windows, air conditioning and long tables for packed lunches. Sometimes I go in and spend a few minutes refreshing myself but the relief has its snag: the transition from the cold to the heat makes me dizzy. The really terrible days are when there's a birthday party. The place becomes an insufferable clamour, which affects the animals' moods. In some cases they break out and have violent fits: bites, kicks, rebellions. I don't have to take care of anything, two girls come especially for that, but all the same it's impossible to block it out. There are unmanageable brats who slip under the fence and find it funny to mount a sheep, pull a pig's tail, throw stones at hens. Then I do have to intervene. Initially I find it difficult, but I soon become tougher and am able to issue frightening shouts. I see Iris everywhere, I mistake her, I imagine her, in some way I miss her.

One Friday afternoon, I open the flat door and I can't understand what I'm seeing: Simón is tied to a chair by his feet and hands, round his waist too, secured to the backrest by a rope. I come out of my daze and make a sign with my hand asking him for an explanation but he can't talk either, in his mouth there's some cloth, a piece of something. I return to the corridor, I lean out into the stairwell, nothing, my head fills with impossible hypotheses. Simón looks me in the eye, inexpressive, with no trace of suffering, nor does he look like he's been crying. I want to believe it's some kind of strange joke, in bad taste, I think about el Buti's brother's gang. I walk over to him and the first thing I do is remove what is preventing him from speaking, one of my socks rolled into a ball, and he goes crazy, he shakes his head biting the air, he wants me to block his mouth again. I understand less and less. I ignore him, crouching to free him from his tethers, and he protests loudly. At that moment, Herbert comes out of the bathroom with a plastic bottle filled with water and a green and black slice of pipe, a garden hose. Before he appears, before discovering that I'm here, addressing Simón, he says: Confess, it's your last chance. The phrase remains unfinished. On seeing me, as well as falling silent, Herbert blushes. I interrogate him in silence, not annoyed, disconcerted. We're playing, Herbert intercepts me and I slap a leg rehearsing a strike

I'm not going to give him. It's a joke, he says. I'm about to say: This is no game, it doesn't look like fun, you might hurt yourselves. But Simón's cries deafen me. Herbert explains the obvious, the inconceivable: He likes being tied up. I stroke Simón's head, I try to dissuade him but he doesn't want to hear it, he rejects me, he kicks, he screams like a savage, he unleashes a new fury. That's what I mean, Herbert insists and raises his shoulders as if saying it's not his fault, he has nothing to do with someone else's whims. I move away a few steps, I allow it without being sure, defeated by the circumstances. Simón calms down as Herbert reties his feet and I cease to hear him altogether with the sock between his teeth.

I drop my things on the mattress, I enter the bath-room and splash my face, my cheeks are flushed, I feel ashamed. I'd like to do something to repair the situation, to go back in some way. I don't know how. I let a couple of minutes pass and go out with the intention of being firm. Everything is the same, Simón tied up, eyes on the ground, waiting to be tortured, Herbert standing with the bottle and the hosepipe, it's clear that he doesn't feel like continuing to play his role in my presence. I try to think of some phrase to befriend Simón, to make him understand. His satisfied and defiant expression suggests I'd best not try. With no way out, I look for an excuse to escape: Be right back, I say, I'm going to the supermarket.

With a sachet of milk, a tin of green beans and a bag of bread in my basket, I stay standing for a while in front of the drinks and liqueurs aisle. An accumulation of superimposed images fills my mind, of those nights in the kitchen at Open Door getting drunk alone: the slits in the oilcloth on the table that I opened with my longest nail, the pile of papers scribbled with illegible notes, the thick glass I filled and emptied without pause, my throat on fire. I stretch out my arm and grab a bottle of gin by the neck, which I hold close to my body as I take it to the checkout.

I return to the building undecided about how to act. How to put an end to the domination game. I even wonder whether it's just a boys' thing that I have no reason to suppress. It could be, I think, and for a while I deceive myself. Right, Simón, it's over. It's that simple, it's a matter of giving a good loud shout and that's it. I rehearse my tone on the stairs, I gather my courage, but there's no need. The chair, the rope and the cords have been cast aside, the torture session is over, Herbert and Simón have returned to car races. I don't know what to say, whether to mention the subject again or let it go. As I hesitate, I serve myself the first measure of gin.

Herbert leaves, Simón falls asleep without eating and drunkenness knocks me out until after midnight. I wake suddenly, the other way up. Between my headache and a very precarious awareness, Tosca appears to me. Monstrous and augmented. And what I remember isn't the morphine injection I didn't give her but what she said this morning: I'm going to die today. Limbs numb, I have no strength to stand, I try to masturbate in search of encouragement but that doesn't work either. Another swig of gin, now from the bottle, and I sit up agonising. I face the stairs with as much impetus as I can, I descend in slow motion. Too late, I realise that I'm in my knickers. Benito opens the door, face more swollen than ever, eyes surrounded by dark circles, haggard. He doesn't need to say anything, I'm about to embrace him, sympathising, but the movement is truncated by a howl from Tosca that hangs paralysed in the air: Beeeniiiiii.

Tosca welcomes me with a reproach: Do you want to kill me? I tell a half-truth: I fell asleep. And I add a stupid excuse: I had a terrible day. Tosca frowns, my breath gives me away. No one says anything about seeing me semi-naked. I stretch my T-shirt and cover myself as best I can. Before I inject her morphine, Tosca uses me as a confidante once more. Like this morning, she wants to tell me something in secret. Come here, she asks, and I obey. You thought I'd carked it, didn't you? It'll come, girl, it'll come, you need to have a bit of patience.

THIRTY-FIVE

March draws to a close without incident. Living in the city isn't that bad sometimes. A week before Easter, when autumn is beginning to make itself felt in the balmy nights, the days gradually shortening and the leaves on the trees fading in swathes, Eloísa reappears. She texts the mobile I'd forgotten existed: axel going to miami, she writes like that, all lower case, a whisper. Not even a minute elapses before she calls me. Did you read it? Yes, yes. I'm alone, understand? No, I don't want to understand, a wave of interference conceals my muteness. She seems to have hung up, Simón shows me a beetle limping across the middle of the room, and entertains himself by finishing it off with several stamps of the feet. Are you at home? Don't move, I'll be there in ten.

Another Eloísa, yet another, jumpy as always. Leather hat, raw silk scarf knotted round her neck, all in denim, looking like I don't know what. That's life, is the first thing she says, not even greeting me. All of a sudden, bish, bash, bosh. Axel's sister got engaged to a Yank and the whole family is getting together in Miami. Imagine the ugly mug to get hooked by that girl. The important thing is that Axel is travelling on Maundy Thursday and returning the following Tuesday. A week and a half to do what I want. Do you realise? She demands that I be the one to translate what's in her head. But she gets impatient and resumes: The jewels, you daft cow, destiny is calling us. We'll sell a couple and we can fuck off. To Miami. No, not Miami, she says, imagine if we bumped into Axel's folks. She spits out a blank laugh. Brazil would be better, a little beach, who's going to waste time looking for us two. It's now or never. Trust me, nothing will happen.

The door opens and Herbert comes to my rescue. I'm going to work, I say. Eloísa suggests accompanying me. I decline, I have to take care of lunch first. We'll speak later, a useless attempt to get rid of her. Impossible. Back me up here, don't be a wimp, she blasts in my ear and I don't understand why she needs me so much, she could do it alone and still come out on top. Fine, let me think about it, I give in just to get her off my back. She corners me: Saturday or Sunday? I hesitate, if I speak I'll condemn myself. She decides: I'll expect you on Saturday at ten. And in my ear: If you don't come, you're dead to me.

The week passes quickly. Tosca feels better and threatens to venture out to the street, Benito manages to get her a tripod walking stick which he retreads with wire and duct tape. During a night of fury Simón bites my breast and leaves me twin scars very near the nipple. The fights between Sonia and Mercedes can be heard as if they were in the flat next door; Herbert makes no comment, he continues with his double shifts at training.

Eva disappears, they locked her up or cleaned her out, according to gossip. Canetti plucks up the nerve to do what I didn't: he gets himself thrown out of the zoo. I'm going to kick up one hell of a fuss, they'll see.

Saturday comes round and, rather than erasing the film of the robbery that keeps playing in my mind, Eloísa's silence functions as a stimulus. I knew it, she says shaking her head and she embraces me as if I'd come back from the dead. You can't let me down, we're practically sisters, aren't we? First, at the door, I bump into Marito, the family's loyal employee. He's leaving as I'm entering. We greet each other as usual, I wonder whether he's in on it, whether he's joined the gang as a necessary accomplice. Eloísa explains without my asking: I made people come and go all day so they're recorded on the cameras, to throw them off. We sit in the dining room, Eloísa goes to her room to look for a joint. I'm such a pot-head, she says. For a while I'm left alone in front of the map of cheeses, which I examine in detail. She returns with a bottle of beer. For starters, so she says, and we make a toast. As I crumble the marijuana, she prepares mini pizzas in the electric oven. She chats to me through the wall, she invents conversations to distract me. How's Simón? she asks as if she cared. I swear I don't know how you do it, there's no way I could have a child. It must be something being a mum, is it? We smoke, we drink, we eat, in that order. My tongue gets tangled round the threads of mozzarella, Eloísa becomes transcendental: Last night I had a vision of cavemen. I pictured them round a fire, partying, half mad, same as us deep down, fucking, chowing, sleeping. Imagine what we would have been like back then. There must have been two girls like us. And Axel? Can you see him hunting? A faggot caveman, she concludes, and releases a cackle I can't replicate.

She coughs, clears her throat, rubs her hands together and emits a man's voice: Let's go for something stronger. From the kitchen to the living room. We put on the slippers and slide over to a false *mappa mundi* next to the piano, which Eloísa opens at Ecuador. Several bottles stand like fish out of water, mouths gaping. To calm me, she says: The fat cow went to visit family in Rosario, so the coast's clear. She closes her eyes and her index finger leaps from cap to cap: Eeny meeny miny moe. We have the dregs of a cherry liqueur.

The bottle empties quickly, we move on to an imported whisky without letting chance intervene. Any idea how much this must cost? She pours two generous glasses which we clink together, To a new life, she says, and I smile thinking that she must have been repeating the phrase all this time. A good pet phrase. The first gulp burns my chest. All this preamble makes me think the plan will come to nothing. And indeed, for fun, and because they are to hand, we start rifling through the pile of vinyl records that Axel's parents keep in a chest. Lots of jazz, some operas and a collection of messianic music: Paul Wilbur, Israel's Hope, Torah Torah. We're flummoxed by the needle and the speeds on the record player but then we manage to get it going. Eloísa dances alone, clapping between her legs tarantella style. Tosca and Syracuse. The Hassidic medley begins with a sugary prologue that makes Eloísa laugh like a madwoman.

Our eternal father lives; the heavens,
the earth, all creation exalts him.
The people of Israel live and, every Shabbat, recall
the miracle of creation and ask for peace and prosperity.
The Lord blesses you from Zion and shows you
the glory of Jerusalem of our days.
May your children's children live to see
true peace in Israel.

At twelve-something we approach the staircase. Upstairs, she walks in front, I linger at the portraits hanging on the wall as if hoping to discover a secret. The hidden intrigue behind Axel's family. I enter the bedroom and in the centre of the dressing room I see Eloísa frozen. Before speaking, as if no words were sufficient, she stretches out her arm and gestures across a shoeless shoe section: That fucking bitch. Certain that she's joking, I smile. But no, she grabs her head, holding it between her hands as if it were about to come off. It's no joke. The bloody idiot went and found out, she says, and points to a shelf above the rail holding the fur coats, the evening gowns and the sheathed suits: piles and piles of identical white boxes.

I say nothing but I think that perhaps Orfe put the shoes away in boxes because Axel's mother asked her to. Or because she does it every so often to give the dressing room a thorough once-over. A cleaning routine. I keep quiet. Her mood quickly changes. Wait here, she says, and shoots off. I crouch down and sink my hand into that thick, soft carpet, like a slumbering beast. Eloísa returns with the bottle of whisky which we left unfinished, an ashtray and cigarettes. We split the task, sharing out the boxes, grabbing three each and putting them back in their places. Before we start, Eloísa reminds me: Red and shiny, spike heels. I wonder what must be going through her head at this point. What will push her to carry on. I can't believe anyone could have so many shoes. After uncovering more than half the boxes and getting nowhere, Eloísa, who was initially taking the search as a game, begins to get annoyed. If I didn't know her better, I'd say she was on the verge of crying. Let's go again, she says. This time the command is to forget the red shoes, which are nowhere to be seen, and check the others one by one, sticking a hand inside, because if someone was suspicious they've more than likely put the key in a different place.

A first piece of carelessness, a box that Eloísa doesn't bother to close, unleashes the chaos. It seems ridiculous to be tidy if she isn't, so I join in. Once again we reach the end to no avail, but worse than before, the mountain of shoes that has formed between us, that brightly coloured monster with a thousand points, is the living image of delirium. It can't be, she says, beginning to doubt herself. I had it in my hands only yesterday, I swear. And once more she rants about Orfe, who must have put everything away that same afternoon before leaving. I think perhaps she's right when she says they found her out, or at least sensed something, and someone took care to hide those red shoes somewhere safe from Eloísa's imagination.

We can still change what is yet to come, we'd have to calm down. Actually, I would have to calm Eloísa down, persuade her that it's nonsense to persist with this, that it was a good idea, but fate didn't want it that way and that's it, we have to resign ourselves to it. Let's forget about it, that's what I would say. Then we'd have to start organising that cluster of shoes, matching pairs, returning the finest to their tissue paper, putting them away in the boxes, piling them on the shelf in rows of three, the way we found them, and carry on getting drunk with no further pretensions. In her anger, incapable of dealing with her frustration any other way, as I mentally rehearse a short speech of persuasion, Eloísa grabs a shoe by the heel, the one closest to her, a suede number, and vents her fury by flinging it through the air. She is, we are, unlucky that the shoe hits the mirror, which breaks the way mirrors break, weaving spider webs without actually falling to pieces. Now there's no going back. That must be why, after a silence that lasts the time it takes Eloísa to form a big, silent Oo, we end up laughing at the absurdity.

Come on, she says. She comes unhinged. She flies downstairs not looking where she's putting her feet, defying gravity, on the verge of an accident. I follow a few metres behind, ornaments whirl across my path, including the urn containing Axel's grandfather's ashes, which scatter over the carpet. She doesn't even turn round, she enters the kitchen and carries on to the basement. But instead of heading for the games room, she opens a small door camouflaged against the colour of the wall: the maid's room. Unstoppable, Eloísa starts going through Orfe's bedroom, swiping blindly, with no real intention of finding anything. Only anger. She opens boxes, hurls clothes over the floor, lifts the mattress, she shows no mercy to a knitted crucifix which she unthreads angrily, she breaks everything she can. On the sidelines, leaning against the doorframe, seeing her in action, I can't find the words to object. I pick up an old ID covered in leather that lands on the floor next to my feet. In the photo, Orfelina de los Milagros, that's her full name, has a cheeky, embarrassed smile, her hair tied tightly back, a white blouse with flounces and a tartan V-necked sweater. I can't and don't want to think about Orfe's life, about the way she's always been, but I can't help letting myself be swayed. Before abandoning the room, when there's nothing left to rip apart, Eloísa lights a match and threatens to burn it all.

It's half three and we are still on an uncontrolled merry-go-round. The alcohol and the hours of madness could make my eyelids droop at any moment. Eloísa is pale, sweaty, she smokes without pause. The plant tattooed on her arm changes colour, from green to black. As if she were going to die. We empty half the bar, we annihilate two bottles of whisky, a half-litre of vodka and one of anisette. Sitting on the armchair in the living room, I fantasise that the remains of Axel's grandfather are resuscitating in search of revenge. I avoid looking at the floor.

What comes next is difficult to relate. Or not to relate but to remember, to give some logical order to. Once again we go upstairs and, faced with the chaos in the dressing room, Eloísa is going to kick doors, smash two bottles of perfume against the wall, pee on the carpet, and I, somewhere between incredulity and fright, have an epiphany. On a partially hidden shelf, on a different level from the rest, I discover about ten shoeboxes we haven't checked. For an instant I don't know what to do, whether to stay silent or cherish one last chance. I'm leaning towards the latter in the hope that everything will be over quickly. Look, I say, and Eloísa pounces on the boxes, causing a landslide. The red shoe, of course, shiny, spike heels, comes to light. Once the euphoria passes, key in hand, Eloísa takes down the broken mirror, which ends up shattering into pieces the minute she rests it on the floor, and opens the safe effortlessly.

The loot, the jewels, are under a pile of files which Eloísa passes to me saying: Chuck these over there, tear them up, it has to look like junkies were here. For the first time she mentions them, the thieves, and then everything else, the destruction in Orfe's room, the stripping of the bar, the wild behaviour, fits perfectly. Creating confusion, that's what it's all about. It's part of a plan that was never revealed to me. For the false clues to be effective we would need to devastate the whole house, set fire to the barbecue area, the rooms, destroy the bunker, the cars in the garage, which would take us a whole day.

I obeyed and ripped to pieces what I assumed to be title deeds, contracts, wills. Eloísa embraced the trinket cases. We examined the jewels as if we knew what we were doing: rings, earrings, chokers. Many seemed to me like cheap bijouterie, fancy dress. With others, however, there was no doubt: a pearl necklace, a teardrop-shaped emerald charm, a star of David adorned with diamonds. Eloísa bagged it all in a crocodile-skin handbag. Weren't we going to take one or two? And what about the ones to plant in Orfe's room to incriminate her? Nothing, no answer, there's no place for discussion and I'm exhausted.

Finally outside, when the gates have closed and I'm hurrying on, wanting to leave the nightmare of the last few hours behind, Eloísa stops short, turns round and retraces her steps. I pay her no attention, I keep walking until my curiosity betrays me and I turn round to watch her. She crosses the small plaza that splits the avenue in two and looks for I don't know what among the bare flower beds. She returns to the front of the house armed with munitions I can't identify because of the night and the distance. She positions herself, measures the angle and throws a stone, a piece of rubble or tile, aiming at the camera on top of the gate. She misses. Three more like that, and the fourth is the winner. She hits the bracket and the camera comes off its axis, lying on its back, filming the sky. Bolts and thunderclaps. Eloísa jogs up to me with the first raindrops, her gaze lost.

The heat means that as the water comes into contact with the pavement it transforms into a thick vapour, a rain of fire that is extinguished on the surface. The downpour is unleashed and we realise that neither of us has money for a taxi. We're rich without a single peso. Not even coins. Eloísa says there's sure to be something in Axel's room. I tell her no. That if she goes back I won't wait for her. She doesn't insist. Several blocks on foot in the rain until a bus driver feels sorry for us and takes us home for free.

We are soaking wet when we arrive. I change in the bathroom, into tight shorts and a blouse stained with ketchup or something red. Eloísa strips off in the middle of the room, she puts on her studded T-shirt and some jogging bottoms, which she rolls up several times so as not to step on them. I'm dead, she says and throws herself down on the bed squeezing the handbag full of jewels to her stomach. She curls up next to the wall below Herbert and Simón, who are sleeping with their arms around one another. I feel equally wiped out but I'm terrified to close my eyes and be trapped in the circles of insomnia. In order to relax, I start tracing what's left of the snake. Its head is never-ending.

The rain seems to have stopped now. A strong wind has got up and the branches of the paradise tree beat against the window like whiplashes. Tzas, tzas, tzas. I find it hard to believe a new life is about to begin.

THIRTY-SIX

Dear readers,

We rely on subscriptions from people like you to tell these other stories – the types of stories most UK publishers would consider too risky to take on.

Our subscribers don't just make the books physically happen. They also help us approach booksellers, because we can demonstrate that our books already have readers and fans. And they give us the security to publish in line with our values, which are collaborative, imaginative and 'shamelessly literary' (the *Guardian*).

All of our subscribers:

- receive a first edition copy of every new book we publish
- are thanked by name in the books
- are warmly invited to contribute to our plans and choice of future books

BECOME A SUBSCRIBER, OR GIVE A SUBSCRIPTION TO A FRIEND

Visit andotherstories.org/subscribe to become part of an alternative approach to publishing.

Subscriptions are:

£20 for two books per year

£35 for four books per year

£50 for six books per year

The subscription includes postage to Europe, the US and Canada. If you're based anywhere else, we'll charge for postage separately.

OTHER WAYS TO GET INVOLVED

If you'd like to know about upcoming events and reading groups (our foreign-language reading groups help us choose books to publish, for example) you can:

- join the mailing list at: andotherstories.org/join-us
- follow us on twitter: @andothertweets
- join us on Facebook: And Other Stories

This book was made possible thanks to the support of:

Abigail Miller

Adam Biles

Adam Lenson

Ajay Sharma

Alannah Hopkin

Alasdair Thomson

Alastair Gillespie

Alastair Kenny

Alastair Laing

Alec Begley

Alex Gregory

Alex Ramsey

Alex Read

Alex Sutcliffe

Alice Nightingale

Ali Conway

Ali Smith

Alison Bennets

Alison Hughes

Alison Layland

Alison Winston

Ali Usman

Allison Graham

Amanda Banham

Amanda Love Darragh

Amelia Ashton

Amy Capelin

Amy Crofts

Ana Amália Alves

Andrea Reinacher

Andrew Clarke

Andrew Marston

Andrew Nairn

Andrew Robertson

Andrew Wilkinson

Angela Jane
    Mackworth-Young

Angus MacDonald

Anna-Karin Palm

Annabel Hagg

Anna Holmwood

Anna Milsom

Anna Vinegrad

Anne & Ian Davenport

Anne Carus

Anne Marie Jackson

Anne Meadows

Annette Morris &
    Jeff Dean

Anne Withers

Anne Woodman

Annie Henriques

Annie Ward

Ann McAllister

Anthony Messenger

Archie Davies

Asher Norris

Barbara Mellor

Barbara Zybutz

Bartolomiej Tyszka

Ben Coles

Benjamin Judge

Benjamin Morris

Ben Smith

Ben Thornton

Ben Ticehurst

Bettina Debon

Bianca Jackson

Blanka Stoltz

Brendan McIntyre

Brenda Scott

Bruce Ackers

Bruce & Maggie
    Holmes

Camilla Cassidy

Cara & Bali Haque

Cara Eden

Carla Palmese

Carole JS Russo

Caroline Maldonado

Caroline Rigby

Caroline Thompson

Catherine Mansfield

Catherine Nightingale

Cecile Baudry

Cecily Maude

Celine McKillion

Charles Lambert

Charles Rowley

Charlotte Holtam

Charlotte Williams

Chris Day

Chris Stevenson

Christina Baum

Christina
    MacSweeney

Christina Scholtz

Christine Luker

Christopher Allen

Christopher Marlow

Christopher Spray
Chris Watson
Ciara Greene
Ciara Ní Riain
Claire Tranah
Claire Williams
Claire Williams
Clare Buckeridge
Clare Fisher
Clare Keates
Clarice Borges-Smith
Clifford Posner
Clive Chapman
Colin Burrow
Collette Eales
Craig Barney

Daisy Meyland-Smith
Daniela Steierberg
Daniel Carpenter
Daniel Hugill
Daniel JF Quinn
Daniel Lipscombe
Dave Lander
David & Ann Dean
David Archer
David Breuer
David Davenport
David Hedges
David Herling
David Johnson-Davies
David Kelly
David Wardrop
Debbie Pinfold
Deborah Smith
Denise Muir

Denis Stillewagt &
    Anca Fronescu
Diana Brighouse

Eamonn Furey
Ed Tallent
Eileen Buttle
EJ Baker
Elaine Rassaby
Eleanor Maier
Elizabeth Boyce &
    Simon Ellis
Elizabeth Draper
Ellie Michell
Els van der Vlist &
    Elise Rietveld
Emily Jeremiah
Emma Kenneally
Emma McLean-Riggs
Emma Timpany
Evgenia Loginova

Fawzia Kane
Fiona & Andrew
    Sutton
Francesca Bray
Frances Chapman
Frances Perston
Francisco Vilhena
Francis Taylor
Freddy Hamilton

Gabrielle Morris
Gale Pryor
Garry Wilson
Gary Debus

Gavin Collins
Gawain Espley
Gemma Tipton
Geoff Egerton
Geoff Thrower
George Sandison &
    Daniela Laterza
George Wilkinson
Georgina Forwood
Geraldine Brodie
Gesine Treptow
Gill Boag-Munroe
Gillian Doherty
Giselle Maynard
Gloria Sully
Glynis Ellis
Gordon Cameron
Gordon Campbell
Grace Cantillon
Graham & Steph
    Parslow
Graham Lockie
Graham R Foster

Hannah & Matt Perry
Harriet Mossop
Harriet Sayer
Harrison Young
Helena Merriman
Helena Taylor
Helen Buck
Helene Walters
Helen Manders
Helen McMurray
Helen Weir
Helen Wormald

Henrike Laehnemann
Hilary McPhee
Howard Watson
Howdy Reisdorf
Hélène Steculorum-
  Decoopman

Ian Barnett
Ian Buchan
Ian Burgess
Ian Kirkwood
Ian McMillan
Imogen Forster
Irene Mansfield
Isabella Garment
Isfahan Henderson
Isobel Staniland

Jack Brown
Jackie Andrade
Jacqueline Crooks
Jacqueline Haskell
Jacqueline Lademann
Jacqueline Taylor
Jacquie Bloese
James Barlow
James Clark
James Cubbon
James Mutch
James Portlock
Janette Ryan
Jane Woollard
J Collins
JC Sutcliffe
Jeffrey & Emily Alford
Jen Hamilton-Emery

Jenifer Logie
Jennifer Higgins
Jennifer Hurstfield
Jenny Diski
Jenny Dover
Jenny Kosniowski
Jenny Newton
Jess Wood
Jill Aizlewood
Jillian Jones
Joanne Hart
Jocelyn English
Joel Love
Jo Elvery
Johan Forsell
Johannes Georg Zipp
Jo Harding
John Allison
John Conway
John Corrigan
John Gent
John Glahome
John Nicholson
John William
  Fallowfield
Jonathan Ruppin
Jonathan Watkiss
Jon Riches
Jorge Lopez de
  Luzuriaga
Joseph Cooney
Joy Tobler
Judit & Nigel
Judy Jones
Judy Kendall
JUJU Sophie

Julia Humphreys
Julian Duplain
Julian Lomas
Julia Sandford-Cooke
Julie Begon
Julie Fisher
Julie Gibson
Julie Van Pelt
Juraj Janik
Justine Taylor

Kaite O'Reilly
Kaitlin Olson
Karan Deep Singh
Karen Badat
Kasia Boddy
Kate Gardner
Kate Pullinger
Kate Thompson
Kate Wild
Katharine Robbins
Katherine El-Salahi
Katherine Wootton
  Joyce
Kathryn Lewis
Kathy Owles
Keith Dunnett
Keith Underwood
Kevin Brockmeier
Kevin Pino
Kim Sanderson
KL Ee
Krystalli Glyniadakis

Lana Selby
Lander Hawes

Laura McGloughlin
Laura Solon
Lauren Hickey
Lauren Kassell
Lesley Lawn
Leslie Rose
Lindsay Brammer
Lindsey Ford
Liz Clifford
Louisa Hare
Louise Bongiovanni
Louise Rogers
Lucie Harris
Lucinda Smith
Lyndsey Cockwell
Lynn Martin

M Manfre
Maggie Peel
Maisie & Nick Carter
Malcolm Bourne
Malcolm Cotton
Mansur Quraishi
Marella Oppenheim
Maria Elisa Moorwood
Maria Pelletta
Maria Potter
Marieke Vollering
Marie Schallamach
Marie Therese Cooney
Marina Castledine
Marina Jones
Marion Cole
Marion Macnair
Marion Tricoire
Mark Ainsbury

Mark Blacklock
Mark T Linn
Martha Nicholson
Martin Hollywood
Martin Whelton
Mary Bryan
Mary Nash
Mary Wang
Matthew Francis
Matthew Shenton
Maxime Dargaud-Fons
Michael & Christine
    Thompson
Michael Harrison
Michael Johnston
Michael Kitto
Michael Thompson
Minna Daum
Monika Olsen
Moshi Moshi Records

Nan Haberman
Natalie Smith
Natalie Wardle
Nicholas Holmes
Nichola Smalley
Nick Sidwell
Nicola Hart
Nicola Hughes
Nina Alexandersen

Olja Knezevic
Omid Bagherli

Paddy Maynes
Paola Ruocco

Pat Henwood
Patricia Hill
Patricia Melo
Paul Bailey
Paul Brand
Paul Cahalan
Paul Jones
Pete Ayrton
Peter Burns
Peter Lawton
Peter Murray
Peter Rowland
Peter Vos
Phil Morgan
Phyllis Reeve
Piet Van Bockstal
PM Goodman
Pria Doogan

Rachel Kennedy
Rachel Parkin
Rachel Pritchard
Rachel Van Riel
Rachel Watkins
Rebecca Atkinson
Rebecca Moss
Rebecca Rosenthal
Regina Liebl
Renata Larkin
Rhian Jones
Rhodri Jones
Richard Carter &
    Rachel Guilbert
Richard Ellis
Richard Jackson
Richard Jacomb

Richard Martin
Richard Soundy
Robert & Clare
    Pearsall
Robert Gillett
Robin Patterson
Rose Cole
Rosemary Rodwell
Rosie Hedger
Ros Schwartz
Ross Macpherson
Ross Walker
Ruth Ahmedzai
Ruth Clarke
Ruth Stokes
Réjane Collard

Sabine Griffiths
SA Harwood
Sally Baker
Samantha Schnee
Sam Gallivan
Sandie Guine
Sandra Hall
Sarah Butler
Sarah Magill
Sarah Salmon
Sascha Feuchert
Saskia Restorick
Sean Malone
Sean McGivern
Seini O'Connor
Selin Kocagoz
Sharon Evans
Shazea Quraishi
Sheridan Marshall

Sherine El-sayed
Sian Christina
Sigrun Hodne
Simon Armstrong
Simon Blake
Simon M Garrett
Simon M Robertson
Simon Pare
Sinead Fitzgerald
Sophie Johnstone
Stefanie Freudenthal
Stephen Abbott
Stephen Bass
Stephen Pearsall
Stephen Walker
Stuart Condie
Sue & Ed Aldred
Susan Bird
Susan Ferguson
Susan Murray
Susan Wicks
Susie Nicklin
Suzanne Fortey

Tania Hershman
Thees Spreckelsen
The Mighty Douche
    Softball Team
Thomas Bell
Thomas Bourke
Thomas Fritz
Tim Russ
Tim Theroux
Tina Rotherham-
    Winqvist
Toby Aisbitt

Tom Bowden
Tom Heel
Tony Crofts
Torna Russel-Hills
Tracy Northup
Trish Hollywood

Vanessa Garden
Vanessa Nolan
Victoria Adams
Victoria O'Neill
Vinita Joseph
Vivien
    Doornekamp-Glass

Walter Prando
William G Dennehy
William Prior
Winifred June
    Craddock

Zoe Brasier

other stories

Current & Upcoming Books by And Other Stories

Title: *Paradises*
Author: Iosi Havilio
Editor: Sophie Lewis
Copy-editor: Ellie Robins
Proofreader: Alex Billington
Typesetter: Tetragon
Set in: 10/14pt Swift Neue Pro, Verlag
Series and Cover Design: Joseph Harries
Format: B Format with French flaps
Paper: LP Opaque 70/15 FSC
Printer: T J International Ltd, Padstow, Cornwall

FSC
www.fsc.org
MIX
Paper from
responsible sources
FSC® C013056